TERRY OF THE DOUBLE C

A CONTEMPORARY WESTERN ROMANCE

REG QUIST

Terry Of The Double C

Paperback Edition
Copyright © 2019 Reg Quist

CKN Christian Publishing
An Imprint of Wolfpack Publishing
6032 Wheat Penny Avenue
Las Vegas, NV 89122

christiankindlenews.com

Paperback ISBN 978-1-64119-502-7
Ebook ISBN 978-1-64119-501-0

Library of Congress Control Number: 2019931365

TERRY OF THE DOUBLE C

Big Mike McConachie stepped out of the cook house door with a satisfied feeling behind his belt and a toothpick squeezed between his lips. He leaned against a roof post, beside the small group of cowboys who had taken up the ladder-back chairs lining the roofed-over cookhouse porch. The afternoon rain was unrelenting, dampening any desire to go back to work, or even to wade through the mud and slop between the cookhouse and the bunkhouse.

The well-fed ranch crew, after taking their evening meal, was content to end their day sitting idly, watching a man splash his way along the ranch road. A small metal suitcase hung from the walker's right hand, and a khaki colored army duffle bag was balanced on his left shoulder. A pair of riding boots, with a thong tied through the boot's pull tabs, hung over his right shoulder

The watchers each had the same question on his mind, but no one bothered to frame it into words. They simply sat and stared, as each step the man took brought him closer to the ranch yard. Rain was dripping from the saturated western-style hat the man wore. The hat sagged at the rain-weakened brim, hiding the walker's face. His pants were muddy to the knees. Each step kicked up fresh muck while the constant rain washed it off in streaks. Everything about the approaching man told of weariness and water.

As the walker neared his destination, he glanced up. One of the cowboys leaned forward on his chair. "Why, that there ain't nothing but a younker." No one had anything to add to that obvious truth.

The young man stopped and glanced at the big ranch house before stepping unhurriedly towards the cookhouse, and the men gathered there, his eyes on the mucky ground. When he was within ten feet of the porch he stopped and tilted his head back, eyeing the men for the first time and forcing the rain gathered on his hat brim to rush back, spilling over, and down his back, much of it beneath the collar of his jacket and shirt. The extra rain water running down his back appeared to have no impact. He simply stopped and stared at the men. No one seemed to know what to say.

Finally, the visitor spoke. "This the Lazy-S?"

The cowboys looked to Big Mike, knowing from experience that it was best to leave these things to the foreman. Mike simply nodded his head while he took in every image of the questioner, from his mud clogged boots to his saturated pants and jacket and to the rain-ruined hat. "You're soaked through there boy."

The young man glanced at his pants and the front of his jacket, as if receiving Mike's statement as some kind of surprising news. Slowly he looked himself over. "Why, danged if you ain't got the right of that."

Big Mike thought that over in his slow, deliberate way

before asking, "You walk from the highway? All the seven miles?"

"Didn't see no other way to get er done." The youngster was showing himself to be a man of few words.

Big Mike wasn't finished with his inquisition. "You walk from Long View too?"

"Old man in a pickup truck gave me a ride. Dropped me at the end of the driveway."

"He offer to run you in?"

"If he did I missed it over the rattle of the truck and the radio blaring."

"You ask him to bring you in?"

"Don't like to ask."

Big Mike seemed to think that was important information. He mulled it awhile before continuing, "That old man have a name?"

"Most likely. Didn't offer it though. Said to say hello to someone named McConachie. That perhaps be you?"

Big Mike might have nodded; the movement was slight and could be misunderstood.

The walker stood in the pouring rain through this entire introduction to the Lazy-S.

One of the sitting cowboys finally ventured an opinion. "Might not hurt none, Mike if'n you was to invite the younker to step out of the rain."

Mike slowly turned and looked at the cowboy before indicating with an uplifted jaw and a swiveled head that stepping onto the porch would be an acceptable move for the saturated walker.

The young man stepped forward and took the two easy stairs onto the covered porch. It was the first relief from the pouring rain in over three hours. With the invite to the porch he made the assumption that he could drop the duffle and suitcase without incurring anyone's wrath.

He propped the duffle beside the wall of the cookhouse and nudged the metal suitcase against it to keep it upright. He slipped the boots off his shoulder and dumped the gathered rainwater out of them before hanging them on a nail driven into the board and batten siding.

He removed his hat and slapped it against his pant leg to shake the abundance of water off, then hung it on the nail with the boots. His long black hair was dry on top where it was protected by the pressed felt of the hat, but was soaked where it hung down, and over his collar at the back. He slipped out of his saturated jacket and draped it over the duffle. His shirt was as wet as it would have been had he not been wearing the jacket.

Big Mike silently studied this new arrival. 'Probably sixteen. No more than seventeen. City kid. Looks tough enough. Big hands, tall as he'll ever be. Still short of six feet.'

With his soaked coat off and his long hair tucked behind his ears, the young man turned to Big Mike, instinctively seeing him as the leader. "Terry Coombs." He didn't offer to shake.

Only then did the young man begin to unwind from his ordeal. Not nearly as sure of himself as he was trying to put on in front of the gathered men, he was shaking with fear, cold and indecision, inside. He only hoped he could keep it inside. He dreaded the thought of shaming himself in front of these tough ranch hands.

As a gust of wind forced its way through his wet shirt, he shivered.

"Mr. Stocker said if I could make my way here by this evening there would be a job waiting. I'm here."

Big Mike might have smiled. Or perhaps he just curled his lips as he slid the toothpick from one side of his mouth to the other. "Yes, I'd say you're here alright. Maybe all of a hundred forty pounds of boy and thirty pounds of wet duds. You're here alright."

'More like a hundred sixty pounds', thought Terry, 'but it ain't worth correcting.'

Big Mike continued his silent assessment of the young man and repeated his original thoughts to himself. What he saw was a well-built, but not tall man. Perhaps five foot ten, with shoulders that spoke of time spent in contact sports or at the workout gym. His eyes confirmed the young man for a city boy, so the shoulders would not likely have come from hard work. Big Mike was only partly right in this.

"You hungry?"

The question from Big Mike was welcome.

"Some."

"C'mon, we'll see if Cookie has any of that prairie dog stew left."

Terry had some ranch experience. He wasn't going to fall for the first jab from this big, slow talking man. Grinning inside at the taunt, and knowing it for a test, he said, "Ain't had a bowl of prairie dog stew for some time now. Cookie catch his own prairie dogs, or will that be one of my jobs?"

Mike had no response.

Terry cleaned up three big bowls of good beef stew and several slices of home-made, whole-wheat bread, wiping out the bowl with the last slice. Two cups of steaming coffee washed it all down.

His saturated clothing was sticking to him and he was feeling chills as his body heat was being used up in drying the cloth. He was about to ask where he might find a bunk and a shower when the cooks helper dropped a big piece of pie in front of him. He looked up at the helper, who was just a bit older than Terry was himself. "Thanks."

After setting the pie down the young fellow said, "Name's Beamer. They give me the swamper 'n bull-cook job here on account'a I don't like horses. Don't trust em. Don't want'a be around em. Like as not ta kill ya, ya turn yer back. I look after the bunkhouse. You put that pie where it'll do some good and then you 'n I'll get ya settled in'ta a bunk."

Beamer, who Terry could now see had a gimpy leg and a slightly twisted spine, struggled back to the wash rack and tied into the dishes again, while Terry dug into the pie. A half hour later Beamer had Terry settled down in a bunk, had shown him where the shower room was and helped him hang his wet clothes from the soaked duffle, on a line stretched across the bunkhouse, where they could dry.

Beamer's work day was finished. After a hot shower and a change of clothes for Terry, the two young men helped themselves to fresh cups of coffee. They relaxed into a couple of chairs in front of the cookhouse. For the next hour Terry listened while Beamer told him about his home, the Lazy-S, the Stalker family and anything else that entered his rambling mind. Terry remained mostly silent, which was his habit.

Beamer didn't offer any information about his twisted leg or spine.

CHAPTER 2

Terry's arrival at the Lazy-S followed a long and difficult discussion with his father. Being the oldest of four siblings, Terry had grown into taking responsibility for the younger ones.

His mother experienced many good days where no one could wish for a better mother. But her bad days were more than a counter balance to those others. The first time Terry heard the term, 'bi-polar', he no idea what any of it meant. He still didn't. Not really, he didn't. He could only shorten a long medical explanation to words like, turmoil, mayhem, chaos, all of which were a mystery to adults and frightening to children. As often as not, they were frightened and crying children.

In spite of his love for his parents and the younger kids, he longed to get away, to get a break, a rest, before another school year started.

With the end of the school year coming, and two free months before him, Terry sought out a ranch job. He had enough ranch experience that he felt confident in applying for work with horses and cattle.

A family friend owned the Double C, a medium sized ranch that Terry had spent several summers at. The first couple of summers were glorious escapes from the city and the turmoil of his home life. He was young, and Old Eli, the ranch owner and friend, let him run and play at will, sliding down stacked hay in the loft and riding a pony chosen for its gentleness.

As he entered his teen years, he was given small chores to do. Although these chores grew in importance and difficulty each summer, they were still not much of a challenge. He knew ranch-born kids were doing these tasks and much more, at that age. And Terry was in a hurry to grow up. To mature. To get away from home. To get off to university. To put away some money towards the costs of education. And he couldn't possibly ask Eli about wages. No, he needed a paying job.

The best memory from those years on the Double C was of Old Eli teaching him to ride. He was given a more challenging horse and had become proficient enough to be trusted around the cattle. Eli kept saying, "You've got the makings boy." Terry didn't fully understand that.

As much as he loved and respected Old Eli, Terry felt he needed a new experience. A truly learning and challenging experience. An experience where he wasn't being protected by his old friend. Eli was a good teacher, but the young man didn't really see that. He couldn't climb over the thought that he was still being treated like a kid, the son of a family friend.

Studying the newspaper, Terry found the advertisement from the Lazy-S. He avoided directly facing the probability that he would hurt Old Eli if he went to work on another ranch. Although his body and a part of his mind said he was grown, his thinking and another part of his mind put a question mark over that.

Although Terry and Eli had largely closed the age gap that separated them, Terry felt he was ready for more challenge.

Then, too, with the Double C, being only a short distance from Terry's disordered home, the young man felt the need for some separation, at least for the summer.

On his first full day of work on the Lazy-S, Terry was led to the horse stable by Big Mike. "I spect you know what a shovel is, and that over there is a wheelbarrow. Spect you know that too. Your job, for now, is to keep this barn clean and the horses fed, watered and groomed. You ever been around horses before?"

Terry nodded, but Mike wasn't looking his way, so he simply followed the nod with "some."

"OK then. Listen up now. The cowboys' horses are in the corral next to the barn or else in the horse trap running off the corral. You don't need to be concerned with them. The riding crew looks after most of what little work need doing out there. Your work is in here. The animals in the open stalls are ranch horses. Daily work animals, including that team of big blacks in the end stall. There'll be different animals in here day by day, as the riders move them in and out. A couple are a bit raunchy to handle. Keep your wits about you. Watch their teeth and hind hooves. You only have to groom and feed them and have them ready. The riders saddle their own animals.

"The animals in the box stalls are family horses. You need to keep them clean and well looked after. Sometimes you'll need to walk them for exercise. Depends on how much riding the kids do.

"Mr. Stocker will be down later to say hello. The two

oldest Stocker boys work on the ranch. The younger three kids are usually not allowed on the working part of the ranch, except to come to the stable for their horses. But that's a rule that sometimes gets broken. They're gett'n older and don't always follow the rules. You'll be getting calls, time to time, to saddle a horse for one or more of the kids. You look, you'll see that all the stalls have a name on the front. In the tack room the saddles are marked. You match the saddle to the horse and lead it out. You might have to help a couple of the young kids mount."

There was a pause of several seconds while Big Mike studied this newest worker.

"You got all that?"

"Got it."

Mike simply nodded and walked away. Terry slowly strode from end to end in the barn, studying the horses and sizing up the work.

CHAPTER 3

THE FIRST MONTH ON THE LAZY-S WENT WELL FOR Terry. The food was good, and he was enjoying a bit of comradery with the cowboys. He did his work, said little, kept to himself except for the few times he and Beamer drank coffee and visited. He mailed his pay check off to his bank. When the cowboys went to town he chose to stay at the ranch. His summer goal was to work towards a degree of financial independence. Going to town would not offer any opportunities towards achieving that goal.

The turmoil and lack of order in Terry's home life led him to early self-reliance. He knew his mother wasn't healthy but until recently he had never heard the term bipolar. Having that condition explained to him by his long-suffering father confirmed for Terry that if he was to reach any reasonable goal in life it was up to him. It was a lesson he never forgot.

The one uncontrollable, but not totally unwelcome distraction in Terry's work world was Cindy, the Stocker's soon to be seventeen-year-old daughter. Terry, at seventeen himself, was a year ahead of Cindy in school. The pretty, but somewhat spoiled young lady had become a bit of a nuisance around the stable, but Terry had no control over that. She hung around, fussing and grooming her horse, although Terry kept the animal spotless and shining. Her efforts to get Terry into conversations had little effect on the young man.

Cindy loved to ride. Terry saddled her gelding and cared for the animal when she returned it. Where she rode or who she rode with was not his problem.

Terry was totally inexperienced in matters of young ladies, except for the casual contacts the school classroom offered, or the occasional school dances, which he enjoyed, held in the gymnasium on some Friday evenings. But even at the dances he had little to say.

He hadn't really thought much about it but if he did he would admit that he was awkward in social situation.

He had no idea what to say or do around the self-assured Cindy. The first time she asked Terry to help her mount her horse he came close to quitting the job. He knew perfectly well that she didn't need help. She was teasing and antagonizing him and they both knew it. With shaking hands and his teeth locked tight, he held her stirrup. He didn't know what else to do. Certainly, he wasn't going to touch her or lift her the way he did with the two younger kids. Cindy lithely placed her foot in the stirrup and swung gracefully to the saddle. As Terry stepped back, the young tormenter giggled and kicked the animal forward.

Terry, just three months before his eighteenth birthday, had trouble sorting out his feelings about Cindy's many visits to the stable, and of her hanging around even when she wasn't riding. She was an attractive and precocious young lady, used to having her own way in most things and uncommonly sure of herself. Terry vowed that he would keep his distance from the ranch-owner's daughter.

Terry also used one of the ranch horses during his free hours, exploring the ranch and a few of the surrounding foothills. He was unsuccessful at changing Beamer's mind about horses, so he usually rode out alone.

The Lazy-S, situated on the eastern slope of the Rockies, with the titled land running well into the rocky and forested foothills, was an almost perfect scene of raw nature. It took no time at all for Terry to feel at home on the far-spreading, windy acres.

In early August Sid Lopez, the straw-boss, the rider Big Mike depended on most, approached Terry in the big stable. "Saddle up young man. Mr. Stocker figures it's time you got a better look at the ranch. See what-all the cowboys do. Get a bit of a break from shovel and wheelbarrow. We'll leave out of here in fifteen minutes. Bring a canteen of water. Miss Cindy wants to come too, so saddle her animal and bring him out.

Sid, a smiling and self-assured man in his mid-thirties, perhaps five foot ten, slim, strong and wiry, led the way out of the yard. A gate was fixed into the wooden plank fence in such a way that it could be opened and closed without dismounting. Sid bent and released the latch, holding it open for the two younger riders.

The three explorers wandered their way through miles of grass and scattered cattle. They waved at a couple of cowboys minding the herd a half mile off. The sun warming the ever-present wind, and shining off the snow-capped Rockies, made it a memorable day for the Lazy-S trio.

As they edged further west Sid pointed into the

wooded foothills, speaking to Terry. Cindy had heard it all before. "The ranch owns or leases land well into the hills. It's those unfenced hills that makes it necessary to carry so many cowboys on the payroll. Lots of grass up there but near impossible to fence. Cows are not noted for brains. They need caring for, else they'll just keep wandering. A good many bears: blacks and grizzlies both, up there. The blacks don't usually bother anything, but the grizzlies will take a calf easy enough or a mama cow too, given opportunity.

"Almost never see them, but there's a few cats claiming territory here and there too. Mostly night creatures, cats are. Seldom seen in the day. Seldom seen at all for that matter. Good at hiding themselves. I expect they see us a lot more often than we see them. Beautiful beasts; bears and cougars both, but deadly. Every Lazy-S rider carries a saddle gun for protection. Not used very often but there's been a few times."

Terry wondered about some of those times, but he let it go.

Riding into the more confining hills, Sid took the lead, followed by Cindy, with Terry bringing up the rear. They followed a trail through the forest for perhaps one quarter mile before the land opened ahead of them again. The forest and rocky hillsides spread out like an hourglass before them, while the grassland slanted upward at an easy slope. There were signs of recent grazing, but lots of grass remained for the early fall weeks that were still ahead of them.

Terry pulled his animal to a halt, letting Sid and Cindy get a short distance ahead of him. He turned in his saddle, first to the right and then back to the left. The young man was awed by all he saw.

Terry was raised in Red Deer, a city where, if the sky was clear he could just see the outline of the Rockies, off into the western distance. Other than a few road trips with the family, he had no knowledge of mountains or wilderness. His inexperienced eyes were overwhelmed, taking in the majesty of his surroundings.

He had just put his horse back into motion when the grassy hillside exploded into a screaming, snarling, shouting, confusing turmoil. He seemed to see everything at once, one image registering in a millisecond before the next image presented itself. With the first scream, his own riding animal started acting up. Cindy's horse twisted into a curl before rising on its hind legs, dumping the rider cruelly onto the grassy hillside, and turning, to run back towards the trail though the bush. Cindy flopped to the ground and bounced once before lying out flat, with a scream of fear and a cry of pain. His own horse was dancing a bit but generally held steady with Terry's firm grip on the reins.

While Terry was struggling with his own horse, Cindy's fear blinded animal twisted on his hind legs and turned to escape the threat. Three frantic steps had the big black smashing into Terry's horse. He came near to knocking Terry out of the saddle. Without even thinking about it, Terry grabbed the frightened horse's reins and held on tightly.

Terry's sub-conscious mind registered the vision of a big cat leaping off the top of a trail-side rock, of Sid flying through the air, arms and feet thrashing, and of his horse screaming in pain, kicking out in all directions. His mind played those couple of seconds back for him.

As Sid fell to the ground, the horse bucked and jumped away. Terry got a clear look at Sid and the attacking animal.

The straw-boss and the big cat were tangled in a heap, with the snarling cougar gripping Sid's arm. Sid appeared to have some fight left in him as the two of them were rolling over and over on the hillside grass. As Terry watched, they came to a stop. Sid was no longer showing resistance.

The big cat clamped his teeth more tightly onto Sid's upper arm and started dragging the unconscious man towards the concealment of the hillside bush. Terry was frozen in fear for just a moment and then the thought came unbidden to him; 'You have to do something.'

With no experience to fall back on, Terry was going by nothing more than guesswork and instinct. Almost unconsciously he thought that he and Cindy were in serious trouble if they lost their horses. His own horse was shaking in fear and only a firm hand on the rein kept the animal partially under control.

Cindy's horse made motions to run but Terry hung fast to the leathers. Fearing the thin rein leather would break, he worked his hands down the reins until he was able to grab the bridle strap. He almost had to drag the reluctant animal back to where Cindy was still sitting on the ground crying. In fear of the cougar, she had skittered backwards with heels and hands propelling her until she was twenty yards from Sid and the cat.

Terry leaped out of the saddle, holding his reins in one hand and the bridle of Cindy's horse in the other. He shouted at Cindy, "Get up, you're not hurt. Get up and grab these horses."

Cindy didn't move. "Get up," he shouted louder. "That cat's going to kill Sid if we don't do something. Get up and hold these horses. Don't lose them." He finally realized that he was shouting. He moved closer to where the girl was sitting in the grass. More softly he said, "Cindy. Cindy. Get up."

The girl was frightened beyond all reason, but slowly, keeping her eyes firmly on the threatening cat, she finally stood to her feet.

"Take these reins and hang on for dear life." He thrust the leathers into Cindy's hands and ran toward where Sid was lying in the grass. The cougar hunched down behind the downed rider, blood covering its face and a snarl on its lips as Terry ran towards it, shouting and waving his arms. The cat snarled and growled louder, forcing his threat. It had let go of Sid's arm.

Terry was shocked by the blood that was covering Sid's arm and upper body. And the side of his head. A lot of blood.

Realizing that the big cat was not going to give up its prey, Terry ran to Sid's horse. The injured animal was standing nearby, his head down, blood covering his chest and shoulder and running down his front legs. It was clear the cougar had done serious damage. The gelding was shuddering, its front legs spread wide apart, trying to remain upright, while its whole body was shaking in shock and pain.

There was no time to look to the care of the injured animal. All Terry wanted was the carbine Sid was carrying in the saddle scabbard. A few quick steps put the young man beside the injured horse. He soon had the weapon in his hands. He knew very little about guns and nothing at all beyond the old .22 he and his father occasionally shot gophers with, or tin cans off the tops of fence posts. He was a reasonably good shot, but tin cans weren't snarling back at you or chewing on your unconscious friend. What he faced was a poor comparison to anything he had done before.

Knowing there was no time to lose, he dropped to his right knee, rested his elbow on the other knee, which was bent close to his body, and pointed the carbine in the direction of the big cat. He wasn't more than twenty-five yards away, but he didn't try to calculate the distance or really even think about it. He accepted the situation as it existed and prepared to take a shot. Idly he hoped Sid carried the gun loaded.

There was little to see of the cat. When Terry was running and shouting at it, the big animal crouched behind Sid, snarling, and threatening the apparition that was approaching. Only its head and shoulders were visible.

As Terry aimed the gun, his hands began to shake. Then his vision blurred as sweat ran down his forehead and into his eyes. Adrenalin and fear were working against each other, causing all kinds of problems for the young shooter. He lowered the gun to the grass and removed his hands. He pulled a handkerchief from his back pocket and cleaned his eyes after wiping his forehead. He stretched out his arms and said to himself, 'settle down'. With the gun again in firing position he took careful aim, raising the target area a bit higher than he thought necessary out of fear of hitting Sid.

He remembered his father telling him, "Don't jerk the trigger. Just press it with an even pressure." Terry wasn't sure how far he'd have to squeeze the trigger on the unfamiliar weapon. He was surprised when the shot went off a bit sooner than he expected, carrying more kick than he was prepared for. It nearly laid him on his back. Over the crack of the shot he heard the big cat scream. Whether from a bullet wound or in anger, Terry couldn't guess. He collected himself and looked towards Sid. A least it appeared that he hadn't shot the downed rider.

In his peripheral vision Terry saw the cat completing a magnificent leap onto a high rock behind Sid and at the side of the grassed area. He had no idea a cougar could leap so far. It was an awesome sight for the young man. The thought flashed through his mind that this would be a story for his grandchildren. If he lived through it. And if he had grandchildren.

Sid was bleeding and he wasn't moving. Cindy was holding the horses but was still frightened beyond telling. Terry had no idea what the cat might do next. He hoped it would turn and disappear into the rocks and forest. It did no such thing. What it did, was, it stood to its feet, and then crouched down again as if it was getting ready to make another leap.

Reluctantly Terry turned the carbine towards the big cat. He had to wait until his hands quite shaking again, but finally he drew a bead on the cat's chest and squeezed the trigger. The effective range of the gun was not a part of Terry's thinking.

The young man wasn't sure if his shot hit the animal or not, but the cougar's reaction was immediate. Identifying a new foe, the cat made another of his magnificent leaps off the rock, this time in Terry's direction. The cat's movements were incredibly fast.

Terry already had the gun pointed in the right direction. After working the loading lever, he sent another shot towards the big cat. The animal had fewer than fifty yards to cover in order to reach the shooter. It would take only seconds.

Terry had no idea how many shells were in the magazine, but he shot again and again as the big cat bounded his way. The cat seemed to stumble once as one front leg folded under him, but it soon recovered. From fifteen feet away, the cougar left the ground in a smaller but still superb leap, directly at Terry.

The young man had time for only one final shot. He tilted the gun upwards, towards the animal's chest as it flew through the air. He heard Cindy screaming again. When he could see nothing in the v-sight but tawny hair, he pulled the trigger. As he squeezed the trigger, he thought a split-second prayer. In his rush and fear and panic he knew there was no finesse to his shooting.

He was starting to jack the loading lever again when he was hit by a freight train. At least it felt like a train. The cougar hit him with his feet first, his deadly claws ready for raking anything they came in contact with.

Terry's felt hat saved his scalp from serious laceration, but one claw found his forehead, opening the skin like an orange peel before raking past his left eye and down his cheek. The momentum of the cat's leap carried it another short distance before it tumbled to the ground. The raking claw slammed into Terry's left shoulder and downward into the top of his arm, shredding his shirt sleeve and tearing flesh and muscle from his shoulder and chest and down his arm, all the way to his elbow.

Terry lay on his back in the long grass, hurting in every part of his body, and bleeding. When the cat slammed into him, Terry was flung several feet to the side. He had never imagined anything to compare with the body slam.

He felt no pain from the claw cuts yet and didn't have time to give thought to it. His forehead was bleeding profusely, as head wounds are apt to do. Because his left eye was closed by the wound, and the blood flowing over it, and into it, he couldn't see the mess the cat made of his shoulder and arm. The pain and the knowledge of the wound would come soon enough.

Afterwards, Terry remembered the stench of the cougar's breath as the big cat's mouth passed close to his own. He remembered, too, Cindy's terrified screams as they seemed to settle into a series of whimpers.

There was no further attack from the cat. Terry rolled over onto his back, raised his head and looked between his feet. Seeing no threatening animal, he sat up enough to prop himself on his elbows. He glanced around with his one good eye until he spotted the cougar lying in the grass a few feet away. Cindy was terrified into silence.

Slowly the young man rolled over and struggled to his knees. He crawled to where the Winchester carbine was lying. He picked it up and jacked the spent shell out of it, leaving the slide open so he could see if there were more shells available. It was clearly empty. His pain was becoming extreme but so was his fear of the cat.

Somehow, he kept hearing Old Eli repeating one of his favorite sayings, "You got er to do boy, ya got er to do."

Keeping his one good eye on the cougar, Terry slowly went to Sid's horse and opened one saddle bag. He found a few loose shells lying on the bottom of the leather satchel and lifted them out. He didn't know how to load the magazine, but he figured he could push one shell into the barrel if he was careful. That's how he loaded his dad's old .22 single shot. He figured it should work on the Winchester. With that done he cautiously approached the cat.

The pain of the claw scratches was now starting. The first sharp stab of pain nearly knocked Terry to his knees. It seemed to come from every part of his body, but his shoulder and arm mostly. Then the shaking started. Fear and shock were taking their toll. Knowing the battle wasn't over yet, he steadied himself as best he could and looked again at the big cat.

Not knowing if the animal was dead or if it was about to leap to dramatic activity again, Terry held the gun at the ready position, as well as he could with one hand. He slowly edged close enough to take another, hopefully, killing shot. His left arm was throbbing in pain such as he had never dreamt of before, but he couldn't handle the Winchester with one hand. He pushed through the agony and lifted his left arm to grip the gun. He held the weapon as steadily as he could.

The cat's eyes were open and watching. Its chest was rising and falling slightly as it struggled for breath. One back leg was slowly, pointlessly, working back and forth. But it showed no menace, beyond its watching eyes. Terry figured it was dying and was surprised to realize that he must have hit it a time or two. Then he noticed the skin and hair gone from the cat's forehead and the groove in the skull bone beneath. 'Must have done that with the first shot', Terry thought to himself.

Needing to finish the horror, Terry continued to ease up to the cat until he was nearly close enough to touch it. He stopped, lifted the gun muzzle until the sights lined up with the side of the cat's head and took the shot. The animal shuddered as a tide of pain rippled through its magnificent body. Its eyes closed, and the chest quit rising. Terry thought he might have heard a final sigh of escaping breath.

The novice rider and cowboy dropped the butt of the gun to the ground, looked over what had become a battle ground, lowered his own eyes and felt a tear run down his cheek. There was time now for fear. It showed itself in a steady flow of tears and a tremble through his whole body, followed by heaving shoulders and an emotional sucking of air into his lungs.

The moisture from his left eye mixed with the blood that was still trickling from his forehead, making the flow even more troublesome. Within a few moments he started pulling himself together. He used his handkerchief again to wipe his forehead. The eye still wouldn't open.

He looked back to where Cindy had been standing with the horses. She was now astride her trusted bay gelding with the reins to Terry's grey wrapped around her saddle horn. "You alright?" Terry hollered back to her.

"I guess so. Is it dead?"

"It's dead."

CHAPTER 4

TERRY WALKED TOWARDS SID AS QUICKLY AS HIS hammered body would allow. The empty carbine was hanging from his right hand. The straw-boss hadn't moved. Terry dropped to his knees beside the injured man, took his hair in one hand and turned his head to the side. Sid's scalp, and the right side of his head were a terrible mess. The flannel shirt common to the Lazy-S riders prevented Terry from seeing how bad the chest and arm wounds were, but judging by the blood and the torn cloth, they too were serious.

The big cat was forcing Terry into a whole new world. A world where he had no knowledge at all of what to do. Over the past year he had been in a rush to reach maturity, to be able to claim full manhood, to be seen as an adult. Kneeling in the grass, his own body wracked in pain, slowly flowing blood blocking the vision of his left eye, and not knowing what to do about the terrible wounds confronting him, he felt young and inadequate. Perhaps he was not as prepared for adulthood as he thought he was.

Terry had less knowledge of wounds than he did of guns, but he knew the bleeding had to be stopped. He pulled off his own torn and bloody, flannel shirt and wrapped it tightly around Sid's shoulder and arm, and then lay one sleeve across his chest. He figured he would be unable to lift Sid to get the sleeves across his back for tying, so he looped the sleeve around the undamaged shoulder and under Sid's arm and pulled it tight. It was the best he could do. The shirt made a poor bandage, at best.

Finally, with the two arms meeting across Sid's chest and with the shirt spread as evenly as possible, he tied them as tightly as his injured arm and waning strength would allow. With nothing else to work with, he pressed the loose end of the flannel onto the bleeding scratches. Perhaps they would adhere somehow and slow the blood flow.

He didn't know if the bleeding would stop but it seemed to be slowing down. Now he needed something for the head wound.

The breeze off the snow-covered mountain competed with the afternoon sun. And won. Terry felt the breeze on his bare back and couldn't prevent the shudders that followed.

He sat back on his heels and trembled in pain, looking at Sid.

He again wiped his forehead and wounded eye with his blood-saturated handkerchief. Both his hands were bloody, up to the wrists. Blood was still flowing from his own head and arm wounds. He waited a moment before again wiping his eye. He then pressed the bloody cloth to his torn forehead and held it there for perhaps thirty seconds while he studied Sid's bleeding head. Without thinking about all that was involved, he shouted over his shoulder, "Cindy, I need your shirt."

Cindy had walked her horse to within a few feet of Sid. The sight of the wounded cowboy nearly made her sick to her stomach, but she remained sitting there. She was still jumpy, and ready to turn her horse towards the ranch at any moment. Her feelings about Sid's injuries were genuine and she might have done something else to help if Terry had asked. But she certainly wasn't about to take off her shirt.

"What? You can't be serious. I'm not going to give you my shirt. No way."

The rapidly maturing young lady was in the full bloom of teen modesty. Conscious of her approaching adulthood, and of the changes in her body and mind, she was a volcano of emotions; coquettish one moment and terribly shy and private the next.

"Cindy, Sid's bleeding badly and has been for far too long. That's more important than your stupid shirt. So, throw it to me. Now!"

Cindy was silent for a few moments. Finally, she said, in a quavering voice, "You can't turn around!"

Between the pain that was racking his own body and having no real idea of what he was doing, and fighting emotion himself, Terry was about at the end of his own rational thoughts. He wasn't concerned about Cindy's modesty. "Oh, for goodness sake, just throw me the shirt. Go hide in the bush if you want." The flannel shirt landed in the grass between Terry and Sid. Cindy was crying again.

A thought came to the young man. "Cindy. Ride as fast as you can and find those cowboys that were working cattle. Tell them what's happened. We need a doctor and an ambulance. Or maybe they could get the pickup truck here more quickly. We've got to get Sid to some kind of help. That horse needs a vet too. Ride. Watch for prairie dog holes but ride. Go. Bring help."

Without looking around, Terry heard Cindy's horse rise to a run. He picked up the shirt and turned to Sid. With the last of his failing strength he folded the shirt and tied it around Sid's head and again used the sleeves as tie straps, tying it as tightly as he could. The wrapping and tying were clumsy, with Sid's eyes covered, and with loose ends of shirt sticking out in several places. Terry didn't figure it would matter. The torn flesh was mostly covered. The marauding flies would have little direct access to Sid's wounds. Terry's own wounds were completely exposed. He could do nothing about that.

When he had done what he could, he slumped onto his back in the grass and allowed his eyes to close. He covered his bleeding forehead and eye as much as he could with his uninjured arm, blocking the flies, and the bright sunlight. He was beyond caring that his arm lay in the still seeping blood. Sleep, and the escape from pain would be a welcome relief.

From such experiences comes maturity. From such actions, a boy starts to grow into a man. From such decisions the spirit of a man is born.

Less than two hours before, Terry was a stable boy, spending his days with shovel and horse brush. But the last hour had changed him in ways he might not even realize and wouldn't be able to explain. He had been tested as few young men are ever tested. A life and death test. That he had passed the test might register in his mind later. For now, it would be enough if both he and Sid could survive. And with that survival would come, within

Terry, a growing sureness, a confidence, a loss of fear. No, this would not come all at once. But it would be a start. These are the things a man needed, to take his place in the world.

He and Sid would face their disfiguring injuries later. But first they had to live through them.

In all likelihood, if Terry and Cindy had turned their horses and run for home, the big cat would have ignored them. The cat had its prey. That was enough. If it was one of the horses the cat had downed, the riders would have been wise to take their escape. But the cat's prey was Sid. And that truth just couldn't be ignored. There had been no thought of escape.

As his eyes closed, with pain and weariness crowding his mind, Terry's last, dimming thought was of the suffering horse, with the flies swarming around the torn flap of skin and the destroyed shoulder muscles. He knew he couldn't muster the strength to do anything about it.

"Sorry horse," was his last semi-awake thought.

CHAPTER 5

It seemed to be only seconds after he lay down that Terry felt a hand on his undamaged shoulder. He struggled to open his eyes. The dried blood on his left side held that eye firmly in its grip. But his right eye, although blurry with sweat, pain and sleep, did open. It took several moments for his awakening mind to pull him back to the present.

He slowly rolled onto his uninjured side, and with his good arm pushed himself to a sitting position. The movement brought new pain as his injured arm and shoulder moved under the dried blood, breaking the seal and starting the bleeding all over again.

Seeing Leon Noble studying him, Terry realized he'd been sleeping. Or, perhaps, more accurately, unconscious.

"You alive boy?"

"Seems like."

Leon waved several flies away from Terry's wounded arm and shoulder. He looked around, taking in the downed cougar, the still standing, but nearly dead horse, the injured and crudely bandaged straw boss, who was still unconscious, and then, Terry himself. "Got yourself a bit of a mess here, son. Looks like ya done good though."

Terry rubbed the sleep from his right eye and looked questioningly around the grassy battle site. Leon said, "No, there's no help here yet. Cindy found us with the cattle. She's sitting over there in the shade. I gave her my vest to take the place of her shirt. Don't rightly know how you managed to get her to give it up. Don't know as how she'll ever get over it either.

"Bull's riding for the ranch. He'll have help out here just as soon as he can. All we can do now is wait."

Terry sighed and lay back down. Again, he thought of the horse. "Can you do anything for the horse?"

"No. I'm not sure even the vet can help that poor brute. Should probably shoot it. But we'll wait and see. That's not my decision to make. You rest."

Terry lay back down and covered his eyes as best he could. Again, he thought it was only seconds before three vehicles bumped over the rocks and clumps of grass, into the battle site. Shouted voices told him that help was there. He sat up again. Mr. Stocker went first to Sid and decided there was nothing more to do without medical help. He then turned to Terry and made the same decision.

The ranch owner took a deep breath and looked carefully at his young worker. "I'll want the whole story Terry, but not now. You rest while we wait. I've phoned Calgary for a medevac helicopter. He'll be well on his way by now. We'll have you with good care just as soon as possible."

He stood in time to catch Cindy as she ran into his arms. "I was so scared Daddy. I thought we were all going to die."

Adam Stocker held his eldest daughter and hugged her

like he hadn't done in years. "You're alright now. Help is on the way and we'll get this situation under control. Why don't you go sit in the car while we wait?"

"I was no help Daddy. I cried and freaked out. Terry did everything while I was too scared to move. Now that we're safe, I'm ashamed of myself."

"We'll sort that all out later too. Don't you be worrying about it. Anyway, you did ride for help. That's no small thing." The thankful father led his daughter to the car and she took a seat.

Adam hollered across the meadow, "Leon, get all these horses out of here. Head back to the ranch. Lead that injured animal slowly. Get it to water as soon as you can. And you men, back those vehicles out. Give the helicopter room to land. I hear it coming now. Clear the area."

A rider who had stayed outside the wooded area waved his hat at the helicopter and pointed the direction to follow. The chopper dropped in altitude to where the pilot could see the clearing in the bush the rider was pointing him to.

As the chopper passed overhead the rider quickly put his hat back on and grabbed for the saddle horn. The horse's introduction to helicopters was proving to have a dramatic effect. He had no idea his favorite mount had that much life held in, just waiting for an excuse to unload. He was glad the short, violent ride was over before his mates arrived. If the other men had seen his off-sided ride, as he lost one stirrup, with his foot waving frantically, trying to get the stirrup back, while he wound up hanging onto the horn for the duration, they would have teased him unmercifully.

The chopper was soon on the ground with the medical team taking control.

CHAPTER 6

SID WOULD REQUIRE MANY WEEKS OF MEDICAL CARE and months of follow-up after he was released from the hospital. His injuries were disfiguring and painful. The doctor explained that wounds as deep as the big cat inflicted took a long time to heal. The worst, most damaging injuries touched muscles and nerves that may never fully heal. Infection was a major concern. The cat's claws and teeth were brimming with filth and bacteria.

One positive note was that the rancher had hauled the cat's carcass to the veterinarian where it was shown to be free of rabies.

During the following weeks Sid underwent many hours of restorative surgery, receiving hundreds of tiny stitches from the patient and thorough plastic surgeon.

Only his head, shoulder and arm were wounded, along with some deep scratches down his rib cage. His legs hadn't been touched by the attacking animal. After the first week in the hospital he was free to wander the hallways, as his strength and pain control would allow. He visited often with Terry.

The body slam from the big cat caused painful bruises over much of Terry's body. They started out a vivid purple-blue, but after the first week settled in to an ugly yellow. Pain kept the young man in bed for most of the first week. By the second week Sid and Terry were strolling the hall-ways together, each with an arm in a sling and with their heads bandaged, one eye covered, and carrying paper cups of coffee to the sun room. There, they sat silently, having already said pretty much everything that needed saying.

The families and crew visited as often as possible, but it was a long drive to Calgary from either the ranch or the patients' homes. On one visit Adam and Cindy arrived at Terry's room together. After the initial enquiries they found little to talk about. Terry, after all, was the stable boy. Adam was the owner and boss of the Lazy-S. They lived in different worlds.

It wasn't long before Adam said, "We'll, we'd best go see how Sid is doing."

With that he turned to the door with Cindy close on his heels. When Adam passed through the door into the hallway Cindy hesitated, and then turned back.

Stepping up beside the bed where the cowering Terry was holding the sheet tightly beneath his chin, as some kind of last line of defense, Cindy said, "You did a wonderful job and I was no help at all. I'm very grateful for my safety and for my life."

With a serious look she continued, "But don't you ever tell me to take my shirt off again. At least not until we're married."

With that she turned again to the door and was gone. Terry let out the breath he was holding and stared at the now empty doorway, his mind full of confusion.

His parents rushed to Terry's side as soon as Adam

Stocker called them. Terry's mother was all set to make a fuss about the rancher allowing her son to be in a place of danger, but Terry's father simply said, "Mother, let it go." The unstable woman said no more.

At the end of the second week Terry was released to home care. His parents drove to the hospital to assist in his discharge details and, perhaps, to take him home.

Adam Stocker and Willard Coombs had a long, private discussion about where Terry should go for convalescence.

Willard was feeling, looking and sounding more haggard than he usually did. Holding the home together, with the younger kids to care for, his demanding job, his unsteady wife, and now the added concern of his injured son, was pushing him to the limit.

"Adam, I'm sure you recognize that Melissa can be a burden. She can't help it, and the medical people offer no solution or relief. Ours is not a completely normal home.

"Obviously, Terry is welcome at home. That goes without saying more. And Melissa will do her best for him. But his preference is to go back to the ranch. He feels he'll be able to do most of his work after a few more days. Of course, the summer is nearly over, and his job was only for July and August. I'm really lacking wisdom on this."

Adam was a while answering.

Finally, he said, "I owe Terry. I owe him something more than just a job. He's done his job well this summer, doing everything he was asked to do. And I'm sure he can still do most of it, even with just the one good arm, once the soreness of those bruises works its way out of his system. But you're right. The summer is nearly over.

"I'm going to break a bit of a confidence here Willard, but I don't think it will matter too much. Terry told Sid that he feels he can't go back to school looking the way he does. He's afraid the other kids will see him as a freak or as something to joke about. Now, we may not agree with that but that's how Terry sees it. Kids, even senior high kids, can be thoughtless and cruel.

"He feels he doesn't want to return to school but he also desperately wants to complete his high school. So, there's a problem. I've taken some liberties that I'll share only with you. I don't want Terry thinking that I'm interfering. I went to see the local school board.

"Of course, the news of the cougar attack is all over the country. It was big news on all the broadcasts. The hospital did a great job keeping the cameras and reporters out of the patients' rooms. We've had something of a mini invasion out at the ranch. I'm proud of the way both Terry and Sid have handled the matter.

"The school board folks were very understanding when I asked them if Terry could stay at the ranch and complete his studies by correspondence. They agreed with just one condition; you would have to approve it, as his parent.

"My wife would help where she could, with bandages and such, and the crew would keep an eye on him. He could keep his job and his pay. There's a small private room in the bunkhouse that's not in use. He could have that for himself, so he could study in the afternoons. By next school year he should be healed up and ready to re-enter the world."

There was a little more discussion, but within a few days Terry was back at the ranch and back at work. His sore, bruised body was healing but his injured arm and shoulder were limiting the amount of work he could undertake. He still carried it in a sling except when he really needed two hands for a particular task. The doctor warned him to keep the bandages clean and to be careful of stressing the injured arm and shoulder. Terry compensated by using a smaller shovel and by using only his right arm in grooming the animals. He protected the bandages with a securely buttoned-up, long sleeved shirt.

He seldom saw Cindy after the new school year started. The few times he did see her she was a much more serious, thoughtful person. There seemed little doubt that the cougar incident had impacted her in ways that did not show up in bruises and bandages.

The long winter months saw expanded progress on the school studies. The cold weather meant the family's riding-animals were only being used occasionally. Terry was easily able to keep up with the work in the stables. The extra free hours he put into his studies. He could often be found sitting on a hay bale in the stable while he read one of his text books.

The injured young man avoided mirrors whenever possible. He reduced his shaving habits to once a week, sometimes even once in ten days. After each contact with a mirror, he found himself with repeated visions of his slowly healing scars, and the deep changes they would cause in his life. What he saw in the mirror in the full light of day he saw in half-awake visions during the night, visions he couldn't turn off.

For much of the school year it took all his determination to fight the discouragement that came with examining his future. He feared that doors would be closed to him. Doors that held good jobs or other opportunities behind them. Doors that led to places where his fellow workers would be uncomfortable looking at his scarred face.

Some days he wondered why he was bothering with

the studies. It might be easier to give it up, to stay on the Lazy-S and work with the regular cowboys. The cowboys accepted his looks and the cattle didn't care. Was that the wise solution?

Then, thinking more seriously and more long-term, he would pull himself back together and get on with the studies.

At the end of the school year the local correspondence students were required to gather at the school board offices to write final examinations. Big Mike loaned Terry the ranch pickup for the drive to High River. There he joined the small number of other students who would be sitting for the tests. Most of the correspondence students were from remote ranches or mining sites. The staring and whispering from the other students were a painful sample of what the scarred young man would face for the rest of his life. It was also adequate proof for Terry, that he was wise in not going back to the public school.

Terry was always a good student. Somewhat against the wishes of his parents, the school had put him a grade ahead in his elementary years. That action made him the youngest in his classes and added social stress to his already taxing home life. Although he was not socially adept, he had no problem with the course work.

When the envelope arrived at the ranch with his examination scores listed, he barely looked at the report. He skipped right to the bottom line where he saw the final grade and confirmation that his formal public-school years were completed. With a small smile of satisfaction, he folded the document and slid it into the pile of personal correspondence.

Terry's many stitches had been removed months before. The bandages were a distant memory. The painful bruising was all but forgotten. His arm and shoulder were slowly regaining their strength and flexibility. Or at least as much as they ever would. He still hung the sling around his neck each morning. Occasionally, after a hard hour or two of work, he liked to rest the arm.

But the facial scars, and the remembrance of the stark terror of the cougar attack, were permanent. So, it seemed, was Terry's reluctance to be involved in any kind of social or personal interaction. He was polite, but distant with Cindy, and the rest of the Stocker family. He never went to town with the men. He continued to send his paycheck to the bank. The balance was slowly growing.

Terry never saw or heard from Sid. When his stay in the hospital and rehab was completed, he went home. Terry wasn't sure where his home was. Sid's actions indicated that he didn't want to work or have fellowship or interaction with the old crew. Everyone seemed to be prepared to honor his decision.

Terry's scars, although serious, weren't as disfiguring as he first feared they would be. The reconstructive surgery had been done well. Still, for a young man to look in the mirror every day and see the remnants of claw marks angling across his face was a heavy burden to bear. He could, and did, hide the shoulder and arm scars with long sleeved shirts. If there was a good side to the whole thing it was that his eye escaped injury, although his eyelid sagged just a bit.

Terry, never comfortable in social settings, was more self-conscious than he had ever been, avoiding strangers and, especially, avoiding Cindy. He was surprised to have her walk into the stable and say, "I hear you did really well on your exams. I knew you would, as hard as you've worked. Good for you,"

Terry just nodded. The silence between them got a bit heavy.

Not knowing what else to say, Cindy asked, "Will you be joining the others at your old school in Red Deer for Grad?"

Terry answered, "That was a month ago. I wasn't invited. Wouldn't have gone if I was."

Again, the silence got heavy.

Cindy stepped a bit forward and placed one hand lightly on his damaged shoulder. "Well, I'll be having a Grad next year. I expect you to be there, with me hanging on your arm."

With both young people somewhat embarrassed, she turned and left the stable. Terry had no idea what to think or do.

Riding among the cattle or working with the cowboys had become his release. He saddled a bay gelding and rode out.

As a totally unexpected graduation gift from the crew, Terry was presented with the tanned hide of the cougar. It showed four bullet holes, plus the skinned notch on the top of the skull. The beautifully tanned, tawny hide was skillfully tied into a wooden frame with strips of leather thong. A plaque on the bottom simply said, Lazy-S and the date.

Although Terry didn't really think of it that way, the graduation, the completion of public school was another step along the way. Each step taking him further down the road to manhood and adult responsibility.

CHAPTER 7

BIG MIKE WAS TRUSTED WITH THE HIRING AND firing on the Lazy-S. Terry approached the foreman when no one else was around who might overhear their conversation. "Mike, I plan to attend college or university but not yet. I need to gain some experience and put away a few more dollars. I'd like to stay on here for the full of next year if you thought you could use me."

Mike, the ubiquitous toothpick clasped between his lips said nothing for a while as he studied the young stable hand. Mike was a good cattle man. Part of what made him good at his job was that he thought before he spoke or took action. A full minute went past, with Mike leaning on the top rail of a corral, staring at the mountains in the distance, and with Terry nervously scratching designs in the dirt of the ranch yard with the pointed toe of his riding boot.

Mike final spoke. "Figured as much. Mr. Stocker put out an advertisement for a replacement for you. Figured it was time you got out of the stable. You think you're ready for a job working cattle?"

"I'm already doing it a good bit."

Mike worked his toothpick while he studied his boots. He finally lifted his eyes to the hills beyond the ranch again. Terry followed the boss's look and knew what he was thinking.

"You'd have to work the back country, time to time. That excitement with the cat going to get in the way of your work?"

"I won't really know until another crises arises, but I don't think so. To have that happen twice seems like a long shot."

"I'll have to ask you to man the stable until we find a replacement for you."

Terry simply smiled and nodded, and the deal was done.

On a chilly October morning, the cook sent Beamer out to find Terry. "Tell him he's wanted on the phone. Long distance."

Terry trotted to the cookhouse and picked up the receiver. After saying hello, he listened as his father said, "Your mother is sick, son. She took a seizure during one of her spells. We nearly lost her last night. You need to come home."

Terry hung up the phone and stood there thinking. Was this the end of his dream for full time cattle work on the Lazy-S? Would he be back, or would his help be required at home?

He reluctantly made his way to where Big Mike was working and explained his situation. Mike listened and said only one word, "Go."

Terry thanked Big Mike, and as the two men were shaking hands Mike said, "It's all about family, Terry. Everything is about family. Go. They need you."

As he walked away Terry asked himself, 'what was that all about'?

Mike seldom left the ranch. Terry had never seen him receive or read a letter, and he never talked about family. Even when the younger riders were laughing and joking about friends and family, Big Mike remained silent. Perhaps that water ran a little deeper than Terry had ever considered before.

Terry had accumulated few possessions during his time at the ranch. Not sure what the coming days and months might entail if his mother's health deteriorated further, he packed everything into the metal suitcase and army duffle he carried with him on his arrival at the Lazy-S. He finished his work and cleaned up his room in the bunk house.

The next morning Adam Stocker drove him to High River, where he would be on time to catch the bus north. Cindy joined the two men for the short trip.

Mr. Stocker shook his hand. "Keep in touch Terry, we'd like to have you back if it works out that way. Be sure to let us know what's happening. And remember to greet your father for me."

Cindy and Terry were both reluctant to show any form of affection. That they had feelings for each other was no secret, but how to express those feelings was something neither one had figured out. Cindy took the lead. She simply said, "Bye. I'll pray for your mother, that all will go well." Terry stoically nodded and picked up his duffle and suitcase. Just before he turned to enter the bus depot, he looked at Cindy. His chin lifted a bit and he pursed his lips. Cindy waited for him to say something. Terry just nodded his head, turned and walked away.

Arriving at the depot at Red Deer shortly after noon,

Terry didn't find anyone waiting to pick him up. Somewhat surprised and disappointed, he flagged a waiting cab and asked the driver to take him on the short trip to the hospital. A foul October wind was driving dust and fallen leaves in a swirling pattern across the city streets. It was not a pleasant day for walking.

The hospital reception clerk let him stash his luggage in the corner of her booth while she directed him to room 278. He climbed the single flight of stairs and started towards his mother's room.

"Terry. This way son." The voice came from behind him.

He turned to see his distraught father walking slowly from the private counselling room beside the nurses' station. Terry thought his father had aged ten years in the few months since he had last seen him.

The two men came together and shook hands. Willard suddenly pulled Terry towards himself and wrapped him in his arms, something that had not happened since Terry was a child. Breaking the hug, Willard kept his arm draped across Terry's shoulders, while he directed him back to the private room.

Once inside, with the door closed Willard said, "Son, I'm just as sorry as I can possibly be. She's gone Terry. About one half hour ago. She had another seizure yesterday. The doctors felt they probably had it under control, but just a short while ago, she had another one. I was sitting at her bedside. She was sleeping peacefully after a pretty good morning. Suddenly, her head jerked sideways, and her whole body shook and trembled. After maybe thirty seconds, her eyes opened, as if in wonder at what she was seeing. Her mouth made a big 'O'. She kept that startled, joyful look on her face until she quit breathing. I don't think she even saw me or knew I was there. It was almost like she was seeing something wonderful and amazing. And then she was gone.

"She had a hard life, Terry. She prayed so often for release from her illness. Now, she's released for sure. I pray it was her reward that she was seeing."

Willard paused to wipe tears from his eyes. In a moment, with his voice halting and broken he continued. "You and I and the kids will miss her, and we'll cry in our hurts, but your mother is at rest. Resting from all her trials and troubles. And all her pain and sadness. I hope you'll come to see it that way."

The two men stood silently for a few seconds. Terry suddenly collapsed into an overstuffed couch that was there for the comfort of those who needed it. Momentarily he forgot the turmoil of their home, and the reason he had escaped to the Lazy-S. He forgot the frantic ups and downs his mother went through as uncontrollable, inner, impulses took control of her actions. Any resentful or hard thoughts he secretly held were forgotten. At least for a while. As the oldest sibling, rightly or wrongly, he often thought he was forced into carrying the heaviest load. Did all that make him strong, or just tough? The two are not the same.

With the challenges of the ranch work, the horrible memories of the fight with the big cat, the months of tedium, grinding his way through the correspondence books, plus hiding his scarred face from any strangers that showed up on the ranch, it felt like he had found it necessary to be strong, sometimes faking it, for too long. With the death of his mother, the last of his strength seemed to ease out of him, leaving him weak and empty. He sank onto the couch without a strong or rational thought in his head.

The silence dragged on until Terry finally looked up at his father. "Is she still in the room? Can I see her?"

"I'll check," answered Willard. He turned and left. but was back in less than a minute. He held out his hand, "Come quickly. The staff were just going to move her, but they'll give us a few minutes."

Terry and his father stood together at the bedside. At first there were no words. Terry lifted her hand and held it. He had never seen nor touched a dead body before. It somehow didn't bother him as much as trying to stem the blood flow on Sid's battered body.

Willard pushed some hair off his wife's face and lovingly brushed her cheek with the back of his hand. Willard again placed his arm across Terry's shoulders. "She suffered so much Terry. She knew when she was acting up. She was aware that she was hurting the ones she loved. But she couldn't seem to control herself. It was as if something was burning up inside, driving her emotions. Afterwards she would feel so guilty. She cried herself to sleep many and many a night, wishing and praying that things could be better. She trusted the Lord and prayed for healing. Healing didn't come. But she kept on praying and trusting.

"In the chaos that we sometimes lived in I know you didn't always see it, or even believe it, but she loved you most of all. A mother isn't supposed to have favorites I guess, but there it is. She loved the other kids, of course, but you were the oldest, the first. My, how she delighted in you when you were a baby. When I came home from work, I would have to listen to the details of all the wonderful things you did during the day. As the other kids came along, she seemed to get sicker, losing control more often, and much of our family joy disappeared. Perhaps we shouldn't have had more kids, but your mother wanted each one of you.

"The only time I heard her angry at God was when you were hurt. I had a hard time settling her down after that.

"You'll miss her Terry and you'll have questions. But don't ever question your mother's special love for you."

As father and son left the room Terry asked, "Do the others know?"

"No, we'll drive together to the school."

CHAPTER 8

THE NEXT WEEK WAS THE MOST DIFFICULT IN TERRY'S young life. The weeping kids. His own troubled thoughts and sadness. The confused and lost look on his father's face. The relatives from near and far coming to mourn and encourage. The funeral. And the questions; so many questions. The biggest question was, 'what now'?

The Lazy-S was at the funeral in some strength. Mr. Stocker was generous in allowing the crew to join the family in showing respect. Sid was not with them.

When the ranch crew were leaving to go back south, Terry shook hands with the men, and even with Mrs. Stocker, but he froze inside when Cindy approached. With no familiarity with death, neither of them knew how to proceed or what to say. They simply looked intently into each other's eyes briefly, before Cindy turned to the waiting car.

CHAPTER 9

TERRY'S TWO BROTHERS, CLIVE, AGE SIXTEEN, Andrew, age ten, and his sister, Sandra, nicknamed 'Sis', born between the two boys, was twelve, going on eighteen, had each lived with the chaos of the home and carried the maturity, the self-reliance and the scars.

It seemed natural that the troubles in the home left their mark on each of the kids.

Clive was a good student, but like his older brother, was socially inept and was finding it difficult to cope in the rush of high school life.

Sis was the social butterfly of the family; pretty and gregarious, but her grades barely met the passing criteria. There were pitfalls in the road ahead for the young lady if she didn't get more direction in her life.

Andrew was smart enough to do well in his studies but was lethargic and largely uninterested in book work.

Willard held a demanding and exacting job as a senior accountant for a local farm machinery manufacturer. He came from work each day, tired and ready for a relaxing evening. It had been difficult enough with his unstable wife running the home. With three younger children in the home and no wife to keep the domestic whirl under some semblance of control, Willard was not at all sure how he would manage. He was a reasonably good cook, but it took more than food to hold a family together. It would be good to have someone take over the major home responsibilities but there was no one. It would be unfair to hold Terry back as some kind of house or family manager, caring for his younger siblings. Terry had to have his chance to move forward.

The solution to the family problems was suggested by Eli Chambly, the owner of the Double C ranch. Eli was an old family friend. Willard's father and Eli went through basic training together in 1939 and shipped out together. Perhaps because they were both at the upper age limit for active duty, the two men, one a city school teacher and the other a rancher's son, became lifelong friends. Both men returned safely and were discharged from the Army. Willard's father died too young but Willard's friendship with the old rancher continued long after his father was gone.

Eli suggested his solution, as he did with ranch matters, in such a way that he was difficult to ignore. He arrived at the funeral looking exactly like what he had always been; a rancher with more interest in land and cattle than he had in his personal appearance. Although his jeans were clean, and he had brushed his hat and kicked the worst off his boots, there was no disguising what he was. Old Eli, as everyone called him, had never heard the saying, "You clean up pretty good." He would have snorted at the idea.

Leaving the cemetery after the internment service, Willard noticed his old rancher friend standing alone, hat in hand, cold rain falling on his balding head. Willard broke stride and motioned for the rest of the family to continue on to the cars. He reached out his hand to Eli, "It's good of you to come Eli."

"Almost didn't." The old rancher still hadn't grasped the outstretched hand. "Thought maybe we wasn't friends no more, you not calling for help and all."

Old Eli was famous for his booming voice. A lifetime bachelor, with no woman to gentle him down, his life had been land, cattle, horses, cowboys and the weather that was a constant challenge. His cowboy or cattle voice could be heard most of the way across a quarter section, but he had never been heard to raise his voice towards a horse.

Everyone at the funeral heard him challenge Willard.

Willard continued to hold out his hand. "It happened awful sudden Eli. There was just no time. But I know you'd be the first here if I'd called out."

Eli completed the handshake with a crushing grip. Willard's accountant's hand was not up to the challenge.

Willard clasped his free hand over Eli's in a three handed gesture that embarrassed the old man. "Eli, can you stay a while. It's too crowded today for a private visit but I'd love to sit with just you, if we can break away from the crowd later tonight or perhaps tomorrow."

"I'm here until you get smart enough to ask an old friend for help." People looked at the two men to assure themselves that the shouting was friendly.

Willard pulled his hand away and gestured at the line of waiting cars. "Come to the house Eli. We'll make a time."

Hours later, the house guests had mostly said their goodbyes, the worst of the noise settled down. Two of Terry's aunts tackled the mountain of dirty dishes. The freezer was full of donated casseroles. The fridge was jammed with desserts. The three younger kids escaped to their rooms. Sis was playing music with two girl cousins that she hadn't seen for a while. Terry escaped to a basement room with a book. He felt that if he had to explain his claw scratches one more time he might say or do something he'd later regret.

Willard made his way to the kitchen where he found Eli slurping coffee at the big oak table, ignoring the critical glances of the two dish washing aunts. Eli, a kind and generous man, but rough around the edges, had little time for fussing. There had never been the need. If the aunts were bound and determined to fuss, he wasn't about to either help nor hinder. Let them do as they wished.

Willard quietly said, "If we were to grab our jackets and sneak out through the garage door, we just might be able to find some peace and quiet at the corner coffee shop."

Eli left his half cup of coffee sitting in a series of brown, concentric rings on the oilcloth table covering, which drew another critical glare from the fussy aunt. Eli didn't notice.

The cold, fall day had turned into a nasty evening, with sleet and high winds. Except for two teenagers sipping sodas in the back booth, Willard and Eli had the place to themselves. Sensible people were home, sitting by the fire.

Willard started the conversation by saying, "Eli, we come here for a meal, on occasion, so the staff know me. Let's keep our voices down. I don't want the whole country knowing my business."

The conversation stopped while the server placed two cups of unordered coffee on the table. The young lady, who knew Willard was a coffee drinker, modestly touched him on the shoulder and said, "I heard. I'm sorry."

When the men were alone again Willard asked his old rancher friend, "So how goes it on the Double C?"

"The Double C and everything about it are doing just fine. But that ain't why we're sitt'n here. We're sitt'n here paying good money for coffee when there's a free pot back at the house because you and I have to talk. Privately. Mostly, I have to talk. You have to listen."

The two men sipped coffee while they studied each other. Between sips, Willard seemed to be holding his breath. Finally, with a great escaping of that held breath, he blurted out, "I have no idea what comes next, Eli. I don't even know where to start."

Eli put down his cup, folded his arms on the café table, looked Willard directly in the eye and said, "Well, do we go around and around with the problem, feeling sorrier and sorrier as we go, or do you listen to my answer?"

"I'd look forward to hearing your answer."

"Alright then. The answer is the Double C, same as it's been the answer ever since Melissa took too sick to give proper care to you and those kids." As Willard opened his mouth to respond Eli held up his hand to stop him. "I know, I know. The ranch is a distance away. But I drove in here this morning in less than one hour. There's folks in the big cities that do that, and more, every day of their lives. On top of that, your office is on the east side of town, which cuts more minutes off your driving time. Were you in Calgary you could sit at red lights for longer than that. So, let it go and let's talk about possibilities."

Willard's shoulders slumped as he gave in to Eli's argument. "Alright. I'm listening."

"Good. Listen carefully. And understand that I'm not saying I have it all figured out. Not exactly, I mean. I figure if we can rough it out and get a start, you and the kids can sort out the details."

Willard waited while his old friend took a big slurp of coffee and then waved his mug at the server, asking for a refill.

"OK. So out on the Double C, there sits a big, mostly empty house. Ain't cost'n me nothing to have it sit there. Wouldn't cost you nothing either, were you to come live there. More room than you have here in this little rented place. In the yard a short jump away is my cottage. Used to be, I had ranch hands hanging their hats in the cottage, but now it sits empty. Only got one hand and he lives on his own small spread a short ways to the south. Nice little home, that cottage. Often wondered why I was holding down the big house for just me. Could have rented out the house and taken up the cottage, many's the time, but didn't do it. Now's the time.

"On top of a big, free house, we got space. Lots of space. You've told me yourself that the kids are doing only so – so in school and not even that well in their out-of-school lives. They're not much interested in sports or other activities. But when they come to the Double C for summers, they're great kids. They love the horses. They're a help with the chores; gathering eggs, cleaning and feeding the horses, and such. They become different people.

"Those kids need to be in the fresh country air with worthwhile things to challenge them when their school day is done. When they come home from school to the Double C, they're not alone. Always folks around the ranch. Be good for you too.

"My friend Bea, old widow Handley, she comes over

time to time to clean and straighten up around, do the washing and such. Sometimes I'm not exactly sure what she does. Maybe just finding excuses to get out for a couple of hours. Near drives me crazy. But I put up with it cause her husband was a great friend for more years than I can count. Can't find a thing after she's done straightening up. Moves stuff around for no reason I can see. Threw away a stack of Ranchers Digest magazines. Never heard the like. Come near to runn'n 'er off, that time."

Willard broke into the conversation with a laugh. "I remember that Eli. You've been standing on that story near as long as I can remember. That's got to be at least five years ago. Are you still grumbling about that with the poor woman?"

"Well, I wasn't happy, you can be sure of that. But I let it go. Old girl needs someone to fuss over I'm thinking. Would probably kick up an awful bother were I to send her packing. Didn't talk to me for a week after the one time I offered to pay her.

"Anyways, the thing is that she would jump at the chance to do for you and the kids as well. Not regular. I don't mean she's going to cook all your meals or noth'n like that. but she'd be a help. Good for Sis too. A young girl needs someone like Bea to help her into becoming a responsible lady.

"You pack up and move to the big house. I'll take my few things and set up housekeeping in the cottage. Bea Handley can fuss over all of us and really feel as if she's doing something. Be good for everyone. The school bus will stop right at the gate. The school is smaller than the big city schools but it's a good school. I know that personally. You'll remember that I served on the school board for nearly twenty years. Only interest outside the Double C I ever had. Worth it though. We've got good schools all over the county."

Again, Eli slurped his coffee. The kids in the back booth both turned to see where the noise was coming from. Eli didn't notice the kids. Looking intently at Willard he said, "Now, I know your tired brain is going in circles trying to find a reason to not listen to an old man, but I can save you all that wear and tear on your grey matter. The Double C is the right solution at the right time. There's nothing else to think about."

The conversation went around and around for some time but finally the two old friends called it a night. Braving the weather, they made their way to the car and back to the now silent house. Eli insisted on pointing his pickup truck towards the Double C. "Got early chores. Can't get no work done lay'n abed in the big city."

Willard didn't argue, even though the truth was that Eli's hired hand did most of the normal work. Other than the horses, which were Eli's first love, the only time he got busy himself was at calving, and that event was some months away.

Just as he was leaving he said, "Willard, I need you to give the car to Terry in the morning. I want to see him at the ranch. He and I need to talk."

Willard looked puzzled. "He's right here. Why can't you talk now?"

"We need to talk at the ranch. First thing in the morning." The rancher left no room for dispute.

CHAPTER 10

Terry drove into the Double C ranch yard at nine the next morning. The weather had not improved. He sat in the car with the wipers slapping mushy snow from side to side while he wondered where Eli would be. He saw no sign of life anywhere. Finally, he decided to take a look in the old hip-roofed barn that stood tall and straight for seven or eight decades and was now fixed up as a suitable stable for Eli's treasured horses. He eased to a stop as close as possible to the barn, jumped from the car and made his way to the door. Just as he was about to reach for the door handle Eli's booming voice shouted out to him from the adjoined corral.

"About ready to give up on you. Thought they might have showed you how to get up in the morning down there on the Lazy-S."

Eli was walking towards the barn while he talked. "Well, anyway welcome. Let's get ourselves into the building and out of this snow." He reached past Terry and opened the door.

Once inside, Eli reached his hand out for a handshake,

surprised at the returned strength from the young visitor. "Well, Terry, by the roughness of your hand and the strength of your fingers, I'd guess Stocker had you doi'n a bit of work the past couple of years. You look good. You've grown well Terry. Glad to see it. You're strong, you stand up straight, and you look a feller in the eye. I like that in a man."

Eli turned and started to walk away. He motioned with his arm for Terry to follow. "Want to show you something."

The two men walked to the end of the row of horse stalls. There were horses tied in most of them. A high sided box-stall held a well-groomed grey mare and a fine-looking colt wearing the identical grey coat. "Isn't that just about the finest sight your eyes ever fell on?"

He leaned on the top rail, smiling as he admired the pair of horses. "You think back some Terry, you might remember the mare. Only she wasn't a mare when you last saw her. I bought her near five years ago. Brought her to the Double C direct from her weaning. You was here the day the breeder drove into the yard with her in the trailer. You remember that? Course, you seen her as a young filly after that too. Now here she is a full grown-up mama with the most beautiful colt at her side."

Terry leaned forward as if to stick his head right into the stall. "I remember. She was so nervous she was shivering and skittish. Liked to of pulled the lead rope right out of your hand. Didn't settle down until you touched her. Seems like after just a minute of patting her and running your hand over her she recognized you for a friend."

Terry looked up at Eli, who was several inches taller than him. "And this is that same little girl all growed up?

What do you call her? Seems I remember you calling her Queenie when she was just a mite of a thing. Did you stick with that?"

"You've a good memory Terry. Queenie she was and Queenie she still is. Never could think of her no other way. Haven't named the colt yet though. I've got some plans for this pair I'll tell you about, but first you and me have to do some talking. There's stove heat and hot coffee at the house."

Within a few minutes they were seated at the kitchen table with steaming mugs before them. When Eli walked past the car and shuffled through the snow-covered grass and gravel of the ranch yard, Terry walked beside him. Terry thought to drive the two hundred feet, but Eli didn't even look at the car.

Terry glanced up as the kitchen door opened. He hadn't seen Mrs. Handley for nearly three years. Still tall and thin, with her hair wrapped in a silver-white bun, she looked about the same as he remembered, just a bit older. He didn't get a chance to say hello or greet her in any way.

"Why, if'n that ain't Terry Coombs, my old eyes are deceiving me. And what a sight for these old eyes." Terry stood up to greet her.

"Why Terry, you're the handsomest man that's been on this sorry ranch for many a year. Ain't he a fine looking man, Eli? Course, why ask you. If'n it don't have four legs and live in a barn you don't have much opinion to judge by."

She stepped the rest of the way into the kitchen and wrapped Terry in her strong arms. She then backed off and gently ran her fingers along Terry's scars. He froze up inside, but he tried not to flinch.

"We all heard the story Terry. We feared for you,

waiting for news day by day. Had a couple of special prayer meetings down at the church hall, praying for God's mercy on you. You and the other injured man, as well. And look at you now. A fine-looking young man, handsome and strong. Why, I had to look twice to see those itty-bitty scratches. Don't amount to hardly noth'n at all."

She turned Terry loose to re-take his seat and turned to Eli after a glance at the floor. "You old coot, I don't suppose it occurred to you to wipe your boots before you slopped yard soil and snow all across this floor. It's a wonder nobody's shot you before now, just on general principles. Might have done it myself but then I'd just have to clean up the mess afterwards."

As she was pouring a cup of coffee Eli winked at Terry. "Don't pay no never mind to the widow, Terry. She's like this most of the time. The mercy is that she's getting senile, so by tomorrow she'll have forgot all about the things she said and did today. I wouldn't keep her around at all except she can turn out a fair feed of beef and mashed potatoes when pushed to it."

When Bea was sitting at the table with her hands wrapped around a steaming mug she looked again at Terry. "Don't be following this old fool's naming of me. Name's Bea. I'd like it if you'd call me Bea."

Terry had no idea how to respond to the back and forth between these old friends and neighbors. He knew Mrs. Handley's late husband had been a close friend to Eli. He suspected there was more behind the banter than met the eye, probably not romance, knowing Eli, but something was there. He just didn't know what it was.

Eli turned to Bea and nodded at Terry. "Tough day yesterday for this young man."

Bea softly touched Terry's arm. "I know. Nothing more difficult than saying goodbye to a loved one Terry. But the sun keeps coming up and God is still in His rightful place, ready to pour out His love on you and the family. I pray you'll recognize His comfort and lean on Him."

After a short pause in the conversation Eli turned to Bea and said, "I'll be moving to the cottage. Not right away. Probably not until the Christmas holidays. If you could find the time to look at what all needs doing, I'd appreciate it."

Suspecting the two men had more to discuss, Bea quietly placed her coffee mug in the sink, slipped into her coat and left to examine the cottage.

Eli leaned back in his chair and studied Terry for a long half minute. "I wondered why you didn't come to me for a job when you went to the Lazy-S, Terry. Care to comment on that?"

"I thought about it. I came up with a couple of reasons that seemed right at the time. Still seem right, I think. I was afraid you'd give me a kid job, just because we were family friends. And then, I really wanted to get far enough away so that it wouldn't be easy for the folks to be on my back. That might seem selfish saying it right out like that. but that's the way it was. I was starting to gather hard feelings towards my mother. I had to get away to let those feeling mellow out.

"The Lazy-S turned out to be a good solution. Of course, I didn't figure to stay so long. That cat changed everything."

Eli was quiet for an uncomfortably long time. When he finally spoke, he started in abruptly. "You like the cattle business? You think you could learn it?"

Terry answered, "On the Lazy-S, I spent more time with horses than cattle, but the answer would be yes. I like it and believe I could be good at the job. I don't know the business end of it though. I expect Dad could help explain that if I needed to know, him being an accountant and all."

"Alright, here's the deal I have for you. Your dad and I talked last evening. He's going to have a family meeting tonight when you're all home. I've suggested that this big house needs a family in it. Your family. Bea would take care of the woman things. I don't mean she'd cook every meal. You'll have to do a lot for yourselves, but she'll watch over things and help Sis become a woman. You live here – the younger kids take their schooling here and you and I work cattle.

"Scotty does most of the hard work now. He's a neighbor. Lives south a few miles. Doesn't live on the CC. He could use some help with the harder jobs. Especially at calving time. I do what I can, but I can't work like I used to. You'd be learning the business and helping me at the same time. You get to know the business you could move on into whatever part of the cattle world you'd want to."

There was silence around the table for a few moments while Terry digested what he had just heard. Finally, Eli continued. "Now, I know you figured on getting more education and that's a good thing. You're still young and you're smart. You help me keep the Double C moving along. I'll pay you a fair wage. You bank your money and in a couple of years you can be off to school. Study whatever you want. And have the money to do it. Maybe you'll marry that pretty little gal I saw making moon eyes at you. I suspect she's Stocker's daughter. You get you some cattle smarts. You marry that gal. Next thing we know you'll be running the Lazy-S."

Terry had no response. He was afraid to comment for fear of exposing the truth of Eli's words regarding Cindy. Some things he hadn't really admitted to himself yet.

CHAPTER 11

At home that evening, Willard placed Eli's ideas before the gathered family. The discussion didn't start well.

Sis didn't want to leave her school friends.

Clive was worried about starting over in a new school, among guys raised on farms and ranches. The academics didn't concern him but being a social misfit concerned him very much. He was already weak in that area. He didn't need another complication.

Andrew couldn't care one way or another. Given opportunity he would have closed his school books and forgotten about them, if he could work on the ranch for wages.

Terry showed his acceptance of the plan by saying nothing.

It took considerable back and forth discussion, bordering on argument, but a decision was finally made.

The family would move to the Double C during the Christmas break from school. Terry would move to the ranch immediately. He and Eli would stay in the big house until the family arrived. The two men figured they could survive on their own cooking.

Bea wasn't so sure. She figured she'd plan for more frequent trips to the Double C than she had before. At least until everyone found out how the arrangement was working. She could keep a few prepared meals in the fridge. And perhaps a dessert or two.

Terry dove into ranch work with enthusiasm, often working more hours than either Eli or Scotty, the hired hand. His familiarity with horses had been well honed on the Lazy-S.

In the early morning dimness of the stable, lit by a single light in the center of the runway, Terry smoothed the hair on the back of a big black gelding. He then went to the tack room and brought out the saddle Eli had assigned to him. Carefully, but quickly, he spread a blanket and checked for wrinkles. He then hoisted the heavy saddle and gently laid that on top of the blanket. A quick wiggle to settle it in place, a smooth tying of the girth strap, and the animal was ready for a day's work. Swapping the halter for a bridle, Terry led the horse outside and swung aboard.

Saddling his own animal in an adjoining stall, Eli followed every move Terry made. Those movements were smooth, the job done with no wasted motions. Eli followed Terry to the door. The big light mounted above the stable door allowed him to watch as the young man trotted his horse across the yard, to the pasture gate. "Going to make a good horseman, that young fellow."

Winter arrived in early November. With a lifetime of cold country ranching behind him, Eli had the Double C ready for whatever the weatherman threw his way. Years before, when still a prideful, self-assured young man, Eli had been caught short by a mid-October blast of winter that settled in and staying until April. It was a lesson to be learned that Eli never forgot.

The last few items needed to prepare for winter could be completed by Scotty and Terry in just a day or two.

Scotty, taking Terry under his wing, patiently showed the young man what had to be done to have the tractor and bale wagon serviced and ready for the long, cold, months ahead.

Together, they completed the last repairs on the feed mangers, replacing a few broken planks. While Scotty replaced a broken plank on the corral, Terry fussed over the two water tanks, lighting a test fire in each small coal and wood burner that would keep the water free of ice in the bitter cold to come.

Assured that all was in readiness, the two men saddled up and moved the animals towards the wintering yard.

The first job facing the riders before winter set in was weaning, separating the calves from their protective mamas.

"We're late getting 'er done this year, Terry," explained Eli. "We had a few late births. Wanted to give them a bit more time to grow on their mama's milk before they left off to be on their own."

Eli manned the corral gate while Scotty, his horse seeming to be one step ahead of the rider, separated the calves from the cows. The calves, one by one, were pushed into the corral. Terry moved the separated cows away from the group, trying to hold them at a distance, to make Scotty's task easier. The bawling and bellowing of the distressed animals made conversation nearly impossible.

At mid-morning, with Terry holding the separated cows back, Scotty rode to the stable and saddled a fresh horse. Only when Scotty returned did Terry go for a fresh ride.

By noon the separation was complete. Three hundred fifty bellowing cows were milling about in the feed yard, held back by Terry, while three hundred forty-two calves were bawling for their mamas in the big corral by the barn.

Terry and Scotty worked together to push the cows into the far pasture. The distance between the two groups of animals would make the pain of weaning a little less trying on mama and baby, both.

For the cows there was a bit of grass for grazing, showing above the inch of snow. The men would deliver a few bales of hay as a supplement. The cows could get by on snow water for a few days, until the weaned calves settled down, and the cows could again be brought to the main wintering yard, where there would be abundant water available.

With the last of the cows moved into the pasture, Terry drew the barb wire gate closed. There was very little slack in the wire-and-post gate. Terry had to wrap his arm around the first gate post and pull the gate toward the fence post. He then was able to drop the wire bale into place. He turned and nodded at Scotty and then climbed back onto his riding animal. The two men were in a happy frame of mind on the ride back to the corrals, satisfied that a big job had been completed.

That changed in a flash of time.

Scotty rode up to the corral thinking to sit a minute and admire the fine gathering of calves. As he approached the corral, he saw a boot protruding from beneath the bottom rail. 'What the?' he thought to himself. He swung down and ran the last couple of steps. Closer, it was easy to see Eli lying in the muck of the corral, one leg curled under him, his hat slanted sidewise across his face and one hand gripping his chest. A couple of curious calves were edging towards him.

"Terry. Terry. Quick. Eli's down."

"What do you mean down?" Terry hollered over the bawling of the calves. Without waiting for an answer, he swung his horse towards the corral gate. He leaped off the animal, not bothering to tie it, opened the gate and knelt beside Eli. Scotty lifted Eli's hat from his face.

The old man's eyes were closed. A look of extreme pain was frozen to his face. He appeared to be unconscious, but still breathing. Neither of the men knew what to do.

Terry's experience with the big cat was a matter of stopping the bleeding. This was a totally different situation. Finally, Terry made a decision. "I'll get the truck."

There was little gentleness in the way the men loaded their boss into the pickup. Terry sat behind the wheel with Scotty sitting on the passenger's side, holding Eli upright between them. He took a grip on Eli's hair to stop his head from flopping around.

Terry eased the truck over the roughness of the pasture and out the gate into the ranch yard. He pulled to a stop, leaped to the ground to close the gate, and had the vehicle moving again in just a few seconds. There was much he didn't know about the Big Valley country. "Is there a doctor in town?"

"There's one moves between here and a couple of small towns in the area. I don't know what day he's here. Better head for Red Deer."

In spite of the slushy snow embedded into the gravel road, the trip took barely one-half hour of sometimes harrowing driving. Scotty held Eli with one hand and braced himself against the dash board with the other. Several times, as the truck slewed around on the wet road, he glanced at the young driver, but he said nothing.

Terry pulled the truck to a stop at the hospital emergency entrance and lay a heavy hand on the horn. He didn't let up until he saw activity inside, as three nurses moved towards the door. He swung out of the truck and around to the passenger side. When he heard the hospital door open he turned towards it. "Got trouble here. Suspect it's a heart attack but I'm not sure."

Two nurses ran inside and were back in a few seconds with a gurney. They pulled the gurney up to the truck door while another girl climbed into the driver's side. The nurse who seemed to be in charge spoke to Scotty. "Ease on out of there while Gail holds him."

Scotty let go of Eli and carefully stepped to the ground. Gail held his head and shoulder, keeping him upright, while the other two nurses slid their arms under his legs and back. They tried to lift Eli, but it wasn't going to work. The cramped space wouldn't allow them to get a firm grip, plus, the old man, as slim as he was, still carried more weight than the two ladies were able to manage. The head nurse let go of Eli's legs, stepped to the propped-open hospital door and yelled, "Toby, get your butt out here."

Toby reached into the truck and gently lifted Eli in his strong arms. He turned and placed the still unconscious man onto the gurney. One of the nurses steadied Eli's head during the transfer. The well-practiced staff soon had the patient inside, an oxygen mask in place, and with a doctor summoned from somewhere in the hospital. Terry left to park the truck while the nurse directed Scotty to the waiting room. "There's nothing more you can do. Leave it to us for now. I'll come find you just as soon as we know anything." She delivered this message with a small smile. Scotty obediently made his way to the waiting room.

The two young men sat for a while, twirling their hats between their fingers and puzzling over what to do next. Terry stood. "I'd better call Dad. He'll want to know right away."

Scotty nodded and said, "When you're finished, I'll call my wife. She can call Bea and a few of the neighbors."

With that done the waiting continued. Scotty found the hospital cafeteria and returned to the waiting room with coffee for the two of them.

Willard left work early and rushed to the side of his old friend. When none of the staff were prepared to comment on the old man's condition, he hunted up a nurse he knew from his wife's several trips to the hospital. He pleaded until she said, "Take a seat in the waiting room. Let me see what I can find out."

She was back in a short while with a brief report. "Your friend is alive. That alone is a miracle, with the seriousness of the heart attack, on top of the way he was handled and the distance the men had to carry him. The staff have done what they can do. The doctor will check him often. He has a nurse by his side watching the monitors. If he survives the next couple of hours, he should be alright. I say alright, but you understand he'll never be truly well again. It was really quite a serious event."

Willard received this news as stoically as he knew how. The injuries to Terry, the loss of his beloved Melissa, the upset in the family, and now this. He was stressed and bewildered. He thanked his friend and took his seat again.

As he sat down, his mind spun to their recent plans. Their time to move to the Double C was fast approaching.

Eli's health crises could easily become the Coombs family crises.

The two ranch hands sat quietly until Scotty finally said, "There's things to be done on the Double C. I'd better get back out there and see to it. Those calves were only weaned a few hours ago too. I wouldn't want anything to go wrong now."

Terry looked over at his father. Willard waved his hand. "You two go. I'll stay close-by here. The kids can make their own supper. Your main job right now is the ranch. Go see to it."

CHAPTER 12

WHEN TERRY AND SCOTTY ARRIVED BACK AT THE ranch, Bea was there. She had coffee ready and a meal waiting. The two men brought her up to date, one talking while the other ate, talking turns as if by design. Bea was clearly distraught, wringing her hands, sitting down and then getting up again and pacing the floor, before sitting down again. Neither of the boys commented.

Scotty and Terry checked the animals, dropping feed where necessary and topping up the water tanks for the calves. Terry said, "Go home Scotty. I'll look after the horses and hang around the corral until dark. If dad phones with news, I'll call you right away."

With the setting of the sun and with Terry not seeing any work left undone, he sat at the kitchen table with Bea. Again, she had food ready. Cooking seemed to be a release for her.

When the phone rang, Terry and Bea both jumped, startled out of their private thoughts. The call was from Willard. He said, "Eli is awake and feeling not too bad. He seems to be aware of what's happened. He asked about the ranch and the weaning, so I took that as a good sign. But he wants to see you this evening Terry. Can you get away from the work and come in here now?"

"The works done. Bea is here. She made supper. Scotty went home. There's nothing stopping me from coming in. I'll throw on some clean clothes and get on the way. Is Eli still in emergency?"

"No, he's in room 352. Come directly there."

When Terry arrived at Eli's room he was met by his father and another man, plus a nurse who continued to keep an eye on the monitors. Terry walked directly to the bed. "How goes it Eli?"

The old man wiggled around on the mattress a bit and made motions as if he wanted to sit up. The nurse gently pushed him back down. Eli gave her a searing look, but finally resigned himself to the restrictions.

"I'm fine Terry. How is it on the Double C?"

"All's well. Scotty went home. He's sitting by the phone waiting for news. Bea came over and made enough food for the whole neighborhood. She's sitting by the phone too. The cattle are fine. Bawling a bit for their calves, but not as bad as this morning. Horses are all cared for."

Eli nodded at all this before pointing at the man standing beside Willard. "This here is young Walpole. His father was my lawyer since back when we first started the Double C. Died couple of years ago. Smart man. Hope the son is just as smart, but I might not live long enough to find out."

Terry looked over at the lawyer who was probably nearing fifty years of age. He couldn't imagine how old the father must have been. He reached out his hand to the lawyer. "Terry. I've been working at the Double C for a short while."

The lawyer completed the handshake. "Bud Walpole. Actually, Dad's been gone for over seven years. but that doesn't make any difference to what we're here for this evening."

Terry looked a bit confused. He glanced from the lawyer to his father and then back to Eli. Eli was lying still, his eyes closed.

The lawyer stepped up to the bed and gently touched Eli's shoulder. The nurse started to scold him. "Mr. Chambly needs to rest."

Eli opened his eyes and said, "Mr. Chambly needs to do some business." He turned his head to the nurse. "This don't concern you, but it's not no real secret either. So, if you can keep your lip buttoned while we talk you can stay."

The frustrated nurse stepped a few feet away. "I can watch the monitors from here, but I don't want you trying to sit up or getting excited."

Eli said, "About the only thing that would excite me at my age is if one of my mares were to drop a matched pair of colts. But that's not likely." He took a couple of deep breaths and said, "Come closer here men so's I don't have to shout. And pay attention. This is important. I don't want to have to say it more than just the once. Bud, you take this all down. We'll need it written out."

The three men waited while Eli gathered his thoughts.

"First, Bud and I drew up my final will a few weeks ago. Could be the Lord nudged me along on that, warned me this was coming. Bud has the original paper. There's a sealed copy in the file cabinet at the ranch. But this here tonight is extra to the will."

Again, there was a pause and several deep breaths.

"Terry, I know your plan was to get an education. That's a good thing, but it isn't always possible, right when you wish for it. Sometimes life has to wait a bit, and sometimes there's another way of doing things.

"I've been watching you carefully the past few weeks. You have what it takes. I thought so back when you was no more than a nubbin, spending your summer holidays on the Double C. Your time on the Lazy-S turned you into a fine horseman and taught you some things about the cattle business. I want you to take over the running of the Double C." The statement was thrown out so matter-of-fact like, with no lead-in, that it caught the men unprepared.

There was a collective intake of breath around the bed. Eli seemed to take a long time before he started talking again. The nurse eased closer in case she was needed. Finally, Eli opened his eyes again and spoke.

"This part's important Bud. Get it down right. Terry, I want you to lean on Bud and your dad. You're young. You'll need an accountant and a lawyer at your side. But the running of the ranch is yours to do. If the Lord gives me more time, I'll be around to talk things over with. But it's plain that I won't be doing any more work.

"You buy and sell as you see fit. Always look'n for a profit. Your dad will help you with the numbers. My advice would be to take a profit when it's offered. If you wait for a bigger profit you may win some, but you'll lose more times than not.

"There's a healthy balance in the bank. It's yours to use for the good of the ranch. On big expenditures you'll need the signatures of both your dad and Bud. Bud has the papers with him here to sign for that. I have my personal funds separated out. What I'm talking about is ranch money."

Eli was silent for so long the men thought he might have gone to sleep. Finally, he roused himself again.

"I'm old Terry. Been old for a long time. Old and stuck in my ways. I don't need anyone telling me that. I know it. Reason I don't change those ways is because I like it the way it is. But you're young. Young and smart. Smarter than me.

"All I had going for me was the strength to work hard. The folks left me that ranch free title, so really, they paved the way for the success of the Double C. All I had to do was work hard and keep it from going backwards.

"You'll want more. In today's world you have to be smart. You'll want to change some of my ways. I'll only ask you to do it carefully and well thought out. Don't be afraid to ask others. You have great neighbors. Talk to them. Ask them questions. Read the ranch journals. Talk to me if I'm still around. And listen to Scotty.

"If the Lord figures I've been on this earth long enough, Bud will give you directions. I won't talk about the will here and now, but I'll tell you this much. The will gives you two years to manage the ranch even if I'm gone. Took a while to work that out. But it's all figured and legal.

"You'll need to hire an experienced man. You'll need him for sure, come calving time. Might as well get a good man now."

Eli was again silent for so long the nurse stepped closer and studied the monitors. There was still a heartbeat and she could hear his shallow breathing. She stepped back again when Eli opened his eyes.

"I'm tired now boys. You get yourselves over to Bud's

office and get that all written up legal and proper. Bring it back here Bud and I'll sign it. Wake me up. It needs signing tonight." He closed his eyes for just a moment and then opened them again. He looked directly at the nurse. "Don't you be giving me any sleeping dope. I've business to do this night."

Slowly he lifted his hand off the bed covers and reached out to Terry. The hand trembled as he held it aloft. The young man wasn't sure if Eli meant to shake, or if it was simply a gesture. "You'll do well Terry. I know you will. And one further thing. Always treat Bea with kindness. She's a fine lady. Her husband was the best friend a man could ever ask for. She's good to have around. Let her fuss over you and the family."

This time he seemed to be truly asleep. The men silently left the room. Eli's slack jaws and grey complexion caused them to wonder if he would be alive when they returned.

As they were adjusting their winter coats before going outside Bud said, "One thing Eli didn't do Terry. He didn't ask you if you wanted the position."

Terry seemed to be struck silent by the events of the past half hour. He found it difficult to wrap his mind around it all. He glanced at the lawyer and then at his father. Seeing the questions in Terry's eyes, Bud motioned to the waiting room. "Why don't we sit here for a few minutes and talk this out."

Willard had said nothing at all in the hospital room. Now he turned to Terry. "Son, this is many things. It's a great opportunity but it's also a great challenge. Eli is placing all his trust on you. If you take up his challenge, you'll bear burdens you can't yet know about. You'll work longer hours and get less sleep than you can picture right now. You'll have to learn fast and thoroughly. But it might also be the future you want for yourself. Or come to want if you're unsure right now.

"There's a purpose in Eli placing this trust in you. He wants the Double C to live on after him. He has no family to leave the ranch to. I don't know what his plan would be if you turn down this offer, but I'm sure he and Bud have a contingency for that. The thing is, you don't have any time to think this through."

Bud broke into the conversation. "I'm going back to the office to write this up. I don't need either of you to be there. Why don't you go find some dinner and meet me back here in one hour? You can make your final decision then Terry. I'll talk with you before I go to Eli's room. You can either sign or turn it down then."

With that agreed on, the men went their separate ways.

Events like those of the past couple of years either made a boy into a whining, complaining, forever feeling sorry for himself man-child, or turned him into a man able to face adversity, growing through the pain.

There was no particular design in Terry's reaction to his experiences. Without thought or any real insight, the young man turned into a more mature, confident adult. Although that maturity put him ahead of most men his age, that still left him with many doubts, many questions.

After Willard and Terry had dinner, they met with the lawyer again. After once again expressing his concern about his lack of ranching experience, a nervous Terry signed the documents Bud had ready. In less than fifteen minutes Bud was back from Eli's room with the final signature. The deal was done. Terry was the manager of the Double C.

Terry was scared half to death. He also knew that the promotion to ranch manager was illogical and unearned. And it left an uncomfortable feeling in his mind when he considered Scotty.

During a coffee break at the big house the next day, with just Scotty and Terry present, Terry broached the subject, although he feared it might be touchy. But he also felt it was unavoidable. In all probability it should have been Eli leading the discussion, but it was plain that wasn't going to happen.

The only thing Terry knew to do was dive right in. He began by telling Scotty about Eli's decision on the management of the Double C. Scotty listened quietly, seemingly without expression. At the end all he did was nod and pick up his coffee mug.

"So, what's your story Scotty? You already know that I have nowhere near your knowledge of ranching or the cattle business. Rightly this should be your job. Yet you don't seem to be resentful. Or am I missing something?"

Scotty twirled his coffee mug for a bit while he studied the table top. He spoke so quietly Terry had to listen very carefully to get the words.

"Eli knows my story. He knows I don't want the job. In fact, I couldn't do the job. Eli knows that too." He paused so long Terry thought he would say no more. But finally, in a quiet voice he started.

"We had a good little ranch up north, the wife and me. Did fine for some years. Wife and three kids seemed to really enjoy the life and I definitely did. We weren't about to get rich, but the bills were paid, and we had what we needed. Life was good."

Scotty was silent for a considerable time while he lifted his mug without taking a drink. He raised his eyes from the table, looking directly at Terry. Haltingly, and with many pauses, he spoke.

"Woke one morning. Didn't want to get out of bed.

"Refused to move when the wife tried to get me up.

"When she asked what was wrong, I broke out sobbing. Couldn't stop myself.

"Didn't know what was wrong. Finally got up and pulled on some clothes. Sat at the table shaking so bad I couldn't keep my coffee in the cup. Still had no idea.

"Long story short – I'd had a complete nervous breakdown.

"It was like the worst possible thunder storm visited just me, during the night. Crashing around and rattling every part of me.

"There's no excuse. No reason. Never saw anything like that coming. There's no real cause. There's no cure.

"I couldn't work. Stared at the wall for hours some days. Was no good to anyone."

Again, he held his silence. Terry was becoming sorry he had started the conversation.

"Wife tried to carry on with the ranch. You never seen a woman work so hard. Kids were young teens. They worked with their mother. I either slept or wandered aimlessly around the ranch. "

It was all a mistake. Ended up losing the ranch and about everything else. The wife held the family together somehow.

"We sold out what was left and managed to scrape up enough to buy this patch of ground down the road, with the pretty little cottage."

Scotty sat silently for so long Terry was tempted to end the matter. Finally, the troubled man spoke again.

"No one else knows this part; Eli helped us when we

needed it the most. A total stranger. Must have heard about us somehow. Just showed up on our door step one day. Without any more introduction than that, he said, "Let's us all have a talk."

Terry was wishing the story would come to an end. Scotty granted that wish by saying, "I'm alright now, Terry. Most days. Can't stand any pressure and can't make big decisions. Don't want to either. Eli knew he couldn't give me this job. He's a good man Terry, better than most.

"So, the wife and I get by. She runs a little café in town. There's no money in it but it gets her out with folks and she needs that. Kids are all married. We have five grandkids. Life is good again. I wouldn't take on a job that might cause that to change. I'd never do anything that might take me back."

There was a long period of silence after Terry re-filled their mugs. Perhaps there was a bit of self-consciousness or embarrassment in the men too. No man had ever laid himself bare before Terry like that. He wasn't sure what his response should be.

Finally, Terry put down his mug and stood. He offered Scotty a handshake, which Scotty accepted. "Thanks for telling me. Your story is safe with me." He was remembering his mother as he said it.

As the two men were pulling on their warm coats Terry said, "Scotty, I'd appreciate if you'd do this much for me. If you see me making a mistake, will you tell me? I promise to listen."

As so often happened with men of Scotty's type, he simply answered with a nod.

CHAPTER 13

KNOWING ELI WAS CORRECT ABOUT THE RANCH needing another experienced man Terry started thinking about Sid Lopez. The Lazy-S straw-boss was an excellent horseman as well as a knowledgeable cattleman. But Sid looked in the mirror after the surgeons completed the reconstruction of his head and face following the cougar attack and decided that he didn't want to be seen in public anymore.

In addition to what could be seen above his shirt collar, the damage he kept hidden under his shirt; his shoulder, arm and rib cage were a dreadful sight. The big cat did terrible mutilation. The surgeons did their best, but their craft has its limitations.

On top of the visual damage, Sid had some restrictions on the use of his right arm. Beyond having limited movement, his muscles had shrunk and atrophied. Regaining his strength would be a long task, if he was able to do it at all. Being right handed complicated everything Sid tried to do. Not that he tried very hard. He could be accused of giving up on life and hope, but no one found the courage to confront him on it.

When Sid was released from hospital, he accepted a ride back to the Lazy-S, where he packed his gear, bid farewell to the Lazy-S crew and went home, feeling as if life had whipped him to the bone. In the case of his arm and shoulder it was the literal bone.

Terry remembered Sid mentioning Rocky Mountain House. He checked the phone book for a Lopez in that area and found a number. He called three times over the next two days without receiving an answer.

Having a pronounced stubborn streak himself and knowing the fear of carrying his scars into public places, Terry made up his mind that Sid was in hiding. He helped Scotty with the morning chores before climbing into the ranch pickup truck. The drive to Rocky was complicated a bit by the snowy roads, but within three hours Terry was parking on the main street of the small town. He walked into the nearest café for a bite of lunch while he tried to figure out who to ask about directions to the Lopez place.

He ignored the troubled stares of the waitress and the few others in the small room as they glared at his scars.

He tried the post office but was told by a harried clerk, "I just pass along the post, I don't ask where they live."

Standing on the wind-swept street, he remembered passing an auction market on the way into town. Sid was a horse and cattle man. The auction might have attracted him sometime in the past, even if not recently. Turning the truck around, he headed to the auction house.

In preparation for the next day's sale, several men were unloading cattle. Terry approached the group and waited for a lull in the activity. When one of the men stood aside to stretch his sore back, Terry called out to him. "I'm looking for the Lopez place."

The man took a long-distance look at Terry and finally asked, somewhat aggressively, "Why?"

"Sid's a friend of mine. Haven't seen him in a while. Thought I'd stop in for coffee and a talk."

As if it was his job to protect Sid the auction worker said, "Could be Sid don't want to see you."

Terry thought for a moment and finally said, "Could be. Might be best to let him make that decision for himself though. Can't hurt to make the offer."

The belligerent man took a few steps towards Terry. The others had quit working too and were crowding around. Terry continued to lean on the top rail of the corral.

Terry made no purposeful move to show his own scars, but the men noticed. The quarrelsome man seemed to soften. He held his eyes on Terry's face while he said, "Would you be Terry?"

Terry said nothing, but as the men looked at the scars they knew.

There was a long pause, with the men studying each other. Finally, the auction man said, "Heck of a thing. Never heard anything like it before. Sid told me the story one evening, us sitting in a darkened room so's to allow him to hide. Mentioned a Terry. Only time I ever saw a grown man cry."

There was a long pause. Finally, "Ya, Sid might make you a welcome. You drive down that road you see right over there. You go five miles and turn two more to the west. Almost hidden drive through the overgrown caragana. Don't be too surprised if he turns you away. Never see him in town. Stays to himself out at the farm. I drop out every once in a while. Always after dark. Take a beer to visit over. We sit in the dark. Have us a short visit. Ya, he may make you a welcome. Say hello from us. Just mention the auction mart. He'll know."

Twenty minutes later Terry parked the truck in front of an old, but well-maintained cottage. The farmstead consisted of a garage, a small barn, and a few smaller buildings, one of which had the appearance of a chicken coup, although the chickens were running loose in the yard. A field of perhaps forty acres adjoining the barnyard was well fenced. The remnants of the summer's hay crop stuck up through the snow. A half dozen horses nibbled on whatever they could scratch up. Surrounding the snowy field was dense forest. Beyond, to the west, would be other small holdings, broken fields cleared out of the forest, and then the foothills, leading into the Rockies.

When there was no sign of Sid, Terry made his way to the house. No one in farm or ranch country uses the front door so he stepped right up to the side, kitchen door and knocked. After three knocks, the inside door opened a crack. The glassed storm door was tightly closed. A woman's face showed through the partially opened inner door. She said nothing.

After deciding the woman wasn't going to speak Terry said, "My name is Terry Coombs. I'm hoping to see Sid. Is he home?"

The door closed and there was silence for perhaps three minutes. The inside door opened again, a bit further this time. Sid was standing there, unshaven, his hair long and disheveled, his clothing wrinkled, the scarred side of his face hidden behind the door.

The two men looked at each other in silence. Terry figured that what was going through his own mind would be going through Sid's mind too. Memories. Wishes. What if's? Self-recriminations. Sid had suffered more from the big cat than Terry did, but the end results were similar.

Terry attempted a smile. He was pretty much out of practice at smiling. It might have looked more like a grimace.

"It's cold out here Sid. How about you invite me in."

Sid opened the inner door a bit wider, reached and snapped the latch on the storm door, and turned away. Terry took that as an invitation.

The house was almost as dark as night. It took a moment for Terry's eyes to adjust from the sun-bright snow outside. When he was able to see properly, he looked around the small cottage. He saw the woman alone in the kitchen. The blind was raised on one window, allowing just enough light in to see without stumbling over things. The rest of the house was closed off with blinds or draperies. Sid wasn't in the kitchen. The woman caught Terry's eye and pointed behind her, across the short hallway and into what Terry guessed would be the sitting room. He turned and made his way carefully in the semi-darkness.

Sid was sitting on an old worn out couch, a cigarette smoldering in a butt-filled saucer beside him. Terry never remembered Sid smoking at the Lazy-S. He took the three steps that closed the distance between them and held out his hand. Sid gave it a quick shake without standing up and then dropped his hand back onto his lap. No words were spoken.

Terry had no clear idea what his next move should be. He'd come to make a big ask. He expected Sid to either say an outright 'no', or to put up an argument. Or a series of arguments. The positions held by the two men at the

Lazy-S, their age difference and his vastly superior knowledge of ranching, might cause Sid to brush him off. But Terry decided to be bold.

Turning to the sitting room window Terry eyed the drawn draperies. Where the draperies didn't quite close, he could see venetian blinds beneath, closed tight. Without a word he stepped over to the window and pulled the draperies open and then reached for the strings on the blinds.

"Don't", Sid squeaked through his tightened throat, almost in a panic. He stood and then abruptly sat down again.

"Can't tell you what I came to say if I can't see you, my friend."

Sid's mother was standing in the doorway with a startled look on her face and her hands clasped at her throat. Terry thought he should introduce himself. He stepped her way and held out his hand. "Terry Coombs, Ma'am. Sid and I worked together some time back. It's good to meet you." There was no response from the lady, although she did shake Terry's hand. She couldn't seem to tear her eyes away from Terry's scars.

Sid again rose from the couch and started towards the windows. Terry caught him by the shoulders, half way across the room. Sid stopped, giving Terry a fierce look. The two work-hardened men, both broken from their former lives through the same violent incident, stood face to face. Before Sid could object, or say anything, Terry said, "Look at me."

Sid's facial expression was impossible to identify; hate? anger? wonder? Or something else altogether.

"Keep looking," said Terry.

Speaking to Sid's mother without turning, Terry said, "Pardon me Ma'am. I have to do this."

He shucked his big coat and dropped it on a chair. He slipped his arms and shoulders out of his suspenders, letting them hang free. He unbuttoned his shirt and pealed it off, dropping it onto the chair with the coat. He then unbuttoned his long-johns and pulled his left arm out of the woolen sleeve. He shrugged his shoulder out of the garment, exposing the worst of his healed-up wounds. His brutally abused shoulder and arm were an unpleasant sight, although he was sure Sid's scars were worse.

Sid stood mesmerized, his lips working. Terry said nothing. He simply stood for a full minute, staring into Sid's eyes, and then pushed his arm back into his long-johns before pulling on his shirt, and then the suspenders. He didn't bother tucking the shirt into his pants.

The two men were standing a bare two feet apart when Terry spoke. "One thing I've learned. Cows don't care what we look like. Neither do most folks once they get past the first look." He paused but Sid said nothing.

"I've been made manager of the Double C. It's a solid ranch in the Big Valley country. The story don't matter right now. I need a good man. You're the best I know. Go pack a bag and dig out your work clothes. I have to be back at the ranch before dark.

"And before you go to thinking up reasons to not do that, forget it. I ain't about to listen to your reasons. I need you. You need a job. You need to get back into the world. Ain't no one on that ranch but me, another hand and a lady who fixes for us. Ain't a mean bone in her whole body. And you'll love her cooking.

"I need to be on the road in fifteen minutes."

Sid said nothing. He simply stared at Terry without moving.

Sid's mother stood the whole time like a statue, still gripping her throat with both hands. Finally, she dropped her hands and spoke for the first time. "I'll pack a bag for you Sid. You dig out your saddle and rigging."

Sid still hadn't moved. After what could have been a slow count of ten, he turned to the door and slipped into his coat. His saddle was in the shed. He took two steps outside the door and stopped. He looked down at his feet and turned back to the door. Inside, he kicked off the carpet slippers he'd been living in. He dug around in the hall closet and pulled out a pair of half-worn-out riding boots, stiff and dry with the passage of time. It took some effort to push his feet into the dry, misshapen leather, but he got it done.

Terry found himself alone in the sitting room. He picked up the saucer of cigarette butts, found the bathroom and flushed the stinking mess away. He then took the time to tuck his shirt in properly.

Driving out the gate twenty minutes later, with Sid's gear in the back of the truck, the two men were silent. As they turned onto the paved highway, and drove past the auction market Sid said, "I owe you. I owe you big, else I wouldn't be here."

Terry glanced over at him. "I don't care what the reason is for you being here Sid. I'm just glad you are. There's work to be done and you're the man for it. I'm going to work both our tails off, but we're going to prove our worth. And you're going to be teaching me all the things I don't know.

"And forget it, you don't owe me. You don't owe me one thing in this whole wide world."

Very little was said during the snowy drive back to Red Deer. Terry was kept busy holding the truck on the snow-covered road and Sid seemed to have sunk into a melancholy.

In Red Deer Terry turned off the main road and swung into the parking lot at the hospital. Sid spoke for the first time in over an hour. "Whoa there, boss. What's this all about?"

Terry shut the truck off, set the hand brake and opened the door. "C'mon. I got someone you need to meet."

Sid didn't move. "Not a chance. I'm not going in there."

"Sid, my friend, this may be the one place where no one cares what we look like. I dare say, they've seen it all before now. And you really do need to meet this man. We need to do it now. I've still got evening chores and dark comes early. And since I'm thinking you've probably forgot how to ride or look after cattle, I'll have it all do by myself." He shot a big, lopsided grin at Sid.

Sid slowly slid off the seat and stood on the snowy asphalt of the parking lot. "Alright, but this ends it. Don't ask me for anything else. We're done."

They took a few steps before Sid said, "Forgot how to ride, you think, do you? You never seen the day." Sid's grin was even more lopsided than Terry's.

Terry smiled to himself and stepped toward to the big front door. Several hospital staff exited the door as the two cowboys were entering. None of them looked their way or seemed to notice the scars they carried. In the elevator there were a couple of visitors. Sid looked away. Terry looked directly at the two, staring them into silence.

Terry didn't feel the confidence he was attempting to

show as he led Sid down the hallway and into Eli's room. It was a bold move, supported mostly by hope and silent prayer. He half expected to find the room empty, fearing the worst for Eli, who really wasn't out of danger yet. Entering the room, he was surprised to see his father sitting in the big chair beside the bed. His two brothers were standing behind the bed, half propped against the window sill. Sis was sitting on the foot of the bed talking to Eli, her gregarious chatter bringing a smile to his face.

At the sight of the room full of people Sid stopped abruptly and let out a gurgle of sound. Terry reached back and took Sid's good arm in his hand.

Willard looked, and then took a longer look. As recognition came, he leaped out of the chair and crossed the room with his hands gesturing a welcome. "Sid? Is that really you? My heavens, man you're a welcome sight. You might not remember me. I'm Willard. Terry's dad. You were pretty groggy the couple of times I looked in on you at the hospital in Calgary."

Sid shook his hand, not knowing how to avoid Willard's overture.

Terry introduced the kids and then led Sid over to the bed. The two boys, being familiar with their older brother's facial scars, just stared at Sid. Sis was less discrete. Shocked by how much more pronounced Sid's scars were than Terry's, she stared at him with wide open eyes. She really didn't mean to be impolite, so when "G—olly" slipped out of her mouth she could've bitten her tongue off. Sid glanced sidewise at her and then looked back at the old man in the bed.

Eli wiggled around until he was sitting up a bit straighter. He said, "Can one of you lazy city kids figure out how to raise this bed?"

Sis was quick to remind Eli that the nurse told him not to raise the bed. "She was quite firm about it, Uncle Eli. Something about posture and pressure on your heart. I'm thinking you're going to get into her bad books."

Eli flipped his hand at the remembrance and pointed to where the control buttons were located. Sis slid off the bed and tried a couple of buttons until the end panel started to rise. Before the motor had time to make more than two or three whirring revolutions, the nurse was storming into the room. Shoving Sis aside, she pushed the other control and lowered the bed. Without a word she turned and left.

"I told you," said Sis.

Eli was working up a retort but before he got it thought out and spoken, Terry introduced Sid. "Sid's the best horse and cattle man the Lazy - S has ever seen. Almost as good as you Eli. He's our new hired hand, foreman and teacher. Not sure how he's going to do it yet, but he's going to teach me everything he knows about handling cattle."

Terry turned to Sid. "Sid this is Eli. He owns the Double C. Had a heart attack a few days back, but I expect he'll be sitt'n a saddle by next week. You couldn't work for a better man, or with better animals; horses nor cattle, either one."

The two men shook hands. Eli took a long look at Sid's face. "I'm guessing you're the other one that went cougar hunting with a willow switch, or some such thing. Welcome to the Double C. You two should make a good team."

No one else had anything to say. The silence became a bit awkward, so Terry said, "Well, I just wanted you two to meet. We need to be at the ranch. I hoped to make it before dark, but judging by what's outside that window, it appears that's not going to happen. I expect Scotty has the feeding looked after, but we'd better make time anyway."

After leaving the hospital Sid was again silent for a while. Finally, he said, "You'd best tell me the story."

Starting with how Eli was an old family friend, how he had spent so many summers on the Double C, why he chose to work on the Lazy-S instead of asking Eli for a job and ending with Eli having a heart attack and assigning Terry as ranch manager, Terry told the tale. He talked about the animals, he told how his family was planning a move to the ranch at the Christmas break and he told about Bea and her helping Eli, and now himself.

Sid was silent, listening intently.

Terry waited for Sid to speak. When that didn't happen, he said, "You're going to like the Double C. I have some thoughts on where I think the ranch should be pointed, but we won't do anything until you've met Scotty and we've all settled in. Then the three of us will try to figure the best way forward."

Although it was too dark in the truck for Terry to see, Sid just nodded.

CHAPTER 14

AT THE RANCH, TERRY PULLED UP BESIDE THE STABLE, so Sid could put his saddle in the tack room, before parking the truck in the garage. Scotty was gone for the day. Terry and Sid took a slow walk through the stable and then spent a long time looking over the corralled calves. The big yard light shone over most of the area.

It was four days since the calves were weaned. All but a few had pretty much settled down. Sid walked along the outside of the corral studying each animal. Only then did he speak. "Good stock. What's the plan?"

Terry answered, "Eli's a cow and calf man. He's never fed his stock to market weight. I have a couple of ideas on that. You'll have to see the place in the light. Look over the land and corrals, the hay and straw stacked up. See what's available to work with. Then we'll talk about those ideas."

Walking up to the big house, Terry pointed over to the cabin. "We'll move over there after the family comes out, but for now there's lots of room in the big house. Let's get out of this cold and see what we can find for supper."

What they found was a small roast of beef in the still-warm oven, potatoes ready for mashing, a pot of carrots cooked, but cool, gravy ready to heat up and a plate of now cold biscuits.

"Terry lifted the pot lids and looked in the oven. "I told you you're going to like Bea."

The next morning Scotty met Sid for the first time. The two men sized each other up as they shook hands. Scotty then walked Sid through their routine with the calves, seeing to their feed and water while Terry dealt with the horses. After that he would then see to the bulls, who were corralled separately.

Lifting the first few hay bales was a challenge for Sid's wounded, and poorly recovered arm and shoulder. It would take some time, but privately he hoped he could get back to something close to his original toughness.

As they were saddling up to check the cows in the far pasture Terry said, "We'll run up the other horses first. Not much left to eat on that piece of scrub ground they're calling home. I'll open the gate on the small corral. We get them boxed, you can pick out three or four for your own string, Sid. We'll put the rest back onto that hay field."

They then brought the cows up to the main yard where they would winter. The mamas seemed to have forgotten that they had birthed a calf some months before.

As they enjoyed a mid-morning coffee up at the big house, Scotty looked at Terry, "What now boss?"

Terry forced a small laugh. "Don't know as how I like you calling me 'boss'. Doesn't feel comfortable."

The three men avoided the coming work while they kibitzed a bit and laughed together. A brief re-telling of their ranching histories helped to break the ice and set a pattern of acceptance among them.

CHAPTER 15

TO GET THEIR MINDS BACK ONTO THE BUSINESS OF the CC, Terry said, "I'd like to separate the calves. The broker will want them separated for marketing anyway. Might just as well get it done.

We don't have another corral though. What suggestions do you two have on that?"

After kicking around some ideas they decided to build a straw-bale separation in the big corral. As well as the stack of new bales purchased from a grain growing neighbor, Eli had a large stack that was a few years old. It had been in the yard so long the twine on the bottom bales was starting to rot and loosen.

Using the tractor and wagon, it took the remainder of the day to pull the old stack apart and build the bale fence across the corral. Sid was out of shape and his injured arm was giving him trouble. After the first hour, he was assigned to driving the tractor.

They left a gap between the bales and the corral fence. The plan was to drive the steers into one side and then close the gap. That was accomplished the next day.

With the morning work done and lunch completed, Terry said, "Boys, I've got to talk with Eli. If you thought you could get through the afternoon without falling off your horses and needing my help getting back on, I'd leave out for the big city."

Scotty just smiled a bit, but Sid snorted some of his coffee back into his porcelain mug. He started to say something to Terry's retreating back but stopped. With the gentle closing of the door Sid instead grinned over at Scotty. "Got to give him credit. He's good at pretending. He's not sure about a lot of things but he's muddling through. I figure sometimes in life a man has to pretend until the real comes along."

Scotty wondered where that pretending was when Sid was hiding in a dark room on a small, bush country ranch. He said nothing.

Terry walked into Eli's hospital room quietly, in case the old man was sleeping. He needn't have worried. He was just in time to hear, "Why you old reprobate, you're sure enough cheat'n. Here I am, crawled out of my death bed to come sit with you, bring'n you a bit of cheer and comfort after yer nearly dy'n, and you whine me into a game of poker. Then you up and cheat, scooping my pennies up as if you won them fair and square. It's a wonder no one's beat you to death with a buggy whip or someth'n before this time. Cheat'n on a friendly game. I ain't never heard the like."

Eli responded, "Stop complaining and deal. There's still eight pennies ly'n there I have to win you out of."

Terry started to laugh. "And here I was afraid I might wake you up, so I came quietly."

Eli looked up and waved one hand at Terry. "Come

and have a seat Terry. I'll be with you shortly. Shouldn't take more than a minute or two to get this done."

The other man picked up his pennies and rolled his wheel chair back a couple of feet before turning it around. "You sit right here young feller. Only leave yer wallet in your pocket and don't deal out any cards, nor let him do it either."

Terry watched the man wheel out of the room, then turned to Eli. Eli was stuffing the cards back into their box. "Poor looser is all. But he'll be back. Old feller's lost both legs to diabetes and now he has cancer. Doesn't have much time." Bouncing seamlessly from one subject to another he continued, "How goes it with you and the Double C?"

Terry brought Eli up to date on ranch matters and then said, "Here's what I'm thinking."

Terry pulled a folded sheet of paper out of his shirt pocket and flattened it on the bed. Slanting it so Eli could see, he fingered a column of numbers. "Steers and heifers together, there's three hundred forty-two animals. One hundred seventy-six steers. One hundred sixty-six heifers.

"Here's last week's auction prices. Steers are selling a bit higher than heifers."

He pointed to the current sale prices, when applied to the Double C animals, and showed Eli the totals at the bottom.

"What I'm suggesting is that we go ahead and sell, like you've always done, but that we take that money and put it right back into unrelated, weaned heifers. We'd breed those heifers when they come to size, in the spring. I'd like to keep our own heifers but that presents all kinds of inbreeding trouble if we use Double C bulls. Might be easier to just buy unrelated animals."

Terry paused to give Eli a chance to speak. When that didn't happen, he continued. "We sell in the fall, a year from now. We keep half the new heifers to build up our cow herd and we sell the rest as pregnant replacement animals. I've checked the prices on replacement animals. If those prices hold you can see the result right there at the bottom of that list." He pointed to the spot.

"We've counted the hay on hand and the bedding straw. I figure there's lots of both. I've done the numbers with Dad. If the market holds anywhere near where it is now, we would increase ranch income quite handsomely." Eli was paying full attention.

Again, there was a long silence, broken when a nurse entered the room. She pressed the button to lower Eli's bed, although he was now allowed to have it raised. She held a small glass out to Eli, which he obediently drank, washing the liquid down with a noisy gulp of water. The nurse spoke to Terry without turning his way. "I have to ask you to leave sir. Mr. Chambly is going to have a rest now. If he gets some rest, I may manage to get some too, so you see how it is."

Eli looked over at Terry. Terry figured the old man was stifling a grin. "This ain't a hospital. It's a prison. These ain't nurses. They're wardens. I need you to smuggle me out of here, get me home. Or at least smuggle in some decent food."

The nurse was tucking in his sheet. "Now Mr. Chambly, is that a nice way to talk after all I do for you?"

Eli ignored her and spoke to Terry again. "The ranch is yours to do with young man. You don't need me." His eyes were closing even as he spoke. The nurse turned to Terry with a smile. She was twirling the little glass in her fingers. "Works every time."

CHAPTER 16

TERRY PHONED THE CATTLE BROKER HE REMEMBERED from his days on the Lazy-S. Within two hours the calves were sold to a feed lot. The price was a little better than the auction price from the previous week. Although Eli had purchased a large scale some years before, it had never been set up to use. The animals would be weighed in at the feed lot. There was a certain amount of trust in the arrangement that Terry couldn't help questioning. He determined to get the Double C scale set up and working before any more animals were bought or sold.

Trucks would be arriving within two days, to load out the animals.

Terry called the broker back. "I want three hundred-fifty top grade, weened heifers. Are you still repping for the Lazy-S?"

When the answer was positive, he placed an order.

Back at the house at lunchtime Sid pulled a small, dirty and much-used tally book out of his shirt pocket. He looked up the number for the Lazy-S cookhouse and placed the call. He didn't recognize the voice that answered but he soon had Big Mike on the line. "Mike. Sid here."

Sid pulled the phone away from his ear as Mike shouted his surprise at the call. Sid listened patiently and then, after assuring Mike that all was well, he said, "Listen, big man, I'm working on the Double C, up by Red Deer. Working with Terry. He's ranch manager."

Mike's amazement could be heard all over the kitchen. Bea smiled at Terry. Sid cut in again. "Mike, the Double C just placed an order with your broker for weened heifers. But the thing is Mike, we want the best. These aren't for feeding, they're for breeding. Can I leave that with you?"

There was a pause, then Sid spoke again. "Thanks Mike, we appreciate it."

Both buyers and sellers could save a bit of money by coordinating the movement of animals; having the trucks bring the Lazy-S stuff north and taking the Double C stuff back south. It took several calls to accomplish, but by late afternoon Terry was satisfied with the arrangements.

At evening feeding time Scotty enquired about spending so much effort over something as simple as trucking. A little out of breath from pitching bales, Terry gasped out, "Hundreds of dollars I'd rather use some other way."

It was a week before all the animals were sorted out and trucked to their new homes. Terry wrote and signed the biggest check he had ever seen. He also deposited a very large check.

The men kept the new heifers in the big corral until the vet arrived. With the tractor, they skidded the cattle squeeze into the corral and built a couple of straw-bale fences to guide the animals into, and out of the squeeze.

The vet arrived the next morning. When a young,

attractive woman stepped out of the pickup truck, dressed for dirty work, Sid stopped in his tracks. "That's the vet?"

"That's the vet," answered Terry, with a knowing grin. "That's Holly. Don't know her last name. Holly and her friend Greta own the vet business in Big Valley. I don't know Greta well, but Holly and I go to the same church in Red Deer, so we've met a few times."

Holly walked over to where the two men were working. She had her eyes on Sid the entire time. Sid shrunk up inside as she approached.

In Sid's mind, working on the isolated Double C was one thing. Standing out in the yard where this beautiful stranger could see his scars was another thing altogether. He wanted to run and hide. He was too late.

"Who's your friend Terry? You two look like the Bobbsey Twins." She said it with a big smile and an outstretched hand to Sid. She was studying his face as she spoke. She made no effort to hide her curiosity. Perhaps her being a doctor, albeit an animal doctor, lessoned the stress for Sid. With no other option available, he shook her hand and said nothing, as Terry introduced him.

Holly held Sid's hand as she carefully examined his partially repaired face. Finally, she let go of the hand and reached to touch his scars. Sid flinched and pulled back. Holly said, "Wait, Sid, let me touch."

Sid was at her mercy, completely unsure what to do. Her beauty and her forwardness held his mind frozen like a mud puddle in January. She softly ran her hand down the disfiguring grooves, stopping at his jacket collar. She lifted his hat and followed the scars to their starting point, then replaced the hat.

Sid stood like a marble statue.

With a studied, doctor's look on her face she said, "Not too different from a barb wire cut."

She dropped her hand, and everyone started to relax. Sid remembered to breath.

Finally, Holly said, "How about you showing me what we're dealing with here?"

Holly examined the newly arrived animals while Scotty and Sid took turns driving the calves into the squeeze and affixing numbered ear tags on each one. Terry wrote down the number on a chart he had created and made a note that it was a Lazy-S animal.

Nudging the heifer out of the squeeze, they drove in onto the portable scale Eli had purchased some years before. It had taken considerable effort to get the scale mounted, leveled and calibrated. But Terry was determined that no Double C animal would ever again be sold, trusting the purchaser's scale. Before an animal left the Double C, it would be weighed fairly and billed out for payment.

Terry made a note of each heifer's weight. The animals were then turned loose to join the herd of cows. Holly didn't turn any of them back. Her single comment when the job was completed was, "Good stock. I like these animals that have been weaned a bit later. Overall, they seem to me to do better, although there are some that question that."

Taking a lunch break at the big house, thankful to get away from the biting cold, Holly somehow convinced Terry and Sid to tell the story of the cougar attack. They were both reluctant, but Holly's pleas finally broke their resistance. She and Scotty listened silently during the telling. At times both Terry and Sid dropped their voices to a bare whisper. Clearly, laying out those dreadful few minutes took a toll on both men.

Sid's part of the telling was restricted to the trio of riders entering the grassy grove and then to waking up in the hospital, and all the horror of realization that confronted him. His mind had somehow blocked out the actual cougar attack.

Everyone but Terry howled with laughter when he told about demanding Cindy's shirt.

Some of the details were new to Sid. He'd been unconscious much of the time. During his recovery he had shown no interest in hearing the full story. From the time he woke up in the hospital he had credited Terry with saving his life. That was as far as he wished to go. The details didn't matter.

In the silence of his own mind and the darkness of the old ranch house, Sid spent months avoiding the words, 'self-pity', but somehow, they kept rising to his conscious thought. Until this day he'd had no desire to hear the full tale, or to confront his true feelings.

When the telling was ended, leaving out a couple of small parts they didn't wish to live through again; the many surgeries, the hundreds of stitches inserted and then, later, removed.

Holly reached across the table and touched each of their hands. "I'm sorry for the event but I'm happy you're both still with us."

Holly pointed to the tanned and mounted cougar hide hung on the kitchen wall. "Is that the animal?"

Terry looked around. It was a nervous reaction only. He knew what the vet was pointing at. "That's the one."

Holly studied it for a length of time before saying, "Amazing."

Terry blew his nose in an attempt to hide the few tears threatening to dribble down his cheeks. Although they seldom discussed their feelings, there was no doubt that for both Sid and Terry, their healing on the outside was much further advanced than the healing on the inside. Strangely, it was just the day before that Sid had broached the subject.

Bea who had arrived just a few minutes before the telling, was spellbound.

Scotty simply sat and stared, casting his eyes between Terry and Sid. He had not heard the story before and it held him in awe. Having suffered so much himself, through his breakdown, he easily saw the parallel between his inner thoughts and fears and those of Sid and Terry. He also saw something amusing in the fact that the three wounded men had been drawn together.

"Well, ain't we a fine, damaged, bunch to be holding down this here ranch?" With that he began to chuckle, and then to laugh, something he did rarely. Before long the seriousness of the past few minutes was broken, and they were all laughing.

Terry watched Sid as the afternoon slid past. On the Lazy-S there was no one with more self-confidence than Sid. No one who stood up and faced the morning quite like Sid. No one who could better answer to any issue that arose on the big ranch. No one better to go to with a question or a problem to sort out. Few men were more handsome. Few men received more attention from the girls at the dances, than Sid. There was no one the young cowboys looked up to more than Sid.

But that was the old Sid. Then came that last fateful ride into the forest clearing. The new Sid was the broken and scarred man sitting on a worn-out couch in a darkened room that Terry had gone to recruit.

Perhaps it was that recruitment that started the change, or perhaps it was the gentle touch of the sensitive young vet. Or perhaps it was finally telling the story to strangers. Whatever was happening inside Sid's mind and heart, Terry took it for a good thing. Sid actually smiled a couple of times during the afternoon and he seemed to be sitting a little taller in his saddle.

Perhaps the injured cowboy had found a release of some kind in having a stranger, a beautiful woman, look directly into his eyes and then look at his scars without judgement. Without revulsion. Perhaps it would be easier to just be who he had always been, acknowledge the physical changes, work to recover from the emotional changes, and let people's opinions fall where they may.

Terry reflected on one question Sid asked the day before. "I would say you're taking your situation a bit better than I'm taking mine Terry. Don't you care how it's all changed your life?"

Terry was slow to answer and careful to try to choose words that would rest easy on Sid's ears. "I care more than I could ever say Sid. Only thing is, it's done and finished and there's not one thing on God's green earth I can do about it. But here's the other thing Sid, just like this earth belongs to God, so do I belong to Him. I don't understand much of that or how it works, but there it lays. I decided to leave it to Him."

Sid listened in silence and then turned away, spurring his horse into a trot.

CHAPTER 17

WILLARD PHONED THE RANCH THAT EVENING. "I WAS at the hospital today. They figure Eli will be in their care for another week. If he doesn't have a relapse, he can come home then. But the thing is, he'll need some care and a clear space of his own. His mobility will be much reduced. He needs to walk some, get some exercise, but we'll pick up a wheel chair for him too. I'm thinking we should have a carpenter come in and turn those two back bedrooms into one large space and put a private bathroom in. What do you think on that?"

Terry kept getting pushed beyond his knowledge and experience. This was no different. He knew exactly nothing about carpentry or plumbing. His first thought was to mentally count the bedrooms, and figure how the family were going to adjust to losing the space. Eli's original plan was to move to the cottage. Clearly, that wasn't going to happen now.

There were upstairs bedrooms in the old house that were used at one time. Perhaps they could be used again.

It had been years since Terry had been up those stairs and he couldn't quite picture the layout.

After a long pause he answered, "I'll see if there's a carpenter in Big Valley who can take a look at it. I'll let you know."

CHAPTER 18

THE DAYS OF NOVEMBER GROUND TOWARDS MID-month, and the true settling-in of winter. Eli was home, enjoying the privacy of his expanded bedroom and the personal bathroom. The kitchen door was removed, and the door frame widened to accommodate a wheelchair.

For a lifelong bachelor who never had to answer to anyone else, he adapted to his limitations with only a minimum of grumbling. Bea was there often, cooking and fussing. Each time she left, there was food enough in the fridge for a couple more days. Terry asked Eli about paying for her help.

"I know what you said before, but it's different now. She seems to be here more and doing more."

Eli's response was, "Don't even mention it. She'd be hurt if you did."

The cattle settled in and the three men developed a pattern of work that suited all of them. When the busy, morning feeding time was over, Scotty and Terry handled the remaining chores while Sid went to the horses.

Although a competent and experienced cattle man, horses were clearly Sid's first love.

In mid-November everything changed. The weather forecasters spread a warning, but even they had no idea of what was to come. It started just after midnight. The temperature dropped suddenly, but it wasn't really the cold that hit so hard. The temperature settled in at around minus fifteen F. That was cold for this early in the season, but it wasn't the first time they had seen those temperatures.

But the wind. Oh, the wind! Even in a country that experienced wind every winter, and in the southern foothills, lived with wind nearly every day, few could remember anything to match or compare. The recently fallen snow was blown into great heaps across roads, farm yards, ranches, and throughout the towns and cities. In places on the Double C, the land was swept clear of snow. The wind would have taken the soil as well, as it did in the dry years of the Thirties, but the frost held it firmly in place.

Where there were obstacles to the movement of the wind, such as buildings, wooden fences, and corrals, the snow broke free of the driving wind and dropped to the ground, creating drifts and burying the feed yard.

The men of the Double C bundled up in their warmest clothing, tied woolen scarves over their ears and noses, pushed heavy cotton mittens inside oversized leather mitts and went to work. The first move would normally be to feed the animals and see to their water. But the feed yard was deep in blown and drifted snow, the feed mangers buried. One look, after the late-rising sun exposed what the yard light wasn't strong enough to show, and the men knew they were facing a long day.

Terry leaned close to Sid, shouting over the howling blast of wind. "I'd appreciate if you would see if the tractor will start. We have to clear out this feed yard." Sid nodded and walked away. The small front-end loader would be inadequate to the challenge, but it was all they had.

The bale wagon had been left in the hay yard, ready for loading. Terry and Scotty plowed through the piled-up snow, leaning into the driving wind. Scotty turned off long enough to pick up a scoop shovel from the stable. Terry scrambled, bale by bale to the top of the stack. Scotty shoveled the wagon reasonably free of snow. With a yell of warning, Terry dropped a bale onto the wagon. Scotty pushed it into position and waited for the next bale of feed to drop.

The three men usually laughed and joked as they did this task each morning and evening, but there was none of that possible over the screaming wind. Sid was soon pulling the tractor into the hay yard, pushing snow before him with the front-end loader. From there he would break a trail through the drifts and into the feed yard. He opened the feed yard gate and left it open, doubting that any of the suffering animals would wander that far and escape. By the time he had a trail broken, Terry and Scotty had the wagon half loaded. The remainder of the loading went faster with Sid's help.

Terry found a second shovel. He and Scotty shoveled the feed mangers clear enough to accept more hay. Shovel work like that sent spasms of agony through Terry's shoulder and upper arm. He could only imagine what the more seriously wounded Sid was feeling.

With the men working as a practiced team, the cattle soon had feed available to them.

The water situation remained to be dealt with. The

wind driven drifts piled up on the little wood stoves faster than the fire could melt them off. Another hour of hard work cleared the stoves and the water tanks. The skim of ice was broken out and the fire was built up in both stoves.

By the time they went into the house for mid-morning coffee break they were exhausted. Their eyes hurt from exposure to the driving snow. Their ears stung with cold, in spite of the woolen coverings.

Eli, moving slowly and carefully, had coffee ready and a plate of homemade rolls sitting on the table, along with butter, strawberry jam and a big plate of sliced cheese. The men shucked their hats and coats and took a seat.

Eli said, "You can thank Bea for the rolls. Done 'em up yesterday." As was his habit, he moved on to the next subject without so much as taking a breath. "Tough morning out there, boys. Did you get 'em fed?"

Anyone who didn't know Eli would think he had little interest in the men's welfare, thinking only of the animals. That perception would be wrong.

The wind blew for ten days. To the men working outside, it seemed like an eternity. Scotty gave up his normal Sunday off, knowing the work would require all the effort the three of them could put together. The Double C didn't lose any cows, but what the wind drained from the suffering animals could only be guessed at.

It was considered close to a miracle that the power stayed on through the storm.

Terry started dreaming of a covered feed and calving yard. He had no idea how to build a cover that large or what the cost would be, so it remained as a dream only. He was tempted to mention his idea to Eli. Worried that Eli might think the young, inexperienced Double C manager was running off on fits of fantasy, Terry said nothing. Always a man of few words, he was becoming a man who also chose his words carefully.

After the storm, with the days on the ranch becoming routine again, Scotty took a week off. Sid needed to visit his family over Christmas so having Scotty taking a break earlier suited everyone well. The plans to move the family to the ranch swung into high gear. Clive would always be the academic, but Andrew and Sis talked non-stop about ranch life and horses. Andrew's interest in horses appeared to be genuine. Sis's interest was perhaps more in the direction of finding a wealthy rancher to marry. Terry stayed out of their discussions.

CHAPTER 19

TERRY WAS STANDING WITH HIS ARMS FOLDED OVER the feed yard fence, as they often were. From there he felt he could keep his eye on the animals, without bothering to saddle a horse to ride among them. He still wasn't totally sure what all to look for, but with Scotty, Sid and Holly pointing out things from time to time, his knowledge was growing.

When he heard a truck crunching its way over the snowy driveway he didn't bother turning around. He was expecting no one so he didn't figure there was anything urgent happening. When the truck stopped almost against the feed yard fence, and only a few feet to his right, with the window rolled down, and the smiling face of their neighbor, Boyce Nugent grinning out at him, he stood where he was, with only his head turned to acknowledge the shouted greeting.

"Morn'n there young man, looks like you got most everything under control on the Double C. As much as I can see from inside this here warm truck cab, anyhow. You've pushed a sight of snow off'n that there feed yard, judg'n by the piles over yonder. Wind blows 'er in, the likes of you'n I dig 'er out. We wait for the next snow fall so's we can do 'er agi'n. How's old Eli doi'n? He up and around some? Come to find out if'n yer com'n to the Cattlemen's Christmas Banquet."

Boyce finally took a breath which gave Terry time to wonder if all the neighbors talked right through, from one subject to another, without needing answers or comments. Eli was well known for that habit, but Boyce just might have him beat.

Terry still hadn't moved. "I don't know about any Christmas banquet, Mr. Nugent. Anyway, if the Double C is going it should be Eli. He's still the owner and boss."

"Na, that old reprobate ain't never come, not that I can think of anyway. He ain't much fer socializ'n. I expect he's afraid he might be gobbled up by some widow who'll take control of his life and he'll be made to wash behind his ears." Boyce had a good laugh at his own joke.

Boyce started his truck again. "Well, I'll go up to the house. Cheer up the old guy for a few minutes. You think about the banquet. It's in Calgary at the Ranchmen's Club. December twelve. Six in the evening. You need to be there. Bring a lady friend if'n ya wish."

With a small grinding of worn-out gears, the neighbor backed his truck all the way to the house before turning it around. Terry could hear the two old friends shouting their greeting all the way from the cattle yard.

That evening, sitting around with fresh mugs of coffee, Eli, Sid and Terry talked all the way through the current situation on the ranch.

Sid said, "So, Eli, what's your plan for the horse business?"

That subject took up the next half hour and was still

going strong when Terry left the table. He could easily see the men both had their hearts more in the stable than in the feed yard. He decided Eli kept cattle to make a living, while giving the best of his mind and heart to the horses.

Terry left the two to their horse talk and decided to make some last-minute arrangements for when the family moved to the ranch. The time was short. Terry had been to the upstairs of the old ranch house only once and only briefly. Figuring that at least one of the boys would be moving up there, he opened the door and climbed the stairs. He knew there were two rooms, but he had never explored either of them.

Pushing into the first old bedroom he stumbled over some obstruction on the floor. Losing his balance, he fell onto the bed. The spring mattress bounced, sending a great cloud of dust into the air. Terry stood, brushing himself off and holding back a cough. He finally found the string hanging from the old light socket in the center of the room. With the light on he could see that what he had fallen over was a misshapen stack of cardboard boxes, also covered in dust. With his foot, he pushed the protruding box out of the way and then looked over the room. Deciding it would be a good bit of work to clean it up for sleeping, but still doable, he moved on to the other space. There was a layer of frost on both windows, but the rooms were reasonably warm.

Curious, when he finished his explorations, he went back to the stack of boxes. Kneeling beside the one he tripped over, he opened the flaps and pulled out a small handful of old papers. The light was poor. He had to get up and take the papers to where he was standing directly under the bulb. What he was holding were sales receipts for cattle sold decades before. He thumbed through some more pages. Some were dated in the last century; in the 1890's. This Big Valley country only opened to settlement a few years before that date. He replaced the papers and opened two more boxes. More of the same plus several stacks of private letters.

Intrigued, he carried a few of the sales receipts down to the kitchen, along with some old letters. The horse talk was still going on. Rather than break into the conversation, he simply dropped the papers onto the table in front of Eli. Eli hesitated in his talking, then glanced at the papers. He picked the top one up and studied it.

Terry said, "Didn't figure to snoop. I tripped over a cardboard box and fell onto the bed. Got curious."

Eli was staring at the papers and nodding. "Forgot about those old papers. No one's lived in that upstairs since I did myself, many's the years ago. Pop, he was one to save things. He'd say, 'you just never know'. Saved just about every piece of paper ever came his way; bills, receipts, bank statements, letters. Hardly ever threw anything away. Course, there weren't anywhere near the paper flying around back in those days. Used to be I could pick up something in the hardware store, tell Old Jimmy to put 'er on my account, and the deal was done. Now it seems we can't go to town and buy a new shovel, but what a man comes home with the shovel in one hand and a bunch of papers in the other."

Sid and Terry sat watching as Eli read over the old document. The horse talk was forgotten for the moment. It was difficult to be sure, but it was possible Eli's face might have taken on a melancholy look. If only Terry could be sure what melancholy looked like. In any case, it didn't seem to be the time for more talking.

Sid and Terry made the outside night-rounds

together, checking the animals and then the water heaters in the cattle pen. Eli always burned wood he cut from bush on the ranch. Terry drove south a few miles to pick up a load of stoker coal, hauling it home in the ranch's one-ton truck with the box hoist. He liked the way the coal lasted through the night, making mornings easier.

After the two young men went to their beds Eli slowly set out to climb the stairs. He knew both Terry and Bea would get all over him if they knew. But his mind had been pulled back to old memories. He wasn't tired. He was sure he could do it just this once. If he took it slow.

In the old bedroom he knelt beside the pile of boxes and started thumbing through the old documents. He gathered some up, and with a firm grip on the hand rail, made his slow way back downstairs. He smiled just a bit as he sat back down at the kitchen table and spread a large handful of papers and a few letters before him. He read until he couldn't hold his eyes open.

At first, in the morning, Terry was shocked and upset when he saw the pile of papers on the table. He was thinking first of Eli's health, and only after that, of what these papers might mean to the old man. Then he relaxed and grinned. "Well, why not?"

Sid arrived, and the men made their own breakfasts; Sid with his bacon and eggs, Terry with his big bowl of oatmeal. Neither of them ever changed much.

After breakfast Terry climbed the stairs and came back with a big box of papers. He went back and picked up a box of old letters and documents. He placed them both on a folding card table he dragged out of the hall closet, leaving them in the kitchen where Eli could get at them without climbing stairs or bending over.

Terry would call his father later in the day to talk about the upstairs bedrooms and the work to be done.

Nothing was said about the Cattlemen's Christmas party until one week before the event. Terry was of a mind to never mention it, but Eli surprised him during their noon meal. "Terry, I've made arrangements for you to go to that Christmas banquet. Got you a ticket and rented you a hotel room close by the banquet hall. I know you think you don't want to go but take it as an order from your boss. I want you to go. I only booked the one ticket but if you wish to invite someone to go with you, we'll fix that up this afternoon."

Terry was silent for a few moments before saying, "I'm told you never went." He left that statement hanging.

"That's true. I never went. Couldn't see the point. But the cattle business has changed. Is still changing. You've already proven that. You've used your connection with the Lazy-S to get us an excellent small herd of heifers, better animals than we would find at most auctions.

"All during my time I just looked after my cows, sold the calves, and did it again the next year. That was enough, way back when. It's about all I could do, mostly by myself anyway.

"Today, the herds are bigger. The CC herd is bigger. Can't do it all myself anymore. Everyone moves around more. The roads and the cars are better. Ranchers and buyers know each other and need to know each other. Ranchers are trying new things. You need to know what those things are."

He paused to look at Bea, as if she might add some words of wisdom. When that didn't happen, he said, "You need to be there. You go to the big city tomorrow and get yourself some new duds. A new hat too. See if you can find some good boots. Spend some ranch money. You've earned it. You need to look good among those big ranchers. Your repp'n for the Double C."

He made that last statement as if it was understood by all, that repping for the Double C was no small matter.

Terry didn't know what to say, so he said nothing.

CHAPTER 20

Seeing how Eli dove into the boxes of old memories, Terry got an idea. When he drove back into the ranch after his visit to the city stores, he had a gift for Eli. He walked through the kitchen without more than a nod at Bea, Sid and Eli and dropped the packages on his bed. Fishing through one of the bags, he pulled out a small box and headed back to the kitchen.

"Got something for you, boss. Take a look."

Eli turned the box over and over in his hands before finally looking at Terry. "What's this?"

"It's a tape recorder. Small. Battery operated. Hand held, like business folks use when they're traveling and such."

Eli snorted. "I know that. I see that written right here. Having a heart attack didn't affect my reading none. What I'm asking is what am I supposed to do with a tape recorder."

Sid caught on immediately. So did Bea. Sid said, "Why I think that's a great idea. You and those boxes of old records take the ranching world right back to the beginning. Why, I wouldn't be surprised if you found a record in one of those boxes that described how those mountains were formed. Or maybe tell who dug Big Valley. You can read it and tell the story right onto that little machine. Some book publisher will pay you a fortune for it and you'll be famous. Yes, sir, I think that's a great idea."

Eli just gave Sid a grim look, while he continued to roll the little box in his big hands. Terry figured he would wait a day or two before offering to show him how to use the recorder.

Bea felt enough had been said. She looked up at Terry, "Supper's still warm. Pull up a chair."

The date for the Cattlemen's Christmas function was upon Terry before he was ready for it. The idea of sitting down with a room full of mature, experienced cattlemen scared him half to death. The matter of the face scars multiplied that fear many times over.

Bea helped him sort out his new wardrobe and adjust the Bolo tie. After looking at a bewildering array of ties in the store, he chose one with leather thongs and an engraved, bone emblem. Not wishing to do anything that would make him stand out in a crowd his choice was one of the more modest on offer.

He set out for Calgary right after noon on the day of the banquet. At the last minute he stuffed an armful of warm clothing into the old truck. In the middle of winter, you need to be prepared.

He asked directions twice in the city and finally found the hotel he was booked at. He checked in, tolerating the stares of the two young ladies behind the counter. He parked the truck in the underground parking garage and carried his new clothes up to his room. When he was changed, he took a last look in the mirror, inhaled some courage and walked the few blocks to the Ranchmen's Club. He was trembling in fear as he approached the big front desk. He wasn't sure he could even talk. He thought about getting back in the truck and driving home, but finally got a grip on himself.

The situation was eased when the lady at the check-in desk proved to be totally professional. She didn't stare at his scars, although she certainly noticed them. She made no obvious reference to his youth or to his clear discomfort. She welcomed him, gave him a name badge and pointed the way to the coat-check, and then the banquet hall, before turning to the next couple in line.

At the entrance to the big hall Terry again stood frozen in fear until a booming voice hollered, "Terry. Ya made it. Come over here and meet some folks."

Terry made his way to the welcoming group and shook hands with Boyce Nugent. "It's good to see you Mr. Nugent. I don't expect I'll know one other person here."

Still shouting, Boyce said, "Well you do now. Meet Cob Madera, Wes Greaves and Hank West."

As the men were shaking hands Boyce advised, "They've all got wives around here somewhere, but I expect they've gone off in search of someone half civilized to visit with." Again, Boyce was loud in the enjoyment of his own joke.

Boyce kept Terry close by him as they wandered the room, meeting folks and shaking hands. Terry was dazed by it all, knowing he would never remember more than just a few of the names. He had never seen such self-assured men or heard so much cattle-talk by men who had been there and done it. He could sense no phoniness among these men.

He was awed by the women, as well. Some were wives. Many were daughters. They all seemed to exhibit the rosy, outdoor, healthy look of country living and riding. He could see that whole ranch families had come together. The way the women were dressed seemed to scream wealth. As little as he knew about clothing or styles, he was careful to keep those thoughts to himself.

The men mostly ignored his scars. They had all heard the story, or at least the bare bones of the tale. No one in ranching country missed hearing about the fight with the lion. Most of them had heard several versions of the event.

The women were less discrete, and some of the younger daughters were openly transfixed. He cringed inwardly as Boyce turned the introductions over to his wife, and tolerated the attention, being careful not to hold eye contact for more than a second or two, not knowing what else to do.

At the call for dinner, Boyce reappeared beside his wife and Terry. He was leading his young charge to a table when a female voice called over the crowd noise. "Terry. Terry Coombs. Is that you?"

Both Boyce and Terry stopped and turned around. Pushing her way through the crowd was Cindy Stocker. A grown-up Cindy, waving and calling out to Terry. They hadn't seen each other for going on two years. Cindy had always been attractive, but the grown-up Cindy was far more than just attractive. She seemed to be a bit taller, and appeared to have put on just a few pounds, in the way a maturing young woman wished to put on pounds.

Like most of the guests, especially those from the old ranching families, her self confidence among the crowd dazzled Terry. She broke free of a few visiting guests and rushed up to Terry. She stopped three feet away and held out both her hands, staring directly into his eyes, flashing a bright smile. He automatically reached to take her hands. He found himself smiling and tongue tied.

Cindy was not tongue tied. "Oh, Terry. I've missed you so. It's good to see you. And you're looking wonderful. Just simply wonderful."

The two young people stood silently, in the midst of the jostling crowd until Cindy started to laugh. "Don't you have anything to say? How about, at least, hello."

Terry shook his mind awake. "Uh, yes. Of course. Hello. I guess I shouldn't be surprised to see you here. But I'm surprised to see myself here."

Following a short, uncomfortable laugh he said, "Cindy, you look great. No. More than great. You look, well, great, I guess."

She laughed at this, stepped close and turned to push her arm under his. When he folded his arm just a bit, she gripped him below the elbow and pulled him tight, still smiling up into his face. "We need to spend just hours talking. There's so much I want to hear about. Come, sit at our table, beside me."

Still stammering for clear thoughts and words, Terry said, "Won't that be pushing someone else out of his place." He was thinking she was probably with a date.

"Just my brother. He can find somewhere else to sit. He really doesn't want to be there anyway."

She dragged him to the Lazy-S table and yelled over the din. "Hey everyone, look who I found." There was no need for introductions to the Lazy-S owner's family. After the handshakes and the words of welcome Cindy half lifted her brother out of his chair. "Go find somewhere else to sit. This place is taken." She knew he would rather be with his friends anyway, so the deed was soon done.

Boyce Nugent who had been watching from a distance smiled and escorted his wife to their table.

Terry's knowledge of buffet dinners was restricted to the small Chinese café the family visited from time to time. It was alright, as far as it went, but the Ranchmen's Club was another world. He didn't know where to start. The choices were overwhelming. He laughed and said to Cindy, "I'll follow you. I'd rather do that than make my own mistakes."

She laughed and smiled and then leaned back slightly, against his chest. They must have turned the heat up. Suddenly he was sweating.

With the delicious dinner behind them the family and a few friends settled in for a time of visiting around the dinner table.

It was probably inevitable. Anyone could have predicted it. While the Stocker family made no mention of the fight with the cougar, one of the visiting couples couldn't hold back their curiosity. It was the mother who first mentioned it, but it was the teen-aged daughter who insisted on hearing the story. She was one of the girls who couldn't keep her eyes off Terry's scars earlier in the evening.

The other thing that was totally predictable was all the pleading in the world wasn't going to get Terry to tell the story.

Adam Stocker knew immediately that the situation was about to get awkward. He said, "Cindy, why don't you tell the story in brief. Just the outline."

After receiving a noncommittal look from Terry, she started the story. A couple from the adjoining table heard what was happening and stood to join the Lazy-S table. They, in turn, waved others over. There was soon a large crown gathered, and the hall fell to a hush, waiting for the story. Terry thought about sliding under the table or running for the door. This plan was thwarted when Cindy again drove her hand beneath Terry's arm.

Cindy rose to the expectations and hopes of the crowd. Forgetting about the short version of the tale, she talked in considerable detail, giving Terry full credit for his courage and his actions. When the story developed to where Terry was trying to stop the bleeding on Sid's head she said, with a radiant smile on her face, "So do you know what this guy did? He made me give him my flannel shirt."

After a stunned silence, the crowd burst into laughter. A couple of the teen age girls looked shocked. One of them said, "What on earth did you do?"

Cindy answered, "Why, of course, I told him there was no way I was taking off my shirt. But this brute didn't even turn around. Still trying to stop Sid's bleeding he said again, 'Give me your shirt.' He actually shouted it at me."

Terry' s head was hanging almost down to the table.

Cindy started again. "Well, I finally told him not to turn around. I started to cry, pulled off my shirt, threw it at him and pushed my horse into a gallop to get away."

She shortened the last part, where the cowboys frantically rode for help. The final part, with the helicopter arrival and the medical people taking over was told by Adam Stocker. When the story was completed the crowd stood in silence.

Adam Stocker wanted to put an end to Terry's misery. He stood to his feet and looked at the gathered folks and then looked at Terry, who was just barely raising his eyes to see Adam. "That's enough folks. This young man saved three lives that day, one of them being my daughter's. The other was my foreman. He's a modest man and I'm sure he doesn't enjoy this attention. In any case, although we at the Lazy-S have all thanked him before, I wish to thank him again."

He then addressed Terry. "Terry, you have our undying thanks and gratitude. You're a credit to your family and to your own name. Thank you."

The applause was spontaneous but subdued, as the occasion called for.

CHAPTER 21

As the music started for the evening's dancing, Cindy pulled Terry to his feet and directed him to the dance floor. Turning and slipping easily into his arms, she was pleasantly surprised to find that he was an excellent dancer. Most riders tend to be light on their feet, but Terry took it further with a natural rhythm and grace, plus a knowledge of the slower waltz steps. Cindy matched him step for step as they circled the small room. "Mr. Coombs, you are a beautiful dancer. How did that come to be?"

"Just always enjoyed it I guess."

"Well, then, we'll just enjoy."

They danced several numbers and then picked up a cold drink and headed for a pair of lounge chairs placed along the adjoining hallway. It was quiet enough to talk.

After a full minute of silence, Cindy said, "I may owe you an apology. I certainly owe you an explanation."

Terry remained silent, waiting.

Cindy tried to cover a self-conscious cough from her constricted throat. Finally, she reached and held Terry's hand. Not looking at him she said, "Terry, I'm sure you remember how I nagged you and got in your way when you were working in the stable. I like to think I was that way because of my youth. But that's probably not really true. I'm only a bit younger than you. And then I remember telling you that I expected to be hanging on your arm at my grad. Well, my grad was a long time ago.

"I don't know how seriously you took my talk back then, but you need to know that I was serious. I really did want you to escort me to my grad."

Cindy was silent long enough for Terry to find the courage to ask, "So what happened?"

Cindy finally lifted her eyes to look at Terry. "Meanness happened, Terry. Meanness and bullying. That's what happened. And I wasn't strong enough to do anything about it."

"Was someone bullying you?"

"No. Well yes, I guess. But only second hand. A couple of the girls, you know the type, the class leaders. By that I don't mean the academic leaders. I mean the sweethearts. The ones who hang with the hunks; the athletes. In our school those are the rodeo guys, not the football guys. The rodeo guys are mostly really good; genuine and respectful. But there are a few of the others. When I mentioned that you were going to escort me, the girls started saying how entertaining it would be and then started foul mouthing and making fun of your injuries. I won't tell you everything they said. The guys picked it up and added some very hurtful names and said how they couldn't wait to see you. You can't believe some of the childish things that were said."

This time there was a long period of silence. Cindy finally gathered her courage and spoke again, in halting steps.

"I guess I wanted to spare us both that experience. So, I didn't go to the grad. Oh, I went and received my diploma.

"Some of the girls got on my back over coming alone, but I still walked up and picked up the document. Then my family and I went straight home. I spent the rest of the evening in the stable plotting revenge, or in my room crying.

"It was a terrible evening. I have wondered a few times since, if I should have invited you and let the idiots do their worst. I'm still not sure. But I'm pretty sure I should have given you the option. I'm afraid I was mostly thinking of myself.

"Anyway, that's why you never heard from me. And I'm embarrassed and really, really sorry that any of this happened. I apologize. Will you forgive me?"

This time Terry spoke fairly quickly. "There's nothing to apologize for and nothing to forgive."

They sat in companionable silence.

Cindy quietly said, "You want to know the really funny thing? Two of those guys and three of the girls are here tonight. They were all at the table listening to your story. I watched their faces. I think I can safely say they will never look down on you or your scars again.

"Kind of late for grad though."

Terry got to his feet. "Forget it. I've had so many people stare at me I've almost become immune. Almost, I say. Not completely. Only a few people have seen my shoulder and arm. I'm sure I could be a big attraction at the beach, so I'll probably avoid that."

Terry took a big breath and sounded sad as he said, "Sid is still working on his feelings. He's got a long way to go. But that's to worry about another time. Let's dance.

They're playing another slow one. I don't do so good on the faster ones."

The two young people both knew they wanted to meet again. Still, they parted with no particular plan. After Terry begged off any further celebrations, they said good-night. Cindy joined her family back at the dinner table where late evening snacks were being set up.

Terry did more socializing in one evening than he had ever done before. He was tired and ready for a night's sleep.

The walk back to the hotel gave him time to consider all that was said and done over the past few hours. With thoughts and questions in his mind that he had no real answers for, he settled into the hotel room and went to sleep.

CHAPTER 22

WHEN TERRY WALKED INTO THE HOTEL DINING ROOM for breakfast the next morning, he recognized several ranch families from the dinner the evening before, but the Lazy-S wasn't there. Somewhat disappointed, he dug into his bacon and eggs and checked out of the hotel.

He had a rough-drawn map directing him to a motor sports retailer. Within a half hour of fighting morning traffic Terry was tired of the big city and its multitude of busy roads.

When he finally found the place, he had to wait a half hour for the store to open. That freed him to think of all the work already done on the ranch by that time each day. Entering the building as soon as the clerk turned the key in the door, he stood mesmerized by the choices of adult toys available.

Basically, it was a motorcycle shop. But in recent years other motorized toys had entered the market. He was there to look over the snowmobiles. His hope was that he could find a machine for the right price, that Eli would be able to use to get around the ranch on. He wanted to find a way to get the old man out of the house and among his beloved horses and cattle.

He followed the clerk around the show room and listened as the young man described each machine. The clerk explained that more features were being added with each year's new models. So far, the offerings were fairly basic. Terry explained why he was interested, and what he hoped to accomplish. The clerk listened carefully before saying, "Let me show you something."

They walked to the other side of the store. The clerk touched the handle of a bright red three-wheeled machine that looked like an overgrown kid's trike.

"This is right out of the design engineers' heads. They've been available in other markets for a year or two, but they just hit this market last week. We got our first stock in yesterday. They're less costly than the snowmobile and easier to operate for someone like the man you're telling me about. They don't go as fast as the snowmobile so they're probably safer too, if the driver doesn't do anything stupid. Plus, they're good for summer and winter, both, as long as you push some paths through the deep snow out on that ranch.

"Maybe this is the unit you're looking for."

Terry walked around the machine several times, studying every part of it. He liked the over-blown tires. They looked like they would handle both snow and mud, in small quantities. He sat on it and held the handlebars. The clerk showed him how it started and then offered to push it outside, so he could try it in the parking lot. Terry readily agreed.

A half hour later, with Terry imagining Eli roaming over the ranch on his new toy, He wrote a check. A couple of mechanics from the back shop helped lift the thing into the back of the pickup and tie it down. When he left the store, Terry was three hours from home. He should get there shortly after lunch.

Looking at the three wheeled machine the next morning, Eli huffed with indignation when Terry suggested giving a lesson on driving the contraption. "I'll have you know young man, that I rode this old ranch on a motorcycle before your daddy was born. Rode dispatch in the army for a while. That's where I learned."

Terry had no response.

Eli stood silently for a bit, looking at the machine, but with his mind far away, across an ocean in a foreign land.

"Those were exciting times. Dangerous too. Had many a shell whiz overhead or explode close by, but my dispatches always got to the front."

There was more silence.

"Only quit riding on the ranch after I dropped the front wheel into a soft spot I missed seeing. Took a trip over the handle bars. Got rid of the bike and its bent front wheel and forks. Used horses ever since.

"I don't think I'll have any trouble getting some use out of this unit."

Terry answered, "I never knew that about the motorcycle, or your part in the war. You'll have to tell me about that sometime. But, for now, I'm going to ask you to promise not to get into a spill on this one. You don't need to cause yourself any more hurts. We need you around here."

The conversation was drowned out as Sid rumbled past with the tractor, pushing snow to create a trail for Eli's new trike.

When the tractor moved off, Terry took up the

conversation again. "And you have to promise to stay away from the cattle."

Eli pretended he hadn't heard. He was busy studying his new toy.

December was a busy month. Sid went home to spend Christmas with the family. Scotty was back on regular duty. Willard and the family moved into the big ranch house. Bea helped Sis with some Christmas decorations.

Christmas Eve came. Bea joined Willard and the family for the evening service at their large city church. When Eli suggested he would go along, no one said a word for fear he'd change his mind.

CHAPTER 23

TERRY DIDN'T TRY TO FOOL HIMSELF OR ANYONE ELSE. He knew next to nothing at all about calving. On the Lazy-S he was pushed into service a couple of times but always with an experienced cow-man.

As the DD cattle started showing signs that their time was upon them, he said to Scotty and Sid at lunch, "I'm going to watch and learn, and you two are going to be the front-line workers, and the teachers. We can't afford to make a mess of this calf crop. I know most of the cows will manage by themselves, but you need to walk me through the rest."

After a short pause he asked, "So, what's the first thing we do?"

Sid spoke up immediately. "Them animals need more space to spread out. All crowded up like they are puts a lot of stress on them when they're calving. Those trails we pushed through the snow helped all winter, but they won't do for calving. I'd suggest you call the corral cleaners. Have them bring a couple of machines over. Clean up the feeding area and push those snow banks back. The ground's all frozen solid now so they won't have any trouble. The manure and straw and stuff should just break up into chunks that they can load up and haul down to the bottom field. Then we can spread a good layer of straw and start again, more or less fresh."

Terry discussed the idea with Eli and it was agreed upon.

With the three men mounted and pushing the cattle out of the way, the corral cleaners, with their big tracked machines and trucks, soon had the area scraped and pushed into acceptable condition. They then broke down the snow banks and greatly expanded the loafing area.

Most of the stack of older straw was spread on the newly cleared area. Eli warned, "You keep an eye out for mold in that old stack. You see any mold you toss that bale aside for burning."

All winter the men kept trails open through the snow to allow the cattle to wander. On occasion they would push a few head onto a trail to relieve the crowding forced on them by the heavy winter snow and the wind-formed drifts. The animals got a bit of exercise and they always found their way back to the feed mangers before darkness took over.

One cow slipped her calf just after Christmas. When Terry told Eli about it, the response was, "If she did it once there's a good chance she'll do it again. We can't afford to keep her around." She was hauled to the packing house in the city.

The first calves pushed their way into the world in mid-February. The weather turned cold, but the calves continued to arrive. At one point, Terry hollered over to Eli, who was sitting on his trike, all bundled up in his warmest clothing, watching through the fence rails, "I don't know how they survive, as cold as it is."

He had no problem hearing Eli's booming reply. "Just see they get a warm drink right soon after they're dropped. They'll be fine."

Two calves were born weak and didn't survive. Their mothers were held over to give them another chance. The men ear-tagged those two cows and made a note of their history. Terry determined that when the rush of calving was over, they'd ear tag all the animals.

By the end of calving, the men had fought through a blizzard of snow and dropping temperatures. Another bitter three-day wind added to their misery. It all meant long days and nights of work, with hands and feet so cold they wondered at times if they could endure.

Then there was the satisfaction of seeing three hundred forty-seven healthy white-face calves following their mothers around the yard.

In April, four mares delivered their young. Eli was delighted. He seemed to spend most of his days in the stable, sitting on his trike, or walking carefully from stall to stall. He spent hours talking to the horses and coaxing the little ones into trust, with soft talk and gentle hands.

Eli's doctor was firm on the patient's need for exercise. He was instructed to walk regularly, but to not overdo it. With the coming of spring he took short walks around the ranch yard, watching the work and talking to the horses in the big corral. When the kids managed to get free of their school work, Eli let them help around the corral and the stable. Their reward was riding. They wished for no other.

The warm spring temperatures and steady winds cleared the snow off the pastures. Abundant green grass seemed to spring up almost overnight. The entire herd of mature cows and calves was turned out to graze. The corral cleaners were brought back in to finish what they started in January.

In late May the bulls were released from their enclosure to join the cows. It had been many years since Eli built the bull pen. Well fenced, with a roofed shelter to protect the animals in the coldest weather, it had proved its worth time after time.

The younger heifers were separated out and held back in the feed yard, to be joined by a group of new, younger bulls that were added over the winter. They would all be thrown together after the breeding season was completed.

During the long winter months, with the birthing season and then the breeding time, the two lady vets were at the CC on a regular basis. Although their services were required from time to time, Terry finally realized the CC was not being billed for every visit. The girls were dropping in to say hello at unplanned and unexpected times. Mulling this over, he started to question if this had been standard practice before his time on the ranch.

Eli laughed out loud when Terry dropped the question on him. "Terry, you're not that young, nor that dumb. Maybe you're just a bit blind. Next time they drop in, keep an eye on Sid and Greta."

Terry couldn't have been more surprised or more unaware. "Sid? Greta?"

Eli simply laughed some more and went back to reading his ranching journal.

Greta was an attractive, though not beautiful, woman, intelligent and competent at her work. Terry never considered asking, but he guessed she was a bit closer to forty than to thirty. She had never married and seemed content with her business and her work. She was active in her church but did very little socializing.

Sid, of course, was just Sid. A cowboy. About the same age as Greta. Good at his work. Happy go lucky before the cat incident. Now, with his scars, both inside and outside, he was a much quieter and withdrawn man. On occasion, when the two vet ladies were present, Terry thought he saw a bit of the old Sid's social skills come to light. He gave it almost no thought.

But now? Sid and Greta? He decided it was none of his business.

A few days later, the plans for the summer work were discussed around the lunch table in the cottage. The big house was now the home grounds of the Coombs family. Although Eli continued to enjoy his private domain at the rear of the big house, with the warming weather he spent more time outdoors and at the cottage.

With all the boxes carried down from the attic and stored in his private space, Eli had spent many cold, winter hours sorting out all the historic CC records. Hours were spent reading old letters. When Eli occasionally lapsed into a melancholy during the readings, even Bea left him alone.

As each box was opened and explored, his excitement grew, finally arriving at the point where he said to Bea, "This is good material. Lots of history. Some I remember, but lots is from before I was born. It would be a shame to lose this stuff."

As he was holding a particularly interesting document in his hand Bea reached over to the shelf above the desk and picked up the never used tape recorder. She held it out to him without a word and left the room.

After swallowing a hard lump of pride, Eli finally

allowed the younger kids to show him how the recorder worked. As he watched the kids, and considered all the paper in the many boxes, he started wondering how to entice them into helping him sort it all out.

The warming weather found the old rancher outdoors more. The history records were not forgotten but they were pushed a bit aside, waiting for a rainy day.

CHAPTER 24

ELI AND TERRY WERE DRINKING COFFEE IN THE QUIET of the evening. "So, Terry, you survived your first full winter and your first calving season. What are your thoughts on the ranching business now? Any bright ideas hatching in that active noggin of yours?"

Terry was hesitant to say anything because of his newness at the cattle game, and because almost anything they did would cost money. Eli was as good as his word on the management of the CC. His original statement that Terry was the manager, with a lot of latitude on the running of the ranch, had become well established in practice. And he was amazed at how the older man was able to keep his hands, and his opinions out of daily operations. But Terry was determined to be cautious.

Still, there were some things Terry felt were worth discussing. A couple were small. One was large and never tried before. He would start with one of the smaller, more easily understood project.

"Well, I didn't try to calculate any exact number, but it seems obvious that we wasted a lot of valuable feed, what with the mangers often full of snow. We spent many hours shoveling snow, and a lot of good hay went out along with the snow. In addition to those hours of work that would have been better spent on other things, all that hay was trampled underfoot. Then, too, the animals were taking in a lot of cold snow along with their feed.

"I'm thinking we should talk to that builder from town. See what it would cost to build some kind of roof over the feed mangers. He's built all kinds of farm and ranch buildings. He might have just the right idea for us."

Eli studied the young man for a full minute. Finally, after nodding his head for a moment he said, "Can't hurt to get a price. You and I both know this can be almighty cold country. Still, this winter was something else. More snow and wind than normal, I'd say. Might not happen again for some years, but it's good to be prepared. You go ahead and give him a call."

Terry heaved a great sigh of relief that his first substantive idea for the CC: the selling of bred heifers, and now this new idea, hadn't been rejected out of hand.

Into the silence of the kitchen Eli asked, "So what else do I see bouncing around in your head?"

Terry flashed a lop-sided grin at Eli. "That obvious, am I?"

Eli sat silently, although his coffee drinking was not silent.

Terry started slowly. "Well, I've been checking around on prices, costs, etc. We know what the cattle brokers' fees costs us. We know what the auction houses' charge for their services. With a big herd, those costs total up to a lot of money, either one of them. Then we have to load and haul the animals. That costs more money."

Terry was a half-minute thinking up his next statement. He covered the time by getting up to re-fill his coffee cup.

"I read about a rancher down in Colorado who puts on his own auction. Right there on his own ranch. Turns it all into a real event. Big tent. BBQ. Western band. Lots of excitement. People come from all over just for the party. His proceeds on feeder steers is nearly twenty percent above the auction price and his returns on bred replacement heifers is even better.

"The purchasing ranchers seem to value buying directly from the source and are willing to pay for what they know are quality animals from a good herd. A few dollars more for a replacement animal that will be a part of the herd for years is a small concern.

"The sales costs are about the same as a broker or traditional auction. And the buyers load and haul their purchased animals themselves, so the selling ranch has no trucking costs.

"The event coordinator pitches a big tent, sets everything up and prepares the food. He covers his costs and makes a profit just from the food and drinks he sells.the possibilities

"I figure someone's going to catch on and do this in our area. The first one in will own the idea and probably no one else close by would attempt to compete. I'd like the CC to hold that position."

When Eli remained silent, Terry continued.

"Holding our own auction would be a lot of work the first year. We'd have to build more corrals, fences, small holding cells, etc. We'd also have to build a sales area. But all of that could stay in place for future years."

Both men were silent while they played with their coffee cups. Eli studied his young protégé over the lip of the stained mug with the photo of a rodeo rider fixed to one side.

Finally, he spoke. "Colorado's a long way away. Where would you find a promoter who could pitch a tent that big and do up the BBQ?"

Terry smiled at him as if Eli had asked exactly the right question.

"I've already found one. Feller in Calgary does almost the same thing at the Stampede, only he's not doing an auction with it. Just the tent, the BBQ, the music and a big dance."

Eli put the mug down. He hadn't taken his eyes off Terry. "You'd have to find a guy who was as much showman as auctioneer."

Terry's grin was about to split his scarred face in half. "Already have a couple of names to research."

Eli struggled to his feet. He groaned and placed his hand on the small of his back. "Comes this time of day, I've about had it. My knees are creaking. My back's sore. If I yawn any more, I'm liable to lose my teeth."

With no further explanation or comment the old man slowly made his way to his bedroom.

Terry figured he was just making excuses to avoid talking any further about the private auction. He would probably sit up for another hour working on the boxes of papers. Terry shut off the kitchen light and left for a last round of the stable and corrals.

As Sid and Terry were readying themselves for bed, Terry asked, "So, what's with Greta visiting so often?"

There was a long period of silence. Sid brushed his teeth and had a good wash, putting time between the question and his answer. He took one final look outdoors, then turned back to where Terry was standing at the kitchen sink, holding a glass of water.

"I like her. She's kind and gentle. And she doesn't make me feel like a freak. I don't know what all that means. I'm just taking it as it is for now."

A few seconds slowly ticked past. "Neither of is what you'd call young anymore. We might want to grab a bit more out of life before we start the downward slide."

With a bit of a chuckle Sid added, "Course she's only seen my face scars. Hasn't seen the mess on my arm or shoulder yet. She may sell the vet business and emigrate somewhere if she should see me with my shirt off. It ain't a pretty sight."

Terry let that comment go, but asked, "Have you gone out together? Away from the ranch, I mean."

"Only for a private picnic, down in the river valley. Place just over here a few miles. Called Dry Island. Old buffalo jump down there. Nice spot. Don't want to get caught in the rain though. The hill apparently gets slick as grease. We haven't gone out in public."

The brief conversation made Terry think of Cindy. He said nothing of that to Sid.

CHAPTER 25

THE SCHOOL YEAR CAME TO AN END FOR TERRY'S siblings, with the long weeks of summer shining their promises ahead of them. That enthused Andrew and Sandra. It left Clive wishing for his old, city life.

A lot was happening on the CC. The Coombs kids, freed from the constraints of school work and early evenings, started to take more interest in the ranching business. Within a couple of weeks, even Clive was perking up a bit.

The calves were growing and, with the help of the vet ladies, staying healthy. A solid spring rain had the pastures and the hay crop both looking green and inviting.

Eli was in the habit of planting a quarter section to horse oats for the past many years. When his old farm machinery started wearing out, he added it to the scrap metal pile that was gathering a few hundred yards behind the old barn. He could recite the history of the CC just by pointing out each rusting piece.

A grain farming neighbor contracted to get the seed in the ground and the oats in a bin at the end of the season.

Eli and the neighbor, both, found the solution satisfactory for their needs.

With Eli's guidance, Terry and the crew organized a pasture rotation system. Eli kept plans like that in his head. Terry made a chart and wrote it all down. Some fencing had to be added to divide the bigger pastures. With the help of a power post-driver a neighbor was willing to rent out, the fencing went together quickly.

Dividing the pastures created a problem with getting water to the animals. Terry drove to Red Deer and purchased a mile of irrigation hose and some fittings. The crew was able to drag it around with the tractor, moving it each time the cattle were moved. They mounted a big, round metal tank onto skids and dragged it from pasture to pasture, along with the irrigation hose.

The Coombs kids rode a few times during the cold months but with summer upon them and with time on their hands, wanted more. Over the years, Eli kept more horses than any small ranch really needed. He just liked to have them around. Sometimes he would simply stand and look at them, admiring each one. That they ate grass better given over to cattle didn't bother Eli.

Sid ran the bunch up from the rough coulee pasture they ran free in. With Sid and Eli giving guidance, the kids each picked out an animal to gentle and hold for their own.

Willard took the family shopping, and, again with Eli's guidance, bought each one a saddle, bridle and some other tack. Eli was acting like a grandfather, a position the old bachelor never thought to attain or understand.

Pairing each young person to his or her chosen animal, showing them how to gain the horse's trust and then to saddle, groom and care for the beast, was a job for Eli. The stable was big enough for each horse to have his own stall. Very patiently, Eli talked the kids through what had to be done. Sis was nipped a couple of times as she was trying to learn how to use the curry comb. Eli suggested they could choose a different animal, but she refused. The old rancher said nothing but privately he admired her spunk.

As much as it hurt him, Eli knew he couldn't ride again. In his place, when Sid could be spared from the cattle work, he led the kids into the big pasture and put them through a thorough learning process. Surprisingly, it was Clive who first became comfortable with the care and riding of his chosen animal.

CHAPTER 26

SID STARTED TALKING ABOUT HE AND GRETA spending a day at the Calgary Stampede. He cornered Terry as they were riding down to the far pasture. "Why don't you come with us? Call Cindy. We can make a day of it. We'll do up all the morning work here before we leave. Scotty can stand in for the one afternoon."

Terry was silent for a long time, thinking about Cindy and all they'd been through together. Her presence caused feelings he was alternately excited by, and terrified of. He hadn't talked to her since the Christmas party. That wasn't because he didn't enjoy her company. He made many excuses to himself over the months since Christmas: he was busy with the ranch, they were a long distance apart, surely, she had a boyfriend by now, he wouldn't know what to say or do.

He'd enjoyed her company at the Christmas gathering but was not totally sure if her friendliness was affection or compassion. Then he decided that perhaps he wasn't quite so over his injuries and scars as he thought he was. It could be that his self-confidence was more designed for the anonymity of the ranch, than for the bright lights of the big city. He wouldn't share that thought with anyone.

He finally answered Sid. "She's probably got a boyfriend by now."

Sid stared at his friend and started to laugh. "You dope. You're dumber than dirt. That girl has eyes for only you. I could see that the first year you were at the Lazy-S. Only you're not kids anymore. And from what you told me of the Christmas party, nothing has changed in her feelings. For months now, I've wondered why you haven't called her."

He let his thoughts roll around in the silence. Then, looking over at Terry he said, "After all you've said to me about my scars, I can see that you're no more over the cat incident than I am. Fact is, with Greta's help, I might be better off than you are now. So, here's the deal. I admit that it took you to come along and drag me out of the house, to get me back into the world. I owe you for that. At first, I thought all I owed you for was saving my life from the cat. But what I really owe you for is giving me back my life, for pulling me here, to the Double C. So, here's some advice as a part of my payback. Go phone that girl."

Nothing more was said as the men went to their work.

They had been there about an hour, circling the herd and looking for problems. At the sound of Eli's power-trike, Terry's head snapped around. Eli promised to stay out of the pastures. The potential hazards to the cattle and Eli, both, were thoroughly discussed. But nothing else on the ranch made that particular sound. It had to be Eli's trike. He turned so he could get a better look. On the horizon, about a half mile away, he saw Eli riding towards him, accompanied by three riders.

Terry sat his horse while the entourage made its way down the sloping grassland, to the herd. They all looked so satisfied with themselves that whatever he planned to say was lost.

Eli pulled up beside Terry's riding animal and shut off the engine. Although the horses were familiar with the sound of the trike, Terry's ride shivered and stamped, before settling down.

Terry flinched when the motor died. Having to pull the starter rope was the part of using the trike that bothered Terry the most. The arm and shoulder action had the potential to put a lot of strain on Eli's back and chest muscles. He was happier when the motor was left running.

Eli grinned up at him. "You know what this rig needs? It needs a back on this seat. A feller might like to lean back once in a while. How are the animals looking?"

Terry was still not quite used to having Eli run his subjects together, as if only the last question or comment mattered.

"Since we isolated that calf with the scours, a while back, there's no sign of any others coming up sick. We've got to credit Scotty with picking out that problem before it hardly happened. He had the calf pushed off by itself within a few minutes. Probably saved us further sick calves. We weaned that little fella, although it's pretty early. But he's coming along fine now. We'll turn him back to the herd in a short while.

"Everything else looks good to me. We're watching them every daylight hour. But you know a lot more about growth patterns. How do the calves look to you for size?"

Eli, leaning on the handle bars, just nodded and said nothing.

Terry and Eli visited while the three younger Coombs kids rode further down the slight hill to where they could wave to Sid. They then put their horses into a slow jog and circled the pasture, ending back up with Terry and Eli.

Watching them, Terry said, "They're coming along. You're a good teacher."

Eli, looking on like a proud parent, made no reply.

It was not easy to find a time when no one was around to overhear, and bother a fella making a phone call. But that evening everyone was outside enjoying the fine summer weather. Almost shaking with fear, Terry dialed the Lazy-S and asked to speak to Cindy.

"This is Cindy, you big dope. I thought you might know my voice when I answered. Of course, it's been a long time. What is it, two years, three years? A person could forget, I guess."

He knew Cindy was teasing but he was still taken aback. The social side of life always seemed to conquer him. When he said nothing, Cindy started to laugh. "Here I sit by this phone each day, for months on end, waiting for your call. And then, when you finally do call you have nothing to say."

"Well, I had it all planned out, what I was going to say. But when I heard your voice my mind went blank."

Cindy laughed again. "I must have that effect on guys. No one ever calls. That must be the reason. I'm thinking of going into a convent. I'll have to find out if they take Protestants. Or maybe a temple of some sort in Tibet. What do you think? Convent or temple in Tibet? Which would you recommend?"

Terry found a little bit of courage. "Could you find time to go the Stampede with me before you apply for the convent?"

After a gasp and a short pause, Cindy asked, "Are you actually phoning to ask me out? Like, you know, out together? As in, do something fun? Together? Is this actually happening? Now wait, just in case I've got this wrong. Let me dream for a moment. Let me just enjoy the concept, the possibilities.

"If this is real, the answer would be 'yes'. Of course, it would be 'yes'. So, tell me, is this real or am I dreaming again?"

"I miss seeing you Cindy." He had absolutely no intention of saying anything remotely like that. Where had that come from? He let the call go to an embarrassed silence.

After more fumbling from Terry and teasing by Cindy it was finally agreed that they would go to the last day of the Stampede. Cindy wanted to see the final-day chuck wagon races. That is, it was agreed, depending on being able to get tickets to the popular event at almost the last minute.

With Terry living the most of three hours north, while Cindy lived two hours south of Calgary, there was a real problem with travel. It was a far distance to do the traditional date pick-up and return home routine. Cindy solved that for herself, at least, with, "My folks are going up too. I'll bunk down on the couch in their hotel room. They're already booked so that's no problem."

Terry silently heaved a sigh of relief. He would have gladly driven her home if that was required but he wasn't happy with the thought of abandoning her to drive home herself, late at night. And the chance of finding a hotel room in Calgary on the last day of Stampede was remote, at best. Now all he had to do was see her safely to her parent's hotel.

With Sid taking a few days off after Stampede to visit Greta's folks, who also lived south, Terry was needed for work the next morning, so he couldn't stay over. He didn't mind the late evening driving to get home to the CC.

Sid and Greta drove to the Stampede together. Terry drove down to Calgary in the ranch truck. Cindy jumped in the car with her folks for the ride to town. The young people managed to all meet up at the agreed-to location, after a time of weaving through crowds and neck stretching, trying to see over and through and around the milling hordes.

Cindy burst past a group of Japanese tourists and grabbed Terry by the arm. "Hey there, big fella, you're here. I was half afraid you'd find some work to do and forget all about our date. It's awful good to see you."

She turned to Sid. "Good to see you too Sid. Who's your friend?"

Introductions were made and the four set off into the maze of side shows, rides, food stalls and come-on games. Cindy had her arm folded firmly through Terry's arm, hanging on tightly. That seemed to be her position of choice.

When Terry showed some embarrassment at her closeness, she smiled up at him and said, "I don't want to lose you in the crowd."

Terry had no logical rebuttal. Maybe he really didn't want one anyway.

There were no tickets available for the afternoon rodeo, so they settled for a few hours wandering the midway. The races would be in the evening.

Over the warm afternoon, the eager visitors gradually turned into a weary and sun-bleached foursome. When Greta spotted a restaurant that offered fare that was several

steps above the midway hot dog and novelty food offerings, she said, "I'm ready to sit down and have some
real food."

Over paper plates of overpriced, but delicious sausages,
grilled potatoes and sauerkraut, the girls started to get
acquainted. The men sat silently, letting them enjoy the
time. After exchanging some information with Greta,
Cindy said, "I'm both envious of you and a bit ashamed of
myself. I had plans to go to university, but I didn't follow
through. Seems there might be other things I've not
followed through on too.

"For you to get a medical degree and offer quality vet
services to farmers and ranchers is a real accomplishment.
Good for you."

Greta paused for a moment, thinking up a response. "I
appreciate the kind words Cindy, but you're certainly not
too old to choose a career and study for it. You could start
this fall if you wished."

Cindy smiled a half-smile and hunched her shoulders.
"I guess. You're right, of course. My heart is really in
ranching though. And with my two older brothers off
starting their own brands, Dad seems to need me on the
Lazy-S. Don't misunderstand. He would never hold me
back. But, oh I don't know, I guess I see myself on a ranch,
with the freedom to either work with the animals or cook
dinner. And having my hands in soapy water never
seemed like a burden either. I see the real me as astride a
horse rather than riding a chair behind some desk in an
office.

"Might like a family too but I'd need to find a
husband for that. You don't know anyone who's available,
do you?"

Three of the four people at the table laughed at the

question. Terry had his eyes firmly planted on his plate while he cut another piece of sausage.

The evening chuckwagon races were all they were advertised to be. And more. The excitement. The roar of the crowd. The shrill enthusiasm of the announcer. The almost frantic pre-race prancing of the thoroughbred horses. The shouting drivers. The agile and athletic out-riders. The neck and neck finishes. All put together, it combined to make the chuckwagon races as thrilling as Terry always imagined they would be. He'd watched them on TV, of course, but to experience the spectacle in person, and live, was many times better than TV. When the last race was ended, and the crowd rose to applaud, and file their way out, Terry was still wishing for another race.

Cindy seemed to have her arm wrapped around Terrys for most of the afternoon and evening. She stood and tugged him to his feet. "It's over big guy. Let's find some place quiet where we can have a late snack. Then you can walk me to my hotel. I don't know about you but I'm starting to feel like it's been a long day." Her smile was intoxicating to Terry.

Sid and Greta said their goodbyes as they left the fair-grounds. They were off to Greta's parents' home for a couple of days. "Looks ominous," said Cindy, with a knowing grin.

Greta just hunched her shoulders, as if to say, 'we'll see', and they disappeared into the crowd.

Terry and Cindy walked towards her hotel, looking for a cafe that wasn't jammed to the rafters with revelers. Every eating and drinking spot was packed, including the outdoor seating that the partygoers were pushing further onto the sidewalks, as more and more people joined in.

Music blared from café and bar speakers. Car horns blew warnings as the party extended itself onto the narrow streets. Traffic was almost at a standstill as merrymakers wove among the stalled cars and pickup trucks.

Looking in wonder at the celebrations, Terry said, with a bit of a chuckle, "Might need a heavy rain to send folks back indoors before this party comes to an end."

They found an eating spot to their liking in the hotel itself. Terry led the way to a comfortable booth and they were just about to order when Cindy's parents walked in. Cindy waved them over. She stood and moved to sit beside Terry, allowing her parents to sit across from them.

"You might just as well join us. My plans are ruined now anyway, whether you're sitting right with us or across the room."

"What plan was that," her mother asked, absently, as if was a small matter. With her attention on the menu she missed Cindy's eye roll directed towards her father. Adam laughed out loud.

"Oh, I was trying to figure out how to trap this cowboy into giving me a good night kiss."

Her mother's head snapped up at that statement.

"Do you know that he's never even tried to hold my hand? How do you figure someone like that?" Terry was looking at the door, as if he'd like to somehow disappear.

Caroline, Cindy's mother smiled a bit and said, "Perhaps it's your aggressive approach. That can be a bit intimidating, if not unnerving."

"Aggressive? Intimidating? Unnerving? Mother, this is a guy who fought a mountain lion. How can a little one-hundred-and-ten-pound girl be intimidating compared to that?" She said this, hoping her arm actions were lending adequate dramatic effect.

Adam said, "You would have to admit there's a sight of difference between the two."

Cindy took a deep breath and let it out with a flourish. "Well, all I know is that you've spoiled my plan and now I'll never know if it might have worked or not. Perhaps I'll have a slice of that coconut cream pie."

Terry privately wondered if somehow, he was the only one who didn't run his thoughts together in the same sentences.

On the slow drive home in the old truck, Terry ran through the evening several times in his mind. Although he wished to die during the conversation in the café, he had to admit that the trio of kisses in the dim hotel foyer were pleasant. "Pleasant. Does that even come close to the appropriate word?" he wondered.

CHAPTER 27

THE SHORT, SUMMER WEEKS WERE BUSY BEYOND compare on the CC. The hay contractor stacked a bumper crop of baled hay in the big, fenced storage yard. Sid plowed a wide fire break all around the yard and between the stacks. The oats went into the bin in mid-August. The oat field was replanted to fall rye for late grazing.

The contractor from Big Valley designed and built a roof system over the feeding mangers. The same contractor was now busy, with an expanded crew, putting together all the corrals, gate systems, loading chutes, auction ring and seating area for the big fall auction. They took great care with the building.

Terry was convinced the private auction would succeed and become an annual affair. These weren't temporary fences.

To ease the loading and unloading they build a gradual, fenced grade, taking advantage of a natural rise in the ranch yard, that would allow the animals to step into or out of the transport trucks without climbing a chute.

Scotty, Sid and Terry kept busy with the cattle and

horses, as well as readying the hay wagons, tractor, and all the other equipment for winter. Special attention was paid to the watering system and the small stoves that burned all winter to keep the water from freezing over.

Contracts were signed for the auctioneer and his crew. BBQ Barnes, who most folks simply called Barny, the organizer for the food and entertainment, moved his tent and furnishing to the ranch early. He had no other fall engagements and he wanted to look the situation over. A contract was signed at that time.

Terry, his mind never far from the thought of a covered wintering yard for the cattle, watched with fascination as the crew erected the big circus tent, readying it for auction day. 'I wonder how big those things come?'

Advertising posters were printed and distributed by the auctioneer.

A long list of names and addresses of ranches was gathered. An attractive brochure and invitation to attend the sale, was mailed to each cattleman.

The biggest single task for the ranch workers, with the assistance of the lady vets, was pregnancy testing the cows and heifers. Terry and Holly ended up working close together for most of the day. The work allowed for little conversation, but Terry found it was not unpleasant being beside the beautiful vet.

They tested the cows for the benefit of the CC ranch itself. Keeping an open cow over the long, winter feeding season didn't make financial sense and was avoided if possible.

The heifers being offered for sale were tested to assure the purchasers that they were buying a calf, along with the heifer. That was the only way to assure the financial success of the auction venture.

By late September the CC appeared to be ready for winter and for the private auction. Bea put together a big lunch, and with Eli's input, all the men carefully went over the work done and the hoped-for results. As was his usual practice, Terry took notes. Some days, it seemed, his shirt pockets were bulging with scraps of paper.

Bea made a few comments along the way. She had a lifetime of ranching experience, along with her late husband. She still owned the two sections of grassland that was now rented out. Eli was given first option to lease the land when Bea's husband died, but he was satisfied with the holdings of the CC. Bea said nothing about it, but when the lease came up for renewal the next spring, she intended to offer it to Terry.

Terry contacted the leaders of the Big Valley riding club. Curtis and Hanna Trembly started the club when their three boys were young. Now that their boys were grown men with families of their own, their grandchildren joined the gathering of local kids who either loved riding or who wished to learn how to ride.

Terry drove the pickup into the Trembly farm yard and waved to Curtis, who was just closing the door on the big stable. "Morning Mr. Trembly. Spare a minute to talk?"

Curtis said nothing until he got closer to the truck. "Sure thing Terry. Got time for a coffee too if you're agreeable to that."

When they were seated across from each other at the big kitchen table Hanna poured the coffee and put out a plate of sweet-rolls. Terry explained the plans for the auction. He closed with, "So, we're going to need riders to push the heifers through. The animals will be separated into bunches of ten, pushed into the holding space and then pushed into the auction ring when the time comes. There'll be twenty bunches of heifers. They won't go on sale until the larger bunch of steers are sold. To have time to get them all through in the one day, things will have to move along quickly.

"When the 'sold' hammer comes down, someone will open the exit gate and the riders will push the bunch down an alley to a holding pen. While the next group of heifers is brought in by a different pair of riders, the first ones will ride around the back into the big corral. Get ready to do it all over again.

"Of course, they'll be under the direction of adult riders the whole time.

"I've hired some local men to help out, but I thought it might be fun for your kids to get their feet wet, herding and driving animals. They'll go home with a few dollars too."

Terry fell silent as Curtis and Hanna studied each other, looking for visual signs or questions. Seeing nothing from Hanna to trouble him Curtis said, "I can't imagine anything the kids would enjoy more. We'd have to get permission from the parents, of course, but I'm pretty sure that won't be a problem. Most of them will probably be at the sale. I know you'll keep the kids' safety in mind the whole while."

Terry nodded and put down his coffee cup. "As I mentioned before, we're only dealing with heifers. They're used to being handled, and none of the animals are horned. Nor will the kids ever be far away from an adult"

Terry stood, and the others joined him. He shook hands with both of them. "I'll leave it with you for now. If you would talk with the kids and their parents and get back to me as quickly as you can that would be great.

Thanks for the coffee and the sweet-rolls. Those rolls are delicious."

Hanna lifted the plate from the table. "Take one with you. You can eat it along the way."

"Thanks. I will."

CHAPTER 28

THE FRIDAY BEFORE THE BIG SALE DAY CAME AND Terry was sure everything was as ready as it could possibly be. The riding club kids were bringing their horses over that afternoon, in readiness for an early start on Saturday. The big tent had already been pitched. The oversized, home built, BBQ pit was in place. The tables and chairs were set up. And best of all, the sun was shining. There was a pleasant, fall, nip in the early morning and evening air. The mosquitos and black flies were gone for the season.

The crew, augmented by four young men and two girls, hired from local farms and ranches, were kept busy for the past week grooming and brushing the bred heifers. It would probably be the first, and only time the animals would enjoy that treatment.

The herd was kept out of the bed ground during the summer months, after the corral cleaners tidied it up. Now it was spread with a good layer of clean straw. The heifers were being kept there until sale time. Hopefully, the animals would maintain a degree of cleanliness until auction day.

The ranch yard and the big pasture adjacent to it was filling up with pickup trucks, horse trailers, three-ton and five-ton farm trucks, motor homes, vacation trailers, and even a couple of tents. One rancher, who obviously intended to purchase more than one lot of animals, pulled in with a semi and a thirty-foot cattle trailer.

Eli was delighted with the happenings. He rode his trike from rancher to rancher, meeting strangers and shaking hands with old friends and acquaintances. When he disappeared for a while Terry began to worry. After asking around and doing a short search, he found the old rancher in the stable, holding forth from the seat of the trike, proudly showing off the mares and foals from the spring birthing.

The horses were turned out to pasture months before, but Eli insisted they be brought in for the weekend. He tried convincing Sid and Terry that it was for the welfare of the animals, that the graze was about gone on the lower pastures. But when Sid reminded him, with a suspicious grin on his face, that the horses were in a half section pasture in the rough land off to the west, and well-fortified with native grasses, the old man grinned back and said, "Just git er done."

The Lazy-S was present. Adam and Caroline Stocker booked a room in Red Deer and would be out in the morning. They had no intention of making a purchase. They simply wanted to watch the spectacle and encourage Terry and Sid.

Cindy arrived by herself on Thursday afternoon. She would share a bedroom with Sis, in the big house. She had come to help. As Terry went over the possible tasks to assign her, the first thing that came to his mind was keeping track of ear tag numbers, as the groupings were pushed through to the auction ring. Cindy just laughed at that suggestion. "So, I'm relegated to pencil and paper, am I? Not likely Mr. Coombs. Not too likely. You give it another think."

As Terry watched her walk off, he thought, 'Oh boy! This man / woman thing is shaping up to be a lot more difficult than I ever imagined. Maybe Eli has had it right all these years.'

They finally settled on Cindy taking charge of the riding club kids. As Terry watched her run the kids through a rehearsal on Friday afternoon, he could see that the young riders hung on her every word. The girls were especially enthralled with the beautiful young lady who rode so well and seemed to know all about horses and cattle. Even the teen-age club kids offered Cindy their full attention. When she asked them to take on some responsibility for helping the young ones, and keeping them safe, the teens seemed to sit a bit taller.

The auction crew blew onto the scene in the late afternoon. They arrived in a noisy throng; three auctioneers, two bid spotters, two record keepers, one pay clerk and a couple of spouses. Loud seemed to be the only volume any of them possessed. From the time they bailed out of their cars they were the centers of attention. It might have been a Vaudeville show. All it needed was music and dancers.

Saturday was going to be a long day. Terry started wondering if the auction crew could maintain that kind of pitch for the entire time. Of course, he reminded himself, that's why there's three auctioneers. They'll spell off.

Evening comes early in October. The sunset on Friday evening was like a signal for things to quiet down. Some went to town, to their hotel rooms, some visited quietly in the big tent, a few were sitting on hay bales in the stable.

Bea fed the family in the big house and it wasn't long before Terry and Sid said, 'good night' and left for their own cabin. At the end of the job assignments it was Willard, the accountant, who volunteered to keep a record of ear tags on each of the sale lots. He would also work with the auctioneer crew to check over and balance the receipts against sales slips at the end of the sale.

To say Terry went to bed was not to mean he went to sleep. Excitement and anxiety were wrestling over which one would keep him awake the longest.

CHAPTER 29

SID AROSE IN THE FULL DARK OF EARLY MORNING ON sale day. He got dressed and ready for the big day and then called out to Terry. When he received no response, he tapped on Terry's door, and finally pushed the door open, to find an empty bed. He stepped outside, into the chilly, early morning air and glanced up at the big house. A light in the kitchen would mean coffee was on. Darkness would mean he had to wait a bit. There was no sign of light.

Arriving at the stable to saddle his first horse for the morning, he almost walked into the door as it swung wide. He stepped back and watched as Terry led out his chosen ride for the morning's work. "Up early, are you? You'd think this might be shaping up to be a busy day or something."

The look on Terry's face as he stepped out the door and into the beam of the overhead light told Sid that whatever he had to say he better say it carefully, and with tact. The pressure building up in the young man was barely being contained.

Sid simply said, "It's going to be a beautiful day, everything's ready and we're going to have a great day and a great sale." He turned just enough to see a light come on in the kitchen of the big house. "And coffee will be ready directly."

There really wasn't much to do before daylight. The two CC men simply walked among the resting heifers, as well as the big yard lights allowed, looking for problems, and then decided that coffee must be ready. As they turned to walk to the house, Scotty drove his pickup into the yard.

They weren't sure who was up in the big house but even Sis could make coffee if it was her. They left their mounts tied to the outside of the corral. Walking quickly, they were soon at the house. Scotty would join them after he had saddled a horse. Along the way they passed a couple of ranchers who appeared to be wandering aimlessly in the before-dawn dark. Many of the motor homes and trailers were showing lights. Ranching, in any country, is an early morning business.

Just then, a light came on in the big tent. BBQ Barnes, a big jovial black man who had made his living cooking and entertaining for many years, had a couple of big steel plates that fit over the gas jets in his homemade BBQ rig. Liberally layered with grease, these plates were soon sizzling with bacon and frying potatoes. Eggs would follow. A huge cauldron of coffee was starting to come to a boil. As the camping ranchers slowly wound their way into the tent, Barny's wife collected the price of breakfast from each one. Coffee was self-serve.

As Terry and Sid opened the house door they were met by the smell of fresh boiled coffee and bacon frying. It turned out to be Cindy who was up and doing. They could have joined the ranchers at the big tent for breakfast but purposely chose to keep themselves apart from the buyers.

The tension at breakfast was palpable. Everyone seemed to understand that being careful with words was the wisest course of action. With breakfast eaten, Sid and Scotty mumbled their thanks and put on their hats. Terry and Cindy were left alone.

Terry was determined to have a last-minute discussion about the riding club kids. With the two of them standing beside the kitchen counter Terry started, "We'll hold the kids back until the heifers go on sale. I don't want them mixed in with fifty range-steers."

He was about to go on with his monologue, but Cindy put her hand over his mouth. "My dear. You've said it all before. No, don't look away. Look at me. I'm a reasonably intelligent girl. I went all the way through high school. I remember little things, like instructions, for at least one day, and one full day is not up yet since you last told me."

At his downcast look she smiled and with her hand still over his mouth, said, "Terry, you've done a wonderful job. No one could have done better. I'll look after the riding club kids. You look after yourself and the Double C. It's going to be a great day."

She removed her hand, lifted his hat, pulled his head down and gave him a long, soft kiss on the lips.

"I saw that," came a voice from the doorway. "That's kind of yucky."

Cindy laughed. "You won't always think it's yucky, young Sis."

Almost before Terry could believe it, the auctioneer strapped on his neck-mic and shouted, "Testing, testing. Everyone of y'all awake and ready to spend some money?"

Even with no more than that small chatter the auction team clearly took control of the day and the excitement started to build. Last minute arrivals were scurrying to find seating. A few vehicles were still wending their way into the ranch yard, parking every which way.

The auctioneer hollered to his helper to adjust the sound a bit and then got serious. He rose from his chair and claimed a spot front and center of the big raised platform. He was to remain standing all day; shouting, fast-talking, pointing, gesturing, exclaiming, making up words, and otherwise keeping the event at a boiling pitch.

The auctioneer arranged for some airtime on the Camrose radio station. They agreed to run with the opening prattle and follow up with live interviews from time to time throughout the day. The announcer was set up on a table right in front of the seating bleachers. At the auctioneer's opening words, the announcer broke in on a country song with a short, voice over introduction and then nodded and pointed at the sales platform. The auctioneer started in immediately.

"All right folks. Welcome to this great fall feeder and bred heifer sale. We're on the historic Double-C ranch in Big Valley, Alberta. Where else would any cow man or woman want to be on a gorgeous October morning?"

Terry hired a photographer to video portions of the action, and snap still photos during the day. He was figuring these would be good for promotions in future years.

The auctioneer kept on with his introduction. "Here's how it's going to go boys and girls. Coming through first, as you can see right before your very eyes, is a group of fifty feeder steers. There's three hundred forty-seven feeders on offer. They'll be coming through in lots of fifty, steers first and then the heifers.

"Following that, you're going to see two hundred of the prettiest little ladies you've ever seen, with their white faces all shined up for the big event. All pregnancy tested and coming at you in groups of ten.

"That's a big day and we've got to move it right along. Don't sit on your hands, men. You can't fill those trucks sitting on your hands. Shout it out, wave, nod, blink, sing a song, do whatever will get the attention of Rose and Gabby down there in front of you.

Your purchases will be professionally weighed on that big scale you see a-sett'n at the end of the runway, before you load out, so everyone can be assured of a square deal, here at the Double C.

"Alright, here we go with the first bunch. Fifty white-face steers ready for you to take home and finish them off. WhatamIbidforthem?"

Terry stood at the side of the outdoor arena, fascinated by the chatter, antics and entertainment value of the auctioneers, and watching the animals move into and out of the ring. Cattle and money changed hands so fast his head was buzzing. Sid and Scotty were in charge of moving the animals, along with some young local ranchers Terry hired.

One thing Terry probably could thank his accountant father for was his skill with numbers. Even in grade school he could do numbers in his head that other kids wore out sharpened pencils trying to figure. He knew the sale prices for the local auctions the past week and mentally compared. The CC sales on the first couple of lots were up by about five percent.

Then the rancher with the semi and cattle trailer

started to bid. No one knew who he was, and he hadn't bothered to introduce himself. In the predawn darkness, another semi had pulled in. The logos on the driver's doors said the two semis were from the same ranch; A bull head. Huge horns. A name. Peacock Cattle Company. No address.

The two men stuck together. They carefully looked over every animal in the big corral, taking notes, before the sale started. Their satisfaction with the offering was shown when the bidding started.

As the third bunch of feeders were driven into the display area the semi-man put in an opening offer five percent above the last closing bid. The auctioneer took a slight pause as silence reigned on the buyers stands. With the leading of the auctioneer, the next minute and a half was filled with frantic, penny by penny, bidding. Three buyers tried to outbid the semi-man. Most others dropped out. The bidding rose in small increments until the auctioneer dropped his hammer at a price increase of another ten percent. The next two bunches were gobbled up by the same bidder. With one hundred fifty animals purchased he dropped out of the bidding but didn't leave the auction area.

Not sure if the semi-man was truly finished or simply lying in the weeds, the bidding remained hot until the feeder steers were through the system and spoken for.

At mid-morning the auctioneer announced a short break before the bred heifers would be presented. There was a rush for the coffee pot and the several port-a-potties strung in a line behind the stable.

In the sorting corral behind the auction ring Cindy was gathering her troops. The excitement among the kids was palpable. The boys tilted their hats at just the right angle and the girls examined their clothing as best they could, without a mirror, and then they, too, adjusted their hats.

The auctioneer called the sale open again. The gate swung wide. Two twelve-year-old boys and one ten-year-old girl swung small, harmless quirts on the rumps of the heifers. With a start, the surprised young cattle lunged for the opening.

The auctioneer advised the crowd that the animals were being handled by the Big Valley Riding Club. There was a solid round of applause, the kids raised their hats in acknowledgement and the sale was on, in full swing. Again, the semi-man was bidding. When the bids reached a bit higher than Terry was hoping for, the semi-man dropped out. Two other ranchers wrestled over the bids until one of them dropped out. The hammer fell, the exit gate opened, and the kids drove their charges into the lane.

The exit gate swung closed while the entrance was opening. The crowd cheered as three girls, perhaps five to seven years old, swung their quirts and yelled at the animals. The heifers slowly made their way into the ring. The three girls were decked out in clothing that was undoubtedly purchased for the occasion. Western hats sat at jaunty angles over well-groomed hair. Brightly colored, sequined and tasseled shirts were tucked into stylish jeans. High heel boots completed the ensemble. Two girls were riding smaller Welsh ponies. The third was aboard a well-behaved bay gelding of perhaps fourteen hands, sitting up there like a cork on a cup of water.

When Cindy rode into the ring behind the girls, talking to them and encouraging them, she was the essence of a rodeo queen. Riding a black gelding that Eli picked out for her, dressed brightly and yet elegantly, every eye swung her way.

Proud parents clicked photos of the young girls. Terry looked at Cindy and wondered how this lovely girl could be interested in him.

The hired photographer was scrambling to get it all recorded.

The auctioneer hesitated perhaps thirty seconds while the kids got the animals positioned and the photos were taken. But he was there to sell cattle, not admire the kids of the riding club. This would be the only time the kids took center stage. And it was the one chance for the little girls to shine. The rest of the heifers would be handled by the older club riders.

With the groupings smaller than the feeder stock, the selling time increased. Only three groups went through before lunch break was called. The auctioneer warned that lunch break would be one hour exactly. "If y'all are not here, someone else will take home the little ladies you have your heart set on."

Barny had mountains of burgers and piping-hot, chili-laced beans ready and waiting. Money changed hands, plates were held out to the servers and the ranchers grabbed seats at the long tables. No one wanted to be late getting back to the sale.

The afternoon's selling was fast and furious. When the hammer fell on the last bunch of heifers, the semi-man had purchased forty animals. Again, his bidding pushed the prices a bit higher, but clearly, he saw the animals he wanted and was prepared to pay to get them. The other ranchers had no choice but to match his bids, or better them, if they wanted to take home any animals.

The sale was completed at four in the afternoon.

Wrapping up the day, the auctioneer thanked everyone for their attendance and for their eager bidding. He was just about to thank the crew when the side gate swung open and the riding club kids rode in. The auctioneer pointed them out and said, "Let's hear it for the Big Valley Riding Club, folks."

The kids quickly formed themselves into two rows, with the bigger boys in the back. They lifted their hats to the crowd and bowed their heads for a moment. It was done just as Cindy had rehearsed them behind the corrals. The crowd roared their approval. Cameras clicked.

As the group turned to ride back out, one little girl couldn't get her pony to budge. She kicked him and pulled up on the reins, but he only dug his front hooves in more solidly. Finally, she whacked him on the rump with her little quirt. The stubborn animal took two reluctant hops and trotted out the gate. The little girl bounced higher with each step the horse took. Again, the crowd roared.

The radio station was keyed to pick up the closing remarks.

The auctioneer held the attention of the crowd for a few more moments while he told about the evening's dinner, the western music and the dance.

He finished with, "Now folks, don't forget about the ten thirty cowboy church service tomorrow morning. We'll have good old country hymn singing, a time of praise and worship and a short time of preaching by non-other than BBQ Barnes, known as Barny to his many friends, your genial chef and dinner-hour host. You really want to be there. You don't want to miss lunch tomorrow either, nor the Blue Grass concert in the afternoon.

"For those buyers who wish to stay over so you can load out and drive home in the daylight, the Double C tell me they can supply you with hay and water. Water is free. You haul it yourself. Just a small cost to the hay. Thanks again folks. When you see someone from the CC, encourage them to do this again one year from now. So long and God bless."

Then came the big job of claiming purchases, weighing out and loading. A few buyers had checked out and loaded while the sale was still proceeding. That eased the time for the others, but it would still be well after dark before all the animals were dealt with. Several strong yard lights were installed during the construction of the pens, in anticipation of the short, fall day and the early evening.

Further relief was gained when several buyers decided to stay over.

Barny again had mountains of food ready. The feature was what he like to call his 'world famous BBQ brisket', along with a mountain of baked potatoes and a creamed cornmeal dish. Somehow, he and his helpers managed to bake a wash tub full of biscuits. Much of the prep work was done the day before, making the big day's work move along more smoothly.

The truck Barny and his wife travelled in boasted a full kitchen in the back. There was a panel that could be raised to create an opening in the side for serving when they were cooking at smaller venues. For the large gatherings they used the tent and the portable BBQ's.

The BBQ man was almost as loud and entertaining as the auctioneers. He loved putting on a show, keeping up a steady flow of chatter as he dished up the fare, banging the back his big carving knife and fork on the grill from time to time, just to make noise, and telling people how fortunate they were to have him cooking for them.

"Ain't no other brisket like this here brisket. Ain't really

BBQ brisket if'n anyone but BBQ Barnes puts er together. No sir. This here is the real McCoy."

If there was a lull in the activity, the genial chef burst into song. With a deep baritone voice, he regaled his listeners with portions of old country hits.

"Ain't gonna have none of this new country stuff around here," he hollered. "Uh, uh. Not while ol' Barny's here. Why that stuff don't hardly even qualify as music. Shouldn't be allowed, what's been done on Music Row, since ol' Hank went to his reward. Uh, uh."

The only relief from old western was when BBQ burst into 'Ol Man River.' He seemed to relish hitting the low notes, holding and stretching them out to almost impossible lengths.

Somehow, during all the noise and excitement of the brisket dinner and the western group tuning up on the stage, Barny managed to tell everyone, "Gonna have ribs tomorrow. You never had ribs till you had Ol' Barny's ribs. The wife's gonna make up a big batch o' the best potato salad this side of anywhere else. And garlic bread. Hmmm. Mmm. I feel sorry for anyone who's anywhere else tomorrow. Hmmmm."

CHAPTER 30

THE CC RANCH LOOKED ALMOST EMPTY ON MONDAY morning. And Terry had never heard it so quiet. At least, it seemed that way. As he strolled the yard just at sunrise, he found it hard to believe that so few hours ago the grass was strewn with vehicles, buyers and visitors. He felt thankful that no one had gone against the advertised wishes of the CC, regarding liquor. What little bit of drinking was done had been confined to the campers and motorhomes. And thankfully, no one was found smoking around the buildings or haystacks.

He was thankful too for the sunshine. October weather was unpredictable. From year to year the country could expect sunshine, rain, heavy, wet snow, and, on occasion, the dry, cold snows of winter. Under those conditions the yard could become a quagmire.

Five hundred new heifers were due to arrive from the Lazy-S in a few days, but for the time being the top pastures were empty. The cows and calves were working over what was left of the summer's graze on the bottom pastures. The fields looked lonesome and deserted. Terry found himself missing the young heifers and feeder stock that had filled the yard for so many months.

He was aiming his slow steps towards the stable when he heard the house screen door slam. Scotty and Sid were both given a few days off to compensate for the rush of the past week. Willard was at work and the kids were at the end of the driveway, waiting for the school bus. Cindy was the only one left in the big house. Except Eli, of course. But Eli went to bed and got up on his own terms. Terry turned and waited while Cindy walked toward him.

He nodded at her. "Good morning. All packed and ready to hit the road?"

She was too far away to make her voice heard. When she got closer, she answered. "Ready. But there's no real hurry. I ate with the kids, but I didn't see you there. Can I make you something?"

"Naw. Won't do me any real harm to step away from the table for a morning. Between you and Bea, and Barny's BBQ's there's been no one around here going hungry for a while now. Anyway, there's not much to do here today. I'm going to pick up a bit of trash the campers left behind and look everything else over. But first I'm going to saddle up and run those horses back down to the coulee pasture."

Smiling at the remembrance, he said, "Eli insisted that Sid and I drive the bunch up here. Made up a couple of strange excuses but the truth is that he simply wanted folks to see and admire his stock. It's been a long weekend for them though, bottled up in that corral, even as big as it is. Won't take but a half hour to push them back down, then check the cows. Will you wait?"

She started towards the stable. "No, I won't wait. I'm not real big on waiting, Mr. Coombs. You should know that by now. But I'll come with you. You might need me.

You know, open a gate or something." Her teasing sometimes came close to sarcasm. Terry had long ago felt it was best to ignore it.

Terry opened the stable door. "Well, I was going to run that black gelding Eli picked out for you down to the pasture too. You're causing me a lot of extra work but, alright. Let's do it."

Humor or teasing was not one of Terry's strong points. She had to look at his grin before she relaxed about his barb. In the same bland tone Terry had used she said, "How would it be if I ride the black down and walk back carrying my saddle? Would that work for you?"

Terry matched her smile and stepped into the stable.

Free of the confines of the big corral, the horses broke into a run, heading for their normal summer pasture. They would be brought back up for winter feeding in a few weeks. Terry let them run. He and Cindy held their horses to a casual walk. "The gates open. They know the way. We just have to follow along and close er up. Rough land down there but pretty too. Just on the edge of the big valley, although they can't get all the way down to the river. Lots of shelter. The horses do well in those breaks and small coulees. We take down a bit of hay from time to time and they're fine until about New Years, depending on the snow buildup. Eli likes to have them driven up to that forty-acre horse trap for the worst of the winter."

Cindy said, "I'd like to see your bad lands. Can we ride around a bit?"

As if on second thought she asked, "Are there any cougars down there?"

Terry laughed and answered, "Not that I ever heard about."

Terry's sense of responsibility caused him to leave the

horses on their own, knowing they would be fine, and turn aside to check the cattle. With that done, they rode into the rough country, closing the gate behind them. There was not a horse to be seen but he knew they would be alright. This was their usual summer home.

An hour later the two young people sat their horses looking at the rough valley hills. Cindy was enthralled with the area. "It's a lot like our foothills on the Lazy-S, but dryer and without the trees. Very rugged. It's beautiful. I love it."

Neither seemed to have anything else to say. Cindy's leaving for home was weighing on Terry's mind. It was hard to tell how long it would be before he saw her again. He had thought through this time over and over and knew what he wanted. The thought terrified him. But the truth was that if he didn't speak now the opportunity might be lost.

He turned his animal to face Cindy, nudging the horse forward just a bit until his knee was almost touching Cindy's knee. He pushed his hat back and gulped down a big breath.

"Cindy, I want to ask you something."

He froze. She sat silently, waiting. Understanding the situation, she didn't tease, as she so often did.

"Well, what it is, actually. I mean. What I want to say is. Uh, uh, Cindy, I really like being with you. No, wait, that's not exactly what I planned to say."

After an uncomfortable pause he blurted out, "Fiddle, why don't I just say it."

He took a deep breath and steeled himself. "Cindy, I love you and I want you for my wife. I don't have anything really to offer. Nothing fancy like the Lazy-S. But whatever

I have I'd like to share it with you for the rest of my life. Would you marry me?"

Somehow, he managed to get it said without choking or running his words together into an unrecognizable blur. He hoped to never have to do anything like that again.

They sat their mounts close enough for Cindy to take Terry's hand in her own. "Terry, I've waited since I was sixteen to hear that speech. Of course, I'll marry you. Silly boy, who in the world did you think I was going to marry? I've loved you, Terry since you were a stable boy on the Lazy-S and I was a spoiled brat of a ranch girl. Yes. Yes. Of course, yes."

There didn't seem to be much more to say and Terry stifled the thought that it might be a good time to kiss her. He was going to have to work on that.

They couldn't ride back to the ranch without Cindy letting go of Terry's hand since they were facing different directions. They finally got their horses lined out and slowly walked them up the shallow grade to the ranch yard.

They had little to say beyond setting a wedding date. "You figure it out," said Terry. "I'll leave that all with you. Just so long as it's not calving time, I'll work it out from my end." After a short break in the talk he said, "I guess I'll have to call your dad. Is that still expected of people our ages?"

Cindy smiled at him. "It's not really required but you should phone anyway. He's expecting your call."

It took a minute for that to sink in. There was a world of information in those four last words. But finally, Terry looked over at her and nodded.

CHAPTER 31

THE CALL TO THE LAZY-S WENT OFF WITHOUT A hitch. Mrs. Stocker answered the phone. Terry introduced himself and asked to speak to Mr. Stocker. Before she passed the telephone to her husband she asked, "Is everything alright Terry? Is Cindy on her way home?"

"She left about a half hour ago. She's fine and anxious to get home."

Adam Stocker came on the line. Terry gulped down a big breath and hesitated, before saying, "Good morning Mr. Stocker. Have you got a minute or two to talk?"

Receiving confirmation of that, Terry stumbled a bit but finally got his thoughts put together. "Mr. Stocker. You know that Cindy and I have spent quite a lot of time together. I'm sure you've wondered where all that was leading. Well, today, before she left for home, I asked Cindy if she would be my wife. For some reason or other that I don't really understand, she agreed. So, I'm calling to ask if you and Mrs. Stocker would give your approval and your blessing to Cindy and I being married."

He let the line go silent. It stayed that way for as long

as it took Adam to relay the short form of the conversation to Caroline. He didn't cover the phone while he was talking so Terry faintly heard what was said. When Adam came back on the line he said, "Terry, we're not at all surprised. We've been expecting this for some time and we couldn't be happier. I'm not sure how I'll replace Cindy on the Lazy-S, but we'll find a way. Our wish is for the two of you to be happy and have a great life together. Mrs. Stocker and I look forward to welcoming you into the family."

A bit more was said but Terry was soon able to hang up and try to breathe normally again.

The new batch of five hundred weaned heifers arrived and the ranch cycle began all over again. The men were pretty sure they were better prepared for winter than they had been one year ago. Terry was looking forward to the challenge now that he had a good understanding of what was required, and what lay ahead. The amazing thing to Terry was that Eli did all this for many years with only occasional help. The herd had grown over the years, of course, but still, what Eli accomplished by himself was worthy of admiration.

Terry and Cindy made their plans by phone. Half-jokingly, they decided that the Lazy-S would run just fine without her everyday presence. If she could get the book-keeping done each month that would be all the help her dad really needed.

Terry approached Eli about moving a temporary mobile home onto the property for he and Cindy to set up housekeeping. Eli gave him a long look, leaned back in his chair, and said, "Let me think that over."

Terry knew not to push, so the conversation moved on to talking about the recording of the CC history.

CHAPTER 32

At Eli's urging, Terry did something that should have been done long before. He covered the cost of installing a phone in the stable tack room. A bell was mounted on the outside of the stable to extend the ring into the yard. A short five years earlier the phone would have been number nine or ten on a party line. With the new cable system buried along the roadways he was able to get a private line. The phone was put to almost daily use. The tack room provided the privacy he desired, away from the family, especially Sis who seemed to be able to hear through walls.

His calls to the Lazy-S were becoming so routine that Cindy's parents and siblings seldom answered the evening calls, leaving them for Cindy. And Cindy no longer waited to find out who was calling. She simply picked up the receiver and said, "Hi."

Cindy and her mother were making wedding plans and talking about dates. Before Christmas would be too much rush. But the two or three months after Christmas were the coldest of the winter and held their own challenges.

Cindy explained that to wait for spring meant moving further towards spinsterhood. Her mother just rolled her eyes at this, knowing there was no logical rebuttal.

After much contemplation and lacing a calendar with crossed-out dates and original thoughts, February four-teenth was chosen. This was partly for its symbolism, being valentines' day, and partly because Terry agreed that they could probably squeeze in a wedding and short honeymoon before calving season got into full swing.

No one seemed to find any serious objections, so the date was set. Cindy wasn't totally sure about the expression, 'squeeze it in.' but she was prepared to take what she was offered.

Being raised herself on a cattle ranch, she was amused to think that Terry, a city raised man, was becoming a typical cattleman; cattle came before love or food or just about anything else that a person could think of.

So, they would squeeze in a wedding and be thankful.

The young couple met in Calgary for a ring shopping trip. Cindy smiled her way from store to store, holding rings up for Terry and hoping for a response. The closest Terry came to a real response was, "Whatever you like".

Eventually the purchase was made, with Terry doing the mental reduction from his bank account and attempting a smile he really had little enthusiasm for.

With a minimum of formality, Terry slipped the ring onto Cindy's finger while they sat in the ranch pickup truck, in the mall parking lot. The wipers were doing their best to hold back the fast falling, slushy snow, while the heater roared, and blew medium warm air. The occasion was sealed with a quick kiss.

With her head resting on Terry's shoulder Cindy tapped the dash board clock to see if it was really working and said, do we have time to grab some lunch before my bus leaves for High River?

Terry's response was, "That clock can't be depended on. I think it's running about a half hour fast."

Cindy started to laugh. "The clock doesn't work. The heater doesn't heat. The wipers mostly smear thing around. The engine sounds like it just might take off on its own at any moment and the transmission clunks every time it shifts. How old is this piece of junk anyway?"

Terry ignored the question. "There's a good pasta joint down by that hotel I stayed in."

Cindy sat up straight. "Well, I love pasta. Then you can drop me at the bus depot."

She was pleased when he didn't just drop her at the depot. He waited with her and made sure she was safely on the bus before he climbed back into the old truck for the three-hour trip home.

CHAPTER 33

IT WAS A SATURDAY MORNING WHEN SIS SCREAMED her way into the stable. "Terry, Terry."

Scotty poked his head out of a box stall. "Hey, Sis, what's all the excitement about."

He barely got the words out before Sis was screaming again. "Terry. Where is he, Eli's sick or something. He's lying on the floor."

Scotty grabbed his coat off the nail on the end of the stall. "C'mon, he's out with the cattle. We'll go find him."

The cattle were wintering in the big feed yard, so it took no time at all to locate Sid and Terry. Again, Sis started to scream the message out. The men understood the urgency immediately. As a group, the three men and Sis ran for the house. Terry's father and two brothers had gone to town for some Christmas shopping. Sis and Eli were alone in the big house.

Oblivious of the snow and muck shaking off his big boots, Terry charged through the kitchen, down the hallway and into Eli's private quarters. He slid to a stop and dropped to his knees beside Eli. The old man had fallen from his chair. In falling, he had dragged a handful of papers and the tape recorder to the floor with him. Unwelcome images of the fight with the big cat flashed unbidden through Terry's mind as he felt for a pulse in Eli's neck. The others stood silently as they waited.

Terry thought he felt a light throbbing in the big neck vein. Without turning his head away from Eli, he said, "One of you get the truck up here."

The race to the hospital was almost a duplicate of the original one about a year earlier. Only this time it was Sid sitting beside the passenger door, holding Eli's head.

The quick response at the hospital was a duplicate also. The old man was alive, but not awake.

Terry and Sid sat in the waiting room hoping for good news. Terry had no idea where to find his father, but he phoned Sis with the little bit of news he had. Within one half hour after turning Eli over to the medical team, a nurse found the waiting men. The news she brought was better than they expected. "Mr. Chambly is fine. He did not have a heart attack. He's awake and talking. A bit groggy but that's to be expected. The best he can figure is that he fell asleep in his chair. He tumbled to the floor, hitting his head on an open desk drawer, and then on the floor. He has some bruising and may have a mild concussion. He'll probably have a headache for a while, but the doctor gave him something he can take. He'll be fine in a day or two."

She started to turn away, others were waiting for her services. Terry jumped to his feet. "Thanks for that good news. Can we see him?"

The nurse simply said, "Follow me."

Eli was sitting on the edge of a gurney in the emergency ward. He was looking sheepish and a bit embarrassed, clutching the flimsy hospital gown as a last defense against impropriety.

Terry and Sid grinned a bit when they saw him. Sid said, "Fell asleep, did you? Oh, well, we had nothing else to do anyway. There's not really much to do on that itty-bitty ranch. A little trip to town was just the thing for this morning."

Eli didn't return Sid's smile. "Toss me them clothes from off that chair and get out of here whilst I get dressed. Don't know why they took all my clothes off anyway. Just a little bump on the head. Why, back in the old days…"

The two men escaped to the waiting room. In less than five minutes a shaky Eli made his slow way down the hallway and went straight to the outside doors. Sid caught up with him just as Eli was about to push the door open. "Hold up there Eli, Terry's bringing the truck around."

Even with the snow falling and the roads in poor shape they had Eli back at the CC and resting in his own bed before lunch time. Bea was in the kitchen with Sis. She looked at Terry, "So the old fool fell asleep and took a tumble, did he? Next time he gets sleepy maybe he'll have sense enough to lie down. Save everyone a lot of trouble."

The men went back to their normal duties, but two days later Eli called a meeting. He set it for the following Saturday morning, so Clive could be there.

Clive, the academic son who hated leaving his city life, had fallen in love with the rural life in general and the Double C in particular. He outshone his younger siblings in horsemanship and was showing considerable interest in cattle. His particular interest was in the improvement of the range stock.

Having completed high school, he signed up for a first-year college course in animal husbandry. If that went well, his intention was to move into a full university degreed program in the same discipline.

Eli wanted the Coombs entire family at the meeting, plus his lawyer. Willard wore two hats; as accountant for the CC and as father to the Coombs clan. Eli gave no hint of what the meeting might be about.

CHAPTER 34

SATURDAY MORNING CAME. SCOTTY HAD THE weekend off. After the morning work was done Terry explained to Sid about the family meeting. Sid nodded and turned for the warmth of the cabin.

Sis had been practicing her coffee making skills. She proudly set the table with mugs and spoons and made the rounds with the big pot, holding it with two hands. A plate of Bea's leftover sweet-rolls was centered on the table.

Everyone took a seat. Suddenly Sis jumped up and went to the fridge. She came back with a small pitcher of coffee cream brought home from the store in town. Eli repeated his oft-told tale; "Milked my own milk for many's the year. Can't seem to get used to having to buy my coffee cream." The others at the table made no comment, wishing to avoid the longer story they had all heard before.

When everyone was settled, Eli started in.

"Bud, here, and me, we've worked something out. Was going to wait till I died and let Bud do it through the will. But I got impatient. Anyway, I kind of want to see how my plan works out. Can't do that if'n I'm dead. At least not so far as I know."

Eli was not one for long conversations. He cut right to the chase.

"Terry, you've been working the Double C for a year now. You've been manager for some months. Done a good job too. Now, I know the other men helped you along, but that's as it should be. I've got no complaint on your work or your decisions. The auction sale put a good deal more money in the bank than a sale through the broker would have done. Kind of fun too. I'm hoping we can do that again and that I'm here to see it. I'm not planning on leaving this old earth for some time yet but that's not really in my hands. Truth to tell.

"A ranch won't run itself and getting a will all worked out can take some time. That might be time for all kinds of mischief to poke its head out of the wood pile. Government folks get involved, there's no telling what all might happen. Figured it might be best to do this while I'm still alive.

"So, here's what I'm going to offer. Bud has it all written up. It's pretty simple, if you like it and we come to an agreement. Terry, I'm going to sell you the Double C." The statement landed like a brick falling from the top of a high wall.

There was a collective gasp from the Coombs family. Terry looked stunned. Eli, looking carefully at Terry, could see a comment or question forming in the young man's mind.

Eli held up his hand. "Now wait, I know what you're about to say. But understand me now. This ain't about money. Not really it ain't. What it's about is keeping the Double C as an active, prosperous ranch, and making a good life for y'all in the process. Holding together what my folks worked so hard to put on the land and what I've held together for the past almost half century. Seems to me that's worth keeping.

"Oh, there's a lot of money involved. A lot more than I ever dreamed of, even way back when I could still dream big dreams. But we'll come to that in a moment."

Eli cleared his throat. Every person sitting around the table had questions circulating through his or her mind, but no one spoke, waiting for Eli.

"I've got enough put aside for myself, and I have no one but a couple of nephews down east that I never see nor hear from. They don't enter in to this arrangement, although with enough money at stake they could decide to challenge the will. Doing it this way stops all of that."

There was another pause as Eli looked the family over.

"So how are you going to buy this ranch? Well, you're going to earn it. The fact is, you've already earned a starting chunk of it. If you hadn't been here the past few months the CC would have been listed for sale. And she'd have sold too!

"You already know Scotty's story. He's a good man but he can't manage this ranch. So, she's yours. If you want her."

The pauses seemed to be getting longer each time Eli stopped talking.

"In those papers in Bud's briefcase is laid out the whole buy-out formula. There's no real price set. How it works is roughly this: you sign the trust agreement Bud has. I've already signed. That agreement says the ranch is yours to run and profit from. The working capital in the bank is part of the ranch. You have access to it for daily operations, up to a certain limit. After that limit you'll need a signature from your dad, and from Bud.

"It's a ten-year agreement. During those ten years you'll be responsible for sharing profits with a few worthy causes. Bud has all that laid out too. If you follow through faithfully for those ten years and Bud is satisfied that our little contract is fulfilled, the ranch will be yours.

"Now I say it's yours. And it is. But there's a few provisions.

"One is, as long as I'm able to more or less take care of myself I live here. You get the privilege of feeding me and hauling me around when I have a doctor's appointment or some such. And buying me a new trike when this one wears out.

"Another is that each of the other kids gets a profit-splitting share. It's one share if they move away. It's another, larger share if they stay and become a working part of the ranch.

"Your dad gets a share right from the start.

"To be able to operate freely, Terry, you'll have the largest voting share after all the others are cared for.

"You will always care for Bea. She has her own family and she don't need more money, so that's not the kind of care she needs. None of her family lives near here, though. She needs an adopted family and she needs to be needed.

"All of that is written out."

This time the silence dragged out until Sis got up and brought the fresh pot of coffee.

Terry sat looking stunned through the few minutes it took to lay out the latest plan. With a quiet voice he said, "I don't hardly know what to say. Thank you, of course. But that don't seem like much is really being said. But I guess I'll have to leave 'er there. For now, anyway."

Terry's short speech broke the log jam of thoughts. It seemed everyone wanted to talk at once. Eli looked as if he was tempted to escape to his own room.

Finally, Bud opened his briefcase. That brought the family to silence. As if they were at a magic show, wondering where the rabbits were coming from, the family watched document after document being pulled from the old leather briefcase.

Bud changed places with Andrew so that he was sitting across from Terry. Willard moved to sit beside his son. Bud laid out the papers, one by one, turning them so Terry and Willard could read them. "We won't sign, Terry, until you've seen the entire agreement."

Terry just nodded.

A half hour later it was done. The papers were signed.

Terry Coombs, young, inexperienced, terribly scarred from the fight with the big cat, with his hopes of an education put on long-term hold, city raised but country trained, a man with a wedding planned in a few months, was now the contractual owner of the Double C. It would take ten years to complete the contract, but for a gift so large as the CC, that seemed a short time and a small price to pay.

The meeting broke up and folks went their several ways.

Terry mounted his favorite gelding and rode out to check the stock. It was a task that didn't really need doing. But the bewildered young man was having trouble thinking straight. Time on the back of a horse was good therapy. He rode for an hour before he made his way back to the stable. He was cold by that time. The warmth of the stable comforted him. From there he phoned Cindy. Relaying the basics of the buy-out plan took almost as long as it had at the kitchen table, earlier in the day.

Of course, Cindy was excited at the opportunity being offered Terry. To both of them, actually. After much discussion she asked, "What will this mean to us, right away I mean?"

Terry responded, "I'm not exactly sure about all of it. But if you're referring to the wedding, I don't see as how it makes any difference at all. The biggest issue that comes to mind is where we will live. Do we move in a mobile for a temporary solution or do we somehow go ahead and build a house? We can't move Eli and the family out of the old house. We'll have to think and pray about that. And none of that has anything to do with the ownership matter anyway."

CHAPTER 35

NOTHING REALLY CHANGED ON THE DOUBLE C. ELI had been allowing Terry to take the full lead on operations for several months. If there were changes, they were within Terry. In his mind. In his heart. In his emotions. In his sense of responsibility. In his expanded work habits.

The new owner of the CC didn't see it in himself, but Sid noticed almost right away. There was a subdued maturity building in Terry. He was never a talkative man. That didn't change. What changed was the thoughtful serious-ness of the few words he did speak. Sid thought it best to hold his observations to himself.

Terry spent a couple of weeks trying to be everywhere at once. Although the late fall days were getting shorter, Terry worked more hours than ever, starting well before mornings first light and extending his day past the normal dinner hour. He then found his way back to the stable to do unnecessary work with the horses.

Sid watched this activity with a feeling of wonder. After a few days he gave up on matching Terry's efforts.

When two weeks went past without change, he finally confronted Terry as he was heading back out after dinner.

With a hand on Terry's arm he said, "Whoa there, big guy. I happen to know from personal experience and observation, that there is not one single thing that needs doing on this ranch this night. It's cold and snowy and miserable out there and I have a nice fire going in the cabin. I'll put the coffee on. We'll put our feet up and I'm willing to bet that whatever you have in mind to do can wait for another time. It's enough for this day."

Sis and the rest of the family stood silently as this little exchange took place.

Terry stood with one arm in his big coat while the other sleeve hung down his back, waiting to be pulled around to the front. He looked at Sid with a dawning light in his eyes and on his face. He expelled his breath, nodded and pulled the sleeve around. Silently he left the big house and headed for the cabin.

When the two men were seated beside the wood stove with fresh coffee at hand, Sid took a long look at his friend. He didn't like the fact that Terry's coffee mug was shaking just a bit. "OK. Talk to me. What's going on. The wedding got you down? You concerned about the responsibilities that come with being married?"

He repeated, "Talk to me."

Terry took the time to kick off his riding boots and slip on the wooly slippers he kept beside the stove. The act of removing the boots was an unplanned signal that he was in for the night. Sid saw that as a good sign. Terry took a sip of coffee and set the mug on top of the stove. He leaned back in the chair, looked at Sid, and seemed to make a decision.

"I wasn't sure how to tell you and Scotty. Wasn't even

sure if I should say anything or not. You both already know that I don't deserve this job. Didn't earn it. Couldn't do it without the two of you. You've kept me from more than one mistake, teaching me all along the way. You and that kind old man up there in the big house.

"Well that old man, beyond teaching me the cattle and horse business, has gone a step further. A big step. Another step I didn't earn nor deserve."

He then explained the situation on the Double C, and how it scared and excited him at the same time. "Don't know what of all the things in the near future troubles me the most. Owning and being responsible for this great ranch? Getting married? Calving again in just a few weeks? Or is there some surprise hiding around the corner, just waiting to catch me half asleep and unaware? It's all smashing together in my head."

Sid stood and took the three steps that would close the distance between them. He held out his hand for shaking. "My young friend. I couldn't be happier for you. And it isn't really a matter of deserving or earning. It's a matter of the right person being in the right place at the right time. Eli believes you've earned his trust. I agree with that."

After shaking Sid's hand and picking up his coffee again, Terry asked, "But will you and Scotty be content to work on the Double C, knowing the owner isn't the cattleman either of you are?"

Sid just laughed at the question. "We both like it here. Scotty ain't going anywhere and my only other options are to go back to sitting on the couch at home or finding another ranch. And who knows, the next ranch might be the worst anyone could imagine. No, I think I'll stay right here."

Terry nodded his thanks. Idly, he wondered about this

business of nodding. Always before, he had been in the habit of speaking his thoughts. It's true his speaking tended to be brief, but still audible. The nodding started with Big Mike on the Lazy-S. But most of the other ranchers had the same habit, so he figured he might just as well leave it alone.

Sid cleared his throat and spoke. "I am going to solve one problem for you though."

Terry lifted his eyes to his friend. "What problem is that?"

"You've been wondering about moving in a mobile home or building another house. You don't really want to do either one in the middle of winter. So, I've decided you can have this cabin. It needs a bit of fixing to make it a happy place for a new bride, but that's easier than building new in the middle of winter."

Terry laughed, not knowing what Sid had in mind. "So what? You're going to roll up in your blankets in the loft?"

"No. I'm moving to town. Greta and I have decided that there are better options than running into old age with no one beside either of us, so we're getting married. Of course, she still hasn't seen my chest and shoulder. Or my arm either, for that matter. I'm half afraid to show her in case she runs for the hills.

"Anyway, she has a nice little house in town and it's only a short drive to the ranch. I'll be available on a moment's notice if a need arises. You and Cindy will be comfortable in the cabin until you make more permanent plans."

Now it was Terry's turn to jump to his feet and shake with Sid. "Good for you. That's a good decision. I'm happy for you. And who knows? It's not too late to start the next generations of cattlemen."

Sid had no follow-up comment on that subject.

CHAPTER 36

TERRY DROVE THE OLD PICKUP OVER TO BOYCE Nugent's ranch. The shouted 'hello' from the feeder pen led Terry directly to where the neighbor was working.

"Welcome there, young feller. What brings ya over this here way on a cold afternoon? Good ta see ya though."

Terry waited until he was a bit closer before talking. He had no hope of matching the rancher's growled volume. "It's good to see you too Sir. It's been a while. You might want to drop over to the Double C if the work ever lets up. I know Eli would like to share a pot of coffee with you. Show you the work he's doing on the ranch history."

"I'll do that. Yessiree, I'll do that very thing. Got a bit to do here first though. Cain't make no promises right this very minute."

"Whenever it works for you. In the meantime, I want to get two tickets to the Christmas banquet. Are you still working on that committee?"

"Just as sure as you know. Got tickets up at the house. I'll drop over in the next couple of days with them. Get you them tickets and swap a lie or two with that old reprobate you work for."

Terry thought it best to leave the ownership issue alone until Eli offered to share it publicly. "Thank you, Mr. Nugent. I'll be getting back."

"Just as sure as you know," Boyce said again, "Just as sure as you know. I'd have you up ta the house fer coffee but when I started 'er, I figure ta finish this little job before dark. Better keep at 'er."

Terry just waved his thanks and walked back to the truck.

Eli was using the trike less during the cold weather and staying by the fire more. His enthusiasm for the history of the Double C was growing with each document he opened and read. He had a small stack of filled tapes sitting on the desk, ready for transcribing. There was no real order or time-line to what he was recording. Sorting it all out once it was on paper was destined to be a major undertaking. Willard promised to find someone in the city who would take on the job of typing it all up.

As the latest small storm passed to the south, the sun came out and the temperature rose a bit. Eli started sensing the urge for fresh, outside air. A lifetime in the ranching world had kept him outside in heat and cold, wet or dry. It was all he knew of life. He was beginning to feel trapped in his own house. He also had a need to see and spend time with his precious horses. The latest newborns, three colts and one filly, had taken on considerable growth since spring. Terry held them in the upper pasture when the riding stock was turned into the lower, rougher land. Come evening, they found their way to the corral, and one of the crew would let them into the barn.

For the past few days, with the wind blowing down off the northern mountains the animals had been left in the stable.

Eli bundled up in his warm clothing and decided to visit his equine friends.

There hadn't yet been a lot of snow, but Sid continued to keep trails cleared anyway. From the house to the barn, to the big corral and the feed lot, the paths were clear enough for Eli's trike to maneuver with little risk, if he stayed to the trails. He made his way down to the stable and let himself in. He could have left the trike outside and walked in, but after considering the wet, snowy seat he would come back out to, he chose to swing the door open and climb back onto the machine. Once inside, with the door closed, he backed the riding machine against the baled bedding straw, out of the way, and shut it down.

Eli spent the full of an hour with the horses and then decided to make his way back to the house. He walked the length of the stable and swung the door open, holding it in place against the wind, with the big hook he attached to the wall many years before. Back on the trike, he squeezed the throttle leaver and pulled the starter rope. When nothing happened, he pumped the throttle again, and pulled the rope twice more. Terry had cautioned him against straining his shoulder and chest. He didn't like the beginning of the pain he felt but he was determined to complete what he'd started.

He could have easily enough walked to the house, taking it slowly, but again he pulled the rope, holding the throttle all the way open, after pumping it twice. The little machine started with a bang and a small puff or grey smoke. Clearly, he had flooded the carburetor.

It popped loudly twice more as it burned up the extra fuel. It then settled down to run normally. Satisfied that it would stay running, Eli put the trike in gear and drove it out of the stable. To close the door, he had to dismount and walk back a few steps. Just as he was about to push the door the last foot or so, he saw smoke curling up off the floor, at the other end of the runway.

Rushing back in, he found the straw the machine had been backed against, on fire. The stacked bales were in no real danger of burning, but around their base was a collection of loose straw, plus two broken bales that were meant to be distributed to the stalls. The overloaded fuel burning off had carried a small flame with it, finding a ready and eager source of fuel for a fire. Although the loose straw was burning freely, it was just starting to flare up. It could have easily been controlled by raking it into the center of the runway. But Eli didn't do that.

He rushed to the hose stand and turned on the water. Aiming the hose at the fire and squeezing the nozzle full open, he was panicked to see the water pressure blow the straw in all directions, carrying the flames with it.

He managed to put out some of the fire with the water, but with the flames spreading around the back of the bale stack at an alarming rate, and with the grey smoke getting thicker, he couldn't get the job done.

There were still no flames showing threat, but clearly, the fire had taken hold behind the stacked bales. Eli was distressed by how quickly the old building was filling with smoke. He started to cough. He dropped the hose and grabbed his chest, gasping for air. It took a few moments for him to get his breath.

He knew he could do no more. The old barn was

going up in flames. With a sad inevitably driving him, the old man turned to the horses. The grey, acrid smoke was taking the place of the clean air in the stable. The terrified beasts, struggling for oxygen that had been replaced by the foul smoke, were backed into the far corners of their box stalls, whinnying and stamping about.

The animals tied in open stalls were squealing in fear, thrashing their heads and pulling back on the tie ropes. The ceiling was now a pall of grey smoke to a depth of several feet. He could hear the terrifying roar behind him as the old wooden structure caught fire, while he tried desperately to loosen the animals. Stepping into a box stall with one frantic mare, Eli, for the first time in his life, feared one of his own horses. The animal was beyond reason. She blindly swung in a circle inside her stall, knocking her colt sideways. The colt recovered and spun out the opened gate. The mare charged the few feet across the stall again, pinning Eli hard against the wooden framing of the pen. He heard something snap and felt a sharp pain.

In fear now for his own life, he wanted only to escape from the maddened mare and the burning stable. The next blind turn of the mare put her right at the door. She lunged through and followed her colt out of the building.

Eli, realizing that his left arm was broken, clutched it with his right hand and staggered for the welcoming sight of the open door, and the snow-covered yard outside.

Two of the cowboys' work-horses broke their halters and were loose. They frantically turned several times in the runway before charging out the door. Sid, working on the tractor in the big shed a hundred feet away saw the horses racing past the shed doorway. He ran out to see what was happening, just as Eli staggered into the yard. The old man took a dozen wobbly steps into the snow of the yard and collapsed to his knees, and then onto his side, still clutching his arm. Sid was beside him within seconds. He knelt down and lifted Eli's head out of the snow. Eli grabbed Sid's jacket front with surprising strength. "Fire. Horses. Help them. I'm alright."

Sid didn't have to enter the old barn to see there was no hope of saving the structure. The job now was to save the horses. And to do that he would need help. He ran to the feed yard, hollering for Terry and Scotty but got no response. Taking a quick turn, he ran to the hay yard and found the other men loading a bale wagon for the evening feeding. He wasted no time on details. "Fire. Fire. The stable."

As if they were tied together, Terry and Scotty's heads snapped up.

"Fire." Sid hollered again, waving his arms. "The horses."

The three men were soon at the burning stable. Risking his own life, Terry took a big breath and charged for the furthest back, box stall. Seeing it empty he went to the next stall. He unlatched the gate and swung it open. Like all the animals trapped in the burning structure, this mare and colt were both frantic with fear and the need to breath clean air. He stepped in, sidled sideways to get behind the twisting mare. With his back against the rear wall of the stall he hollered and made pushing motions with his arms, trying to force the mare out. He tried to holler louder but with each deep breath his lungs filled with more smoke.

Bits of half burned straw were floating in the inferno. The stench of burning white-wash and smoldering flecks of old paint added to the dense smoke Terry was gulping down.

In the stall with Terry, the terrified mare's eyes were rolled back in her head and there was no sign of reason in her actions. She swung around in the stall, knocking both her colt and Terry flat to the floor. Terry leaped to his feet and managed to get hold of the mare's halter. She leaned back onto her hind legs, lifting Terry completely off the floor. When she came back down, he made another effort to get her out. He wasn't exactly able to lead her. It was more like directing her leaps towards the runway and safety. The colt followed.

Going to the third box stall, Terry, now coughing and gasping for air, and fighting down the temptation to let it all go while he ran to safety, managed to open the gate and again make his way inside. The filly was down. Ignoring her, Terry repeated his actions from the previous stall and the mare surged towards the door.

With the fire behind them, the animals break for freedom and safety pushed them naturally towards the big, open door.

Sid managed to get the fourth box stall emptied and some of the working animals loose and out the door. Terry stepped outside, took several big breaths of clean air and lunged back into the stable to help Sid.

Scotty was running back and forth as fast as his legs would carry him, dragging saddles and tack into the safety of the snow-covered yard. The fire had not yet broken through to the tack room, but it was filling up with smoke anyway.

Several minutes passed, with Terry kneeling in the snow-covered yard, catching his breath. His attention was drawn to a couple of vehicles bounding dangerously over the rough, gravel driveway. Pausing to watch while he coughed and gasped for air, he saw neighbors and a few men from town stop a safe distance from the fire. Men poured out of each vehicle, running to help.

Scotty staggered out with the last of the leather gear. He had a big armful of old harness that Eli kept draped on pegs in the wall, the last remnant of a by-gone era. He dropped it onto the growing pile of tack and knelt beside Terry.

He coughed a couple of times and gasped for air, before saying, "I managed to get a call off to the wife in town. She was going to make some calls. Looks like she connected alright."

Terry was bent over, coughing and retching. He nodded at Scotty's words, reflecting on the benefits of ranching so close to town, and mumbled, 'thanks'. His coughing was bringing up all kinds of black sputum and gobs of messy saliva. His hair was singed, and his scarred face was almost unrecognizable with smoke and grime plastering him from head to foot.

Sid was on his knees in the snow a few feet away. He was coughing up the same kind of mess Terry had spit to the ground. Sid reached for an untrammeled patch of snow and scooped great handfuls into his mouth. He waited a few seconds for it to melt. He then swished it around his teeth and gums before spitting it out. He couldn't seem to stop coughing and spitting. The sputum was an awful, unnatural sight.

The newly arrived men looked to Terry for direction. He struggled back upright before saying, "Thanks for coming men. There's nothing can be done anymore except try to protect the rest of the buildings and the hay stacks. Maybe someone can take a look at the stacks. They're all layered with snow, so I don't think there's much danger. We couldn't afford to lose them."

Between fits of coughing and throwing up he continued.

"If some of you could round up those loose horses that would be a great help."

Another pickup drove too fast into the melee. With the breaks locked, the truck skidded sidewise on the snow and finally came to a shuddering halt. Bea bailed out while the truck was still rocking on its springs, defying her known age.

Before she had a chance to say anything, Terry was at her side. "Everyone is alright I think. Well, we're all alive anyway. Except Eli breathed too much smoke and he broke his arm. He has to get to the hospital. Scotty took in a lot of smoke too. If I send him along to help Eli, do you think you could make that trip?"

"Of course. Where is the old fool?"

Eli had dragged himself to the corral fence. He was sitting in the snow, still clutching his arm, his back to the corral. The pain of the broken arm was now showing on his face. A neighbor was squatting beside him. As Terry and Bea approached, his first question was, "You men all OK? What about the horses?" The two question came as one.

Terry saw no point in lying to try to protect the old man. "Lost the bay filly. The rest are fine. Just scared a bit."

Eli let his chin sag to his chest at this news. When he looked back up there was the tracks of tears etched through the dirt and grime on his filthy face. He truly loved his horses. He couldn't seem to keep his eyes off the burning remnants of the old barn. "My father built that barn. Known it all my life as a happy place to work and dream."

After a short pause he continued. "That was a pretty filly. Shame. My fault. Stupid."

Terry put his hand under Eli's good arm. "C'mon, we have to get you off that cold ground. Bea and Scotty are going to take you to the hospital. Sid and I'll be along shortly, just as soon as we're sure this is all under control. The doctor will splint up that arm for you and he may want to do something about the smoke we all breathed too much of."

Bea moved her truck closer to where Eli was standing. With the neighbor helping him balance and with the assistance of the late arriving Boyce Nugent, the two men lifted Eli into the vehicle. Scotty, still coughing up smoke and ash, climbed in beside Eli. With several men's voices in her ears, admonishing her to drive carefully, Bea left for the hospital.

Terry and Sid sat side by side in the snow, their back against the corral. The fight with the fire was over. The fire, of course, won. A couple of men managed to drive the, now settled down, horses into the cattle pen. The first attempt to drive them into their own paddock proved the animals would go nowhere near the still blazing fire, or the horse yard attached to the old barn. They would be safe with the cattle and there was time enough to gather them up when things settled down.

The town men and the neighbors took charge of the situation. A couple of them staked out the hay yard, watching for troublesome sparks of fire brands floating in the wind. As close as it was to the barn, the tool shed could not be saved. Three or four men rushed to carry arms full of shovels, brooms, pry bars, digging tools, fence post diggers, and a lifetimes collection of miscellaneous gear from the shed to the machine shop a short distance away. A few old cream cans and some miscellaneous keepsakes from the previous generation were carefully carried out.

With the fire roaring its deadly message and with the weight of the old cream separator, the men gave up on it. The machine Eli spent so much time turning the handle on, as a boy, was not to be saved. The blacksmith forge and tools were left where they were. The anvil was too heavy to even consider. Boyce Nugent expressed his opinion. "Them there is all metal. They'll still be some use when ya'll dig them out'n the ashes."

Thanks to the snow on the roof, the machine shop would be safe.

When the fire broke through to the loose hay in the loft, it took on new, expanded life, virtually exploding with vigor. The decades old structure was fully engulfed at this point, with the cedar shingles curling in the heat before bursting into flame and flying off with the fire generated wind. It wasn't long before the roof fell, and then one wall collapsed outward, draping itself over the recently cleaned out tool shed. The other three barn walls fell inward, sending thousands of flaming fire brands into the air. Most landed harmlessly in the snow.

Eli's overlooked trike was lost. First the vinyl seat melted and sagged. Then the tires burst into flame and exploded. Terry looked over at the sad spectacle and thought how easy it would have been to move the little machine.

The men at the hay stacks were extra diligent until everything settled down again.

As the fire slowly burned itself out of fuel, and with

the blaze concentrated on the piles of half burned timbers and outer wall structure piled up on the old concrete floor, the stench of burned flesh was added to the smoke. Every man there knew the smell and where it came from. No one saw any need to comment.

CHAPTER 37

BY THE TIME THE SCHOOL BUS DROPPED THE TWO younger Coombs kids off at the end of the driveway most of the neighbors and town men had left for home. Willard had been called at work. He arrived home just as the walls were falling, leaving the old building as a burnt-out relic.

Rushing to Terry's side Willard said, "What…?"

Terry cut him off with a flick of his hand, sensing the urgency of his and Sid's medical needs. He bent towards the ground, his face almost in the snow, while he coughed horribly, sucked air deeply, and then struggled to his feet. Between gasps for air, he said, "Later Dad. Can you stand by and see to the rest of this? There's no more danger unless the wind comes up, but it should be watched anyway. Sid and I need to get to town."

With that agreed, Willard rushed to the house to change from his suit and tie to his work clothes.

It was early in the day, but Bryce Nugent was doing the evening feeding with the help of two other neighbors. Terry waved his thanks at them before he and Sid left for the hospital. Had Terry thought about it, or had anyone pointed it out, he would have realized that he was beyond helping anyone on the CC. Staggering with weariness and sickness, he finally got the old truck turned around and on its way to town.

Both men were still coughing up smoke and digging charred bits of straw and wood out of their mouths. Sid especially seemed to have a serious reaction to the smoke. Under the grime on his friend's face Terry thought he could see a grey paleness he had never seen before. It worried him.

About a mile down the road Sid looked over at the struggling Terry. "You alright to drive?"

Terry nodded. "No option."

But there was an option and it showed up a few minutes later in the form of the two lady veterinarians. Terry recognized their station wagon with the vet's sign painted on the side, from half a mile away. He had lots of time to slow and come to a stop on the side of the road. He rolled down his window and flagged the girls to a stop.

Holly was driving. In her concern for the men, she misjudged her stopping distance, turned sideways on the remnants of snow the plow left behind and stopped just inches from colliding with the old pickup. Both vets piled out of their car and rushed to Terry's open window. Both started talking at once, but Terry held up his hand.

Sid was in the middle of a coughing spell. He was too slow rolling down his window. He ended up spitting on the floor. Terry coughed again, but not as much as Sid. He found his breath and said, between gasps, "Gotta get to the hospital. Sid needs help."

He was about to shift back into gear when Greta said, "Shut that old piece of junk off and get in our wagon." Her tone of voice didn't seem to leave much to discuss.

With the windows rolled down and the keys still hanging from the ignition, the Double C ranch pickup was left where it stood.

There was little talking on the drive to town. Greta sat in the back with Sid, holding a bundle of clean cloth for him to spit into. At one point his coughing turned into a violent spray of vomit. The experienced vet didn't flinch at the sight or smell. "That's good Sid. Do that again if you can. But I may have you clean up this car later on."

At the hospital, the efficient staff soon had the situation under control. The four men were lying on gurneys in the crowded emergency room. For all Terry's concern about Eli, it turned out to be Sid who had the full attention of the medical staff.

Eli's arm was set and in a splint. A cast would be put on as time allowed. Although he still had the oxygen mask in place, he no longer really needed it. He had far less exposure to the fire than the other three men. Being aware of his previous heart attack, the attending physician did a thorough examination of his pulse, blood pressure and heart. He was declared fit to leave for home a soon as his arm was stabilized in plaster.

An orderly helped him to the shower room so he could clean up before the cast was applied.

Holly went to the nursing station and asked if Eli could stay on the oxygen until they knew about the other three men. He couldn't get home anyway, unless Holly drove him, and she wasn't offering to do that. Not right away, anyway. She was unaware of Bea's involvement. The nurse said, "Alright, unless another case comes in. Then we would need the space."

The vet went back into the ward and with a smile said to Eli, "Looks like we either have to put up with you a while longer or give you a tap behind the ear with a chunk of firewood. Seems like you're tougher than any simple fire."

Eli ignored her.

The doctor addressed the other three men all at once. "Fellas, there's no obvious reason you won't all be just fine in a few days. We're going to keep you overnight just in case something shows up that we don't see right now. With an old building like that barn you tell me about, there's no saying what all might have been in that smoke. Could be old chemical sprays. Could be toxins from treating horses over the years. Some of those old medicines were more toxic than the disease they were designed to treat. And who's to know how many layers of lead base paints burned off?

"You stay and rest. Keep the oxygen going. Lift the mask only for drinking. And drink all the water you can. Gargle and spit it out. Drink it and throw up, swallow it until you bloat. It'll all help. The nurse has gone to find you each a toothbrush. Clean your mouths as well as you can. The nurse will show you where you can have a shower. Clean as much of that smoke and grime off as you can. Then lay back down and rest. We'll see what's next, in the morning. I'm glad you're all alive. Be thankful. And take your rest."

Terry broke away long enough to find a telephone. He dialed the Lazy-S and asked for Cindy. He told the short form of the story and when she finished asking her few questions he said, "I've got a big ask. You have a good crew there. Do you suppose the Lazy-S could spare a couple of men for a few days? I'm going to need some help tomorrow with the others laid up."

Cindy's response was immediate. Without asking her

father or Big Mike, she said, "I'll have three men geared out and on the road in an hour. I'll come with them. The least I can do is put some food on the table. And listen up, my hero. You will do no work for the next few days, either. That's an order and you might just as well start getting used to it since we're to be married shortly."

Greta walked into the ward and lifted the oxygen mask from Eli face. C'mon, big guy, time to go home."

She helped him up and then turned to Sid. "You rest easy now. I'll come by in the morning unless we get an emergency call of some sort."

Sid lifted the mask and thanked her. The other two men followed suit. As she was nearing the door Sid called her back. "Appreciate if you'd go by the ranch and get me and Terry some clothes."

A few minutes later Scotty's wife rushed in. "I had trouble getting away from the shop. Tell me."

Greta caught up to the slowly walking Eli. She took him by the arm and said, "Holly's gone for the car. We'll wait at the door."

Eli was looking all around the entranceway and waiting room. "Bea is here somewhere."

Bea arrived just at that time with two take-out cups of coffee. "Got you some pain killers too. Wait while I get the truck."

Eli thanked Greta and turned to Bea.

CHAPTER 38

WITHIN ONE WEEK THE DOUBLE C WAS SHOWING signs of normality. There had been no new snow to cover the remains of the fire, so that ugly display lay there for all to see and remember. The insurance agent spent a few minutes looking at the mess without getting out of his car. He then waved at Terry and left.

The men loaned by the Lazy-S did a more than satisfactory job. After sincere thanks and firm handshakes from Terry, Cindy motioned everyone into the car and they left the Double C. The car was loaded with saddles and gear plus a small duffle of clothing for each man. Terry and Cindy had found no time to be alone, but with work to do on both ranches they reluctantly parted.

In a phone call to the Lazy-S, Adam accepted Terry's emotional thanks for the loan of the men but refused any thought of payment. "There might come a time when I'll be calling you for help. Glad we were here when you needed us."

Terry called the corral cleaners and explained about the fire. "What's the chance of you bringing that big track-loader of yours over here, along with a dump truck? We'd like to have this mess gone before it snows again."

The arrangements were made and the next day the men were hard at work. Their attempt to separate out the remains of the burned filly were hopeless. The fire hadn't left much to sort out.

The Double C had been slowly filling a hollow in the bottom lands for some years. The debris from the barn was hauled there to add its grim reminders to the detritus of the past.

Terry again called the builder in Big Valley. He was starting to think he might as well put the man on the payroll, he was there so often. Within two days the builder and a couple of men were busy turning the machine shed into a make-shift stable.

The Cattlemen's Christmas banquet came and went. Terry stood aside as the ladies and teen-age girls oohed and awed over Cindy's engagement ring. A few men shook his hand and offered congratulations, but most ignored the announcement, preferring to discuss cattle, feed and sales prices, or the ever-popular topic of the foolishness of politicians.

CHAPTER 39

THE NARROW, TWO LANE PAVED ROAD WAS IN WHAT the highways department would describe as good winter driving conditions. That meant the recent snowfall had been cleared off, and the road was open to traffic. What it didn't mean was that there was no need to be cautious.

In this constantly windy country there was always a need to watch for wind driven snow and for sudden cross-winds that could catch a driver unaware.

Adam and Caroline Stocker were nearly home. The turn-off to the ranch was one mile ahead. The bed of the pickup truck was piled carefully with boxes and crates of food and supplies for the cookhouse, as well as for their own use. The full morning of shopping had procured the needed supplies for the next two weeks. The lunch in High River was much to their liking. Now they were looking forward to a quiet afternoon in the warmth and comfort of the big ranch house, with the wood stove adding greatly to that comfort.

The slight downward slope in the road was familiar, as were the several small hills and rises skirting the roadway.

But the driving and swirling wind can catch the best of drivers off guard. Perhaps Adam relaxed his vigilance as they neared home. Perhaps his mind wandered for just a moment. Perhaps he took his eye off the road to look at the cattle in the adjoining field. No one would ever know for sure.

People driving two lane roads are so familiar with sharing the space with others that no extra thought is really required. But Adam's slight bit of inattention coincided with a gust of wind that drove through the little valley between two small hills, sending a blast of blinding snow ahead of it and pushing the pickup into a sideways drift, and across the center line. Adam immediately made the necessary correction. He had done it a thousand times before.

But in that fraction of a moment the wind changed again. Not much, but enough. Making the correction against a wind that was no longer there, on a road laced with frost and a skiff of light snow, caused the truck to side-slip, turning crossways on the road.

The timing was unfortunate, to quote a police officer at the scene. The road was not busy. At any other time, the truck would have spun and settled, allowing Adam to get it back under control. But there was no way, and no time to avoid the one-ton delivery van approaching from the other direction. The impact was more violent, and more damaging than the average driver could ever imagine.

The full force of the collision landed on the driver's door. That anyone survived was credited to the fact that it was a somewhat angled, glancing blow. The delivery van drove its front fender hard into the pickup's door, pushing the full force of the collision into Adam's space. The van then bounced off, fish-tailed twice as it passed the damaged pickup, flipped onto its side and slid into the snow-filled ditch. The driver's head hit the steering wheel, splitting his forehead open. He lay unconscious in the turned over van with the engine sputtering to a stop while the one exposed rear wheel spun freely, and final came to rest.

The van driver had serious injuries, but he would survive.

In the split second before the window exploded into a thousand pieces, Adam's head swung sideways, hitting the window frame with a sickening thud that no one heard.

No one heard Caroline's scream either. As Adam's head rebounded violently, the full force of the impact drove the door partway into the truck's cab. The truck swirled in several circles on the slippery road and finally came to a stop.

Adam and Caroline were both wearing seat belts but there were no shoulder harnesses. The two victims bounced helplessly inside the truck's cab. Adam was unconscious from the first blow to his head. He offered no resistance to what followed. His forehead hit the steering wheel and an instant later the back of his head hit the rear cab window.

Carolyn's smallness of stature prevented her from hitting the dash, but the extreme forward motion caused terrible bruising on her chest and stomach, while the return to an upright position left her with whiplash that would cause her grief for the remainder of her life.

Still held in place by his seat belt when the truck came to a stop, Adam slumped sideways, his bleeding head flopping onto Caroline's lap. His body was twisted and torn, trapped between the crushed door, the bent seat and the steering wheel.

Caroline was unconscious. The impact of the collision pulled her towards the driver's side of the truck. Her head didn't hit the side window until she rebounded to the right. Although her collision with the glass was enough to cause a concussion and drop her into unconsciousness, she was not hurt nearly as seriously as her husband.

No one moved as the two trucks lay hundreds of yards apart on the road. The morning's purchases were strewn from ditch to ditch across the pavement.

It was perhaps ten minutes before another vehicle arrived at the wreck scene. The driver pulled to a stop, ran first to the van and then to the pickup truck. Seeing blood but no movement, he climbed into his car and frantically swung into the first travelled road he saw. It happened to be the road to the Lazy-S. Pulling to a stop and running towards the cookhouse with his arms waving and hollering for help at the top of his voice, he soon had the attention of the cook, and then Big Mike.

CHAPTER 40

CINDY DROVE TO BIG VALLEY TO SPEND CHRISTMAS with the Coombs family. She planned to stay over until New Year's, but just two days before that time, the phone rang. Sis answered, listened for a moment and then called Cindy to take the call. Cindy said 'hello', listened for a moment, gasped, and put her free hand to her face, shielding her eyes as if there was something she didn't wish to see. As she continued to listen, she slowly sank to a chair. She was soon crying, her shoulders rising and falling with horrible sobs. Without saying a single word, she hung up the phone. She turned to Terry with a drawn, tear streaked face.

"There's been an accident. Dad's pickup turned sideways on the icy road. A truck coming the other way T-boned him. Dad's seriously hurt. They're not sure he's going to make it. Mom's hurt too but not as badly. They're in the hospital in Calgary."

Terry stood immediately, turned for the door and said over his shoulder, "Get your things together."

Terry found Sid in the temporary stable, working with the horses. He quickly explained the situation.

Without even waiting for Terry to finish. Sid waved his hand towards the door. "Go. Get that girl down there. She'll be in no condition to drive herself. We'll make out here."

Terry said his thanks over his shoulder as he charged out the door. A quick change of clothes, a few things thrown into a bag, and he was ready. Cindy came out of the house, still weeping. Andrew was carrying her bag. Terry held out his hand and she dropped the keys into it. He opened the passenger-side door for her and within a minute they were on the road to Big Valley. It was silent ride, except for the low music playing on the radio and the occasional sob from Cindy.

At the hospital the news was grim. A doctor took Cindy and the other gathered family members, into a private room. With the men doing their best to look stoic and with the women holding back tears, the doctor explained the situation.

"Mr. Stocker's injuries are quite serious. It's too early to predict if he will survive. He has a broken left arm and a broken left leg and hip. There's damage to his spine. The impact of the collision pushed him sideways, while his seat belt prevented him from sliding across the seat. The result is that his left side is seriously damaged.

"He has internal injuries. There's no way to know how serious they are yet. If we can hold him stable until tomorrow, we will do more tests."

He paused to let the family adjust to this news, before continuing.

"Broken bones heal, so that is not a big concern. The concern is the spine, the internal injuries and the impact damage to his head. His head hit the window frame, according to the police. That's where they found blood and hair. There's skull damage but, again, it's too soon to know the extent of the injury. Certainly, he has sustained a serious concussion, but if that is the extent of it won't be known for some time. He's unconscious. Whether he will awake soon or not at all we don't know. I have to be honest with you on that.

"Whether he will be mobile again, or not, if he does awaken, won't be known for several days. Right now, the challenge is to keep him alive. I wish I could be more specific. But as I've said a couple of times, the testing takes time. I know you're impatient for exact news. You're simply going to have to wait a few days. We will deal with the broken bones immediately. The internal injuries, and the head injuries will take longer. Please try to be patient. In the meantime, he will remain in intensive care. We'll let you know when you can see him. It won't be tonight."

He waited a moment to allow the stunned gathering to voice questions. No one spoke. The doctor then turned to Caroline Stocker's report.

"Mrs. Stocker was badly shaken up. She sustained some whiplash and small head injuries from hitting the window. We don't think that is too serious at this point.

"Although she's bruised and in considerable pain, she has no broken bones and no internal injuries that we have discovered so far. She should be up and around within one week. Unless there's something we haven't seen yet she should enjoy a full recovery."

When it was clear the shocked family had no immediate questions, the doctor left the room.

A couple of the women sunk into chairs while others were hugging and crying. The men silently looked at the floor. One by one they left the room and slowly found their way to the sun room to wait and talk.

Terry stood aside as Cindy joined the family during this time. He found a chair near the elevators. Within one half hour Cindy left the family group and walked over to where Terry was sitting. "I've got to get back to the Lazy-S. There's nothing to do here and the men will be wondering. Can you come with me?"

Terry stood and put his arm around Cindy's shoulders. "I can stay for a couple of days. You can tell me all about it as we drive."

At the ranch, the crew waited for news. After getting Cindy to the house and unloading her suitcase, Terry went to the cookhouse. It took only a few minutes to bring the men up to date. Terry left them with solemn looks on their faces and returned to the house.

The next day Cindy had a long discussion with Big Mike. The main concern on the ranch was the impending calving season. Mike assured Cindy that all was in readiness or would be in a few days. The crew was well experienced and dependable. They could work without daily supervision.

Cindy had been slowly taking over the management of the Lazy-S during the past two years as her father eased away from the daily ranch tasks. He had been taking on some responsibilities with the Cattlemen's Association and was considering a run at politics. But he had always been there in the background, ready to assert his authority.

Cindy had taken over all the bookkeeping matters and the handling of the finances.

She wasn't sure how the crew would take to having her stepping in as sole manager. Her concern wasn't because she was a woman supervising men. She had been around the men from when she was a child. She had ridden with them and gradually taken on bits of responsibility in recent years. She was comfortable around the men and they with her. No, whatever issues there were in that regard could be dealt with.

What concerned her was that most of the crew were long term on the ranch. That was both good and not so good. They remembered her as a young girl. Several of them assisted in teaching her to ride. They had put up with her youthful antics and covered for her when she might have gotten into trouble if her parents knew everything she did.

Now, after all those years, would the men recognize her as an adult, with knowledge of ranching that was adequate to manage this large spread? For the first few days after the accident, hoping to avoid any potential conflicts or doubts about her management, she carefully phrased her desires as suggestions, or as questions, seeking Big Mikes input or approval. The arrangement couldn't stay that way over time, but she felt it was best to tread lightly, at least until Adam Stocker's situation clarified itself. Terry purposely stayed in the background.

Cindy and Terry made another trip to the hospital. There was no new information from the medical people, but Cindy was anxious to see her mother and to look in on her father, even if he was unconscious.

Terry would be taking the bus north to Big Valley after the hospital visit.

At the hospital, Cindy and her mother wept together while Terry stood back. Caroline Stocker finally held out her hand to Terry and said, "Come here, Terry."

As he stepped close to the bed, she grasped his hand and held on tightly. It seemed a natural thing for Terry to slip his other arm around Cindy's shoulders. The three of them remained there in silence for a few moments before Caroline said. "Thanks for standing beside Cindy and our family at this time. I suspect you're needed back at your own ranch. But please know that your concerns are greatly appreciated. I don't know where the Lazy-S will lie in the future. Cindy may well be needing your help again. Thank you."

Terry, ever awkward in social situations didn't know what to say. Finally, he gently pulled his hand free of Caroline's grip and reached for his hat that he had laid on the bed.

"Actually, I have to get back today. Cindy has her car here, so she can get home alright. I'll take a cab to the bus depot now. A bus leaves about an hour from now. But if there's more I can do, Cindy knows she only has to call."

After a short moment of quiet he said, "I'll be praying for all of you. "

The women both had tears in their eyes. "Thank you," said Caroline.

With the busyness on both ranches and with the trauma still being dealt with in the Stocker family, the phone calls grew fewer over the next weeks. Nothing more had been said about the wedding.

CHAPTER 41

SIS TORE OFF THE PAGE TILTED 'JANUARY', ON THE BIG kitchen calendar, the calendar all the family and ranch dates and events were recorded on. She took a moment to look at the red circling around Feb. 14. Turning to the dinner table where the family was gathering for the evening meal, she snuck a quick look at her big brother.

Terry noticed her action. He couldn't help but see the red circling. There had been no real cancellation of the wedding. It simply was never mentioned again, after the accident. As Terry had done with the high school grad, he turned the wedding planning over to Cindy and her mother. He now made the assumption that if the wedding wasn't cancelled, it at least was seriously delayed. He was deeply disappointed in Cindy. He thought the very least she could do was call and discuss the matter with him. The last couple of times he called the conversation was short and desultory, as if Cindy was too preoccupied with family matters to delve into anything personal.

He kept his feeling to himself. It was not Coombs family or Double C business.

To make the management of the Lazy-S more efficient Adam had given Cindy signing authority on the bank accounts and with the few suppliers the ranch depended on. Almost as if he had a premonition of coming disaster, he had also given her power of attorney, to manage ranch matters in the event of his absence, temporary or permanent.

Following the accident, Cindy and the ranch lawyer appeared before a local judge. Within five minutes the power of attorney was confirmed.

Cindy was now fully in charge of the Lazy-S. She was careful to respect the crew and to impose small changes slowly. The crew adapted to her changes without comment, although she noticed a few of the men glancing sideways at her from time to time. Cindy had long felt that her father was a bit lax in some of his management practices. She intended to tighten things up, but she knew she had to do it carefully and gradually.

Caroline was home and recovering. She was badly bruised from the thrust against the seat belt during the collision, and the bouncing and rattling she endured, but those ugly black and blue marks were gradually dissipating. Most of the soreness was gone. Only the soreness in her right arm and shoulder, where she slammed against the door were still painful. Her concussion was serious, but the healing was slowly getting under way.

Cindy was no longer concerned about her mother's survival or her physical healing. What concerned her the most was her long periods of silence, followed by tirades about slippery roads, careless drivers and the weather. It was as if Carolyn needed to find something or someone to blame.

In her quiet times alone, Caroline thought about the

accident. She sometimes came close to re-living it. Feeling the truck swerve sideways on the icy road. A quick glance, seeing the frantic look on Adam's face. The useless spin of the steering wheel as Adam tried to correct. Seeing the oncoming truck and knowing it was too late, no matter what either driver did. Feeling the first shudder through the metal of the vehicle as the two trucks came together.

The noise and speed and violence of the collision were beyond her wildest imaginings. The crazy, high speed spin of the pickup as it separated from the other vehicle. Feeling the shower of broken glass from Adam's side window. Feeling her body first lurch violently towards her husband and then, as the seatbelt grabbed her, and the two trucks separated, even more violently whipping back to the right.

Seeing Adam flopping sideways, as a puppet without strings might do. The blood pouring from his head wound. The sensation as her husband's head flopped loosely on her legs, as if there were no longer any muscles holding it or controlling it.

Her screams. The same scream that echoed in her mind some nights and woke her up. Her shoulder crushing against the door. Finally, her head slamming against the window. Knowing she was losing consciousness.

The way her brain told her, in the last split second of consciousness that she was going to die. Waking up cold and hurting with Big Mike leaning over her, calling to her to open her eyes, and assuring her that help was on the way.

All this, and more, Carolyn re-lived in her dreams, and in her quiet, solemn moments through the day.

The first week after the accident she suffered terrible

headaches. She still had headaches, but they were minor, and she was learning to live with them.

What was new, and totally unexpected, was the melancholy, leading to bouts of serious depression. Some days were almost lost in feelings of overwhelming sadness, that were like a heavy weight, dragging her down, spinning and spinning into a dark hole of her own making. It took all she had, internally and spiritually, to drag herself back. A few times the thought entered her troubled mind; 'why bother'?

As a believer since her early childhood, she knew she should be able to call on God. She heard all the right words many times over the years from faithful teachers and said them herself. Now, put to the test, those words sounded like a child's Sunday School lesson. She realized that she really had no clear understanding of how to apply the lessons of a lifetime. That thought added to her melancholy.

But now her needs were serious. Adult needs. Having lived a controlled and almost charmed life, where she was seldom put to any serious test, it had been as if God was there 'just in case', and like a gentleman, He hadn't interfered too much with her life.

It was as if someone who had never climbed a mountain suddenly needed to climb the highest mountain anywhere around and had no real idea how to start. She wondered about many things, and then found herself quietly praying, hoping God would answer.

There was little to do, with just the two women in the house. To simplify things, they were taking their meals at the cookhouse.

Legally, Carolyn and Adam were co-owners of the ranch, but her actions showed total disinterest. She was terribly disappointed in her two older sons. Their father took out a huge loan, risking the Lazy-S, to set them up on their own ranches. She thought they might have shown their gratitude by taking on more of the load at the home place after the accident. That they hadn't done so, left her with deep feelings of failure as a parent. It also left her concerned about Cindy.

In one of her deeply melancholy times, thinking of her sons, the thought entered her mind; 'they had it too easy. They didn't earn all their father gifted them with. Unearned pride is blinding them, and it's too late for any teaching from me'.

Cindy was focusing all her attention and energy on the ranch. She was forcing herself into working long hours, sometimes doing things best left to the crew. She was losing weight and wasn't caring for herself as she had always done. Her previous talk of a February wedding seemed to be forgotten.

Terry visited just once. The visit was uncomfortable, the relationship strained, Cindy preoccupied. He drove home without ever having removed his overnight bag from the truck.

The phone seldom rang. It was as if the Lazy-S was cut off from the world. Terry never called. Cindy never called the Double C. Caroline wanted to give advice to Cindy but wasn't exactly sure what to say, and Cindy never brought the subject up.

Adam had still not awakened. He was on life support, showing no signs of improvement. The medical reports were tediously repetitive. The one report none of the family would ever forget came about two weeks after the accident.

Cindy and her siblings were asked to come to the

hospital. Again, the doctor gathered them in a private room. "Thank you for coming," began the doctor. "I know it's a long drive, but this is important." He looked over the small gathering, seeing several competing emotions among them.

Putting on his most professional, but compassionate manner, he said, "We have done extensive tests and now have the results back from the labs. The bottom line is this: although your father's body is healing, and most functions are returning to normal, his brain functions are not doing as well. When his head struck the window frame the damage was quite severe. His skull was fractured. A few sharp pieces of bone entered his brain. Surgery is not the answer at this time and may never be the answer. Whether or not he will come back to consciousness is unknown. At this point he shows no awareness or reaction to any stimuli.

"The unfortunate news is that even if he does wake up it is unlikely his brain will ever return to normal. He may well live for many years, but he will in all probability remain in a vegetative state." He paused to look eye to eye with the family.

"I am aware that you don't want to hear that. We'll keep watching him closely. If there are improvements, we will let you know immediately, and we will rejoice with you."

After a short silence he concluded. "I truly wish the news could be better." He folded his notes and quietly left the room.

Driving home, Cindy's overriding thought was, 'what now'?

CHAPTER 42

ON A TRIP TO RED DEER ON A COLD, BLUSTERY, February day, Terry was shocked from his thoughts about the ranch, and his cancelled wedding, by a vibration that ran through the old pickup. He felt it first in his foot, as if whatever was happening in the old engine was transferring its distress through the carburetor linkage and on to the gas pedal. The engine quit momentarily, backfired, coughed a couple of times and then seemed to smooth out again. Terry managed to nurse the ancient machine into the city where he joined the normal, slow traffic on the snowy streets.

His original reason for the trip was forgotten. He now thought he had better head for a garage where he could find a mechanic. When the truck coughed and jerked again, he made a quick left turn and headed for a dealership instead, sensing that he probably needed more than a mechanic.

Slowing for the turn over the slightly raised entryway into the dealership, the engine coughed once more, a great cloud of blue smoke escaped the tailpipe, and the whole machine seemed to shudder. With the rear half of the truck still jutting into the traffic lane, it stopped. Terry had to press the brakes to keep it from rolling further back into traffic. He knew there was no point trying to re-start Old Eli's pride and joy, so he sat there for a moment wondering what to do next.

A yard man, dressed for the weather while he swept snow off the display of new vehicles, had seen the whole arrival. He wandered over to where Terry was still sitting in the stalled vehicle. Terry rolled down the window and the two men looked at each other. The yard man had a big grin on his face. "Ya mighty near made er all the way there buddy. Gotta give this old, blue machine a 'A' fer effort. Cain't leave ya on the street though. You hold tight fer a few minutes while I get the wrecker from the shop."

It wasn't long until the old truck was pulled to safety and parked out of the way, at the edge of the big lot. Terry was inside the showroom with a cup of coffee steaming on the low table before him while he blew warm breath onto his cold hands. A salesman was rapidly talking about possibilities.

Most city dealerships displayed cars in their show-rooms. But this was farm, ranch, and truck country. There was no need to wander around in the snow looking at the choices on offer. The trucks were right there in the warm showroom.

Terry had never made an automotive purchase and didn't really understand the system. But, of course, he had heard the talk of discounts and hard bargaining.

He was uncomfortable with the clipped chatter of the salesman and was starting to think of walking over to a different dealership. But where he stopped was the brand of vehicle he wanted, to match the old work-horse and make Eli happy if nothing else.

He sized up the three units on display, first looking at the load capacity of the box, then at the interior of the cab. The one that caught his eye was almost the same blue color as the old truck that had served the Double C for so many years. It came with a radio, which Terry didn't care about. What he did care about was that it came with a four-speed transmission, suitable to both ranch and highway needs. Only when he was satisfied at the choice he preferred, did he take a slow, careful look at the price sticker. He had nothing to compare to, but instinctively he felt the price must have some wiggle room.

He stalled for a moment, gathering his thoughts. Finally, he turned to the salesman. "Well, clearly I need a truck. I like the looks of this one. All except for this here sticker. There's a couple of other shops in town. Can I leave the old truck sitting where it is for a while? I'm thinking I need to take me a walk. See what else might be available."

The salesman quickly grabbed the printed price card off the windshield. "Let's not be hasty, my friend. It's possible I could do something here for you. So, what would I have to do to get you into this baby today?"

Terry almost laughed out loud. The verbal skit was so practiced and worn that even a novice shopper could see right through it. He lifted his hat and scratched his head. He walked around the truck once more, not really looking at anything particular, just thinking.

"Well, I'm thinking what you need to do is put a good set of winter tires on those back wheels. You need to see that the gas tank is full to the top. You need to do whatever it is you do to get it ready for the road and have it sitting outside for me in two hours. I've got work to do back at the ranch. And you need to take a serious bite out of that bottom number. You do those simple things and I'll write you a check."

The salesman shrugged off the tires and gas and honed in on the price. "How big a bite did you have in mind?"

Terry almost laughed out loud again. "Well, it's you thats doing the biting. The old man I work for told me one time that I can't be both the buyer and the seller. Since I'm the buyer that leaves you as the seller. You go ahead and take your bite. I'll let you know if you need to take another."

Two hours later, after Terry did his other business, including getting license and insurance for the new truck, he was ready to go. The salesman shook his hand and passed him the keys. As he was walking towards the new truck he stopped and turned, as if remembering something. "Double C ranch is just south of Big Valley. Have your tow driver haul that old truck out there. We'll add it to our collection."

The salesman said, "Sure enough. Probably about a fifty-dollar haul.

Terry shrugged, although with his big coat on the salesman might have missed it. "I expect the dealership will be more than happy to absorb that. Just to get the thing off the lot if nothing else."

As the salesman watched the new truck disappear in traffic, he was mentally calculating his commission, minus the tow bill.

It was Sis that started giggling at the dinner table as

Terry told the story. Terry was the furthest thing from an entertainer, but soon the whole table was roaring with laughter. Even Eli seemed to enjoy the tale, although he had been pretty despondent as he stared out the window earlier, watching the wrecker back the old truck into a spot beside the garage.

There was more news to come that evening.

The family was still sitting around the table when there was a tapping on the door and Sid poked his head in.

"Can I interrupt you for a moment?"

"Come in," answered Sis. "We're just having dessert. Will you have some?"

"I'll pass on the dessert. But thanks. I just wanted to give you a bit of news."

Everyone put down their forks and their coffee cups, giving their full attention to Sid.

Without dragging the situation out Sid started right in.

"Just wanted to let you know that Greta and I were married last evening. We kept it small. Just the two of us and the pastor of Greta's church. A couple of friends of Greta's stood up with us.

"We'll have a gathering and a bit of a celebration after the weather breaks. Her folks were afraid of the roads and Greta and I are both too busy to take time off for travel, so we arrived at this solution."

For a long moment there was silence around the table. Sis broke the spell by saying, "Does this mean I'm going to have to find someone else?"

With the room breaking out into laughter, Terry jumped to his feet and gave Sid a handshake. Everyone else joined in on the congratulations.

After a suitable time, Sid bid them all good night and closed the door behind himself. The room was again silent. The silence was broken by Eli saying, "Might a known it. Saw it com'n."

Between the truck and the wedding news there was much to discuss and laugh about that evening.

CHAPTER 43

CINDY WAS DOING THE JANUARY, MONTH-END BOOKS for the Lazy-S. The original plan was that she and Terry would be married just two weeks from that date. She pushed that fact to the back of her mind. If questioned, she would have quickly confirmed her love for Terry, although they hadn't talked in some time and their last visit didn't go well, with each of them burdened with their own matters.

The load thrust upon her from the truck accident was all she could think of. In her singleness of purpose, she thought no further than the Lazy-S and the account books lying before her. The ranch was so much a part of her, and a part of the Stocker family, that she hadn't opened her mind to a life without the ranch being a big part of her existence.

Before the accident she had easily pictured leaving the Lazy-S herself. Life with Terry, on the Double C, would demand that. But there would still be the well-loved home ranch, where her parents could be found living in the big, old house, and where she and Terry could visit and, eventually, bring their children.

That her emotional remoteness and her seemingly fickle heart was causing Terry to think of his unstable mother, and make comparisons, was unknown to Cindy.

Terry too, was firm in his vow of love. But that position was set against the remembrance of a chaotic home. He would rather remain single than repeat his family's experiences. If Cindy could come and go so easily in her affection, Terry could see nothing in the future but grief.

Cindy made out the pay checks for the crew and then turned to the utilities and other invoices in the accounts file, as she did each month. It was all pretty repetitive. When she was done and was putting away the re-filed, paid accounts, she found herself concerned, as she had been for the past couple of months, about the diminishing cash on hand. Even when her father was there and in control, she had worried. Now, unless she ordered the sale of some animals, she would have to negotiate an increase to their operating loan.

But the bank had total control. And the decisions made in the high towers of big banks were not always completely rational; certainly not always in the interests of the client. The animals were pledged to the large collateral loan. If she sold some, they would expect her to use the money to reduce the loan.

Her father always took a casual approach to ranch finances, never seeming to lose sleep about accruing an ever-larger operating loan. Nor did a new loan for purchasing a piece of machinery or a group of bulls, bother him. A single check to the bank made it all go away after the fall feeder sale.

The Lazy-S handled a lot of money. With a single large

payday each year, bank loans seemed to be a part of the operating procedure. Cindy suspected that a portion of her father's attitude simply reflected his easy-going nature. But another portion was the result of years of prosperity, creating a laid-back boldness.

It was certainly true that cattle prices fluctuated year by year, sometimes, alarmingly so. But the Lazy-S had always shown a profit. Sometimes the margin was slim, but they had never suffered an actual loss.

What had long bothering Cindy, and had caused her to lose sleep, was the large collateral loan that funded her brothers into their own ranching businesses. That action had always troubled her. A large portion of the income from the Lazy-S feeder sale went towards that loan, leaving less on-hand funding for the next year's operations.

The re-payment plan was having a serious impact on the operation of the ranch. If cattle prices fell off and held low for any length of time, the ranch would be in serious jeopardy. She thought her father had been foolish but, being young, her advice was not sought.

Now, all her fears became reality. She was just putting the paper work away when the bank phoned. The loan manager, the one that Cindy had never liked or felt comfortable around, said, "Good afternoon Miss Stocker. Herb France here, from the West Country Bank."

Without preamble or even a polite greeting the man continued.

"We have just recently been reviewing the Lazy-S position with the bank. I'd like it if you could make an appointment to come in for a consultation. It's time we looked at your loans in light of the situation with Mr. Stocker."

Cindy wasn't sure how to respond. To say something

impolite would undoubtedly hurt the ranch. Carefully she said, "It's a two-hour drive to your bank, Mr. France. Could we not discuss this on the phone? The line is private."

The bank had the entire Lazy-S at their mercy. It was clear the cattle alone were more than valuable enough to secure the collateral loan, but that was not how it was structured. The cattle, the land, the horses, the buildings, the machinery, it was all tied up as collateral. So far it had not proven to be a problem, but technically the Lazy-S needed the bank's permission to complete the fall feeder sales. Moving any animals off the Lazy-S property was, by the fine print of the bank contract, reason enough to call the entire loan. Adam ignored this stipulation and so far, the bank had accepted the practice. But with Adam no longer in charge of ranch matters there was no guessing what the bank might do.

The ranch lawyer informed the bank of Adam's injuries and of Cindy's irrevocable power of attorney. Herb France was a city man. As far as Cindy knew he had little, if any, knowledge of ranching. Anything beyond his book learning moved him to think the worst. Having someone as young as Cindy in charge of such a large ranching client may have made him nervous.

The banker continued. "Well, I'd rather speak in person, but I suppose we could save you the trip if you insist. What I need to tell you Miss. Stocker is that the bank is concerned about its exposure. Because of our long relationship with Mr. Stocker the loans committee extended overly generous terms on the collateral loan. Taking your father out of the picture has put the Lazy-S above our risk comfort zone. We will be requiring either more security or a large reduction of the outstanding principle."

Cindy couldn't breathe. Not only was there no collateral available that the bank didn't already hold, clearly there would be no new operating loan. She couldn't make the February payroll or expenses with the cash on hand. All those facts rattled through her mind like a flash of lightening.

Sensing that there would be little purpose in talking more, Cindy bit off a hostile retort and simply said, "Thank you for your call Mr. France. I have just written the payroll checks. There's enough cash on hand to cover those. I'm assuming you will honor those checks and give the ranch thirty, or perhaps sixty days to satisfy your demands."

"Thirty. Not Sixty." Was the terse response.

Cindy quietly hung up the phone and stood there trembling. With one hand still holding the telephone receiver and the other leaning on the kitchen counter she thought, "Father. How could you be so stupid?"

Tears of frustration and tension rolled down her cheeks.

Her mother wandered into the kitchen on one of her pointless ramblings around the big house. She looked at Cindy, noticed the white knuckles holding the phone receiver and then saw the tears on her daughter's cheeks. "What's wrong dear?"

Cindy had never in her life spoken harshly to either of her parents. She was already in mid-speech before she realized how unforgiving her words were. "Well, our world is just falling to pieces, mother. But don't you worry about it. Cindy will take care of it. Cindy takes care of everything while her useless brothers live the good life. You go rest mother. Or do whatever it is you do."

She grabbed a jacket and swung the door open before her startled mother could respond. Cindy then did something she hadn't done in weeks.

The day was cold. The wind was whipping around the hills, pushing snow before it. But she went to the stable and saddled a horse. The wrangler saw what she was doing and offered to help. She didn't bother to answer.

Within a short few minutes she was astride the gelding and was disappearing over a small rise into the empty pasture, with snow throwing off the horse's hooves as it ran. She hadn't grabbed a hat before leaving but she didn't care. She crossed the reins over the gelding's neck, spread her arms wide and tilted her head back, exposing herself to the cold wind, as if inviting it to wash some of the anger and frustration out of her.

Without even thinking, she let out a primal scream. A scream that came from the very depths of her troubled soul. A scream of anger, frustration and defeat.

The startled horse missed a step, wobbled on the snow, and then carried on.

She rode until she started feeling the cold through her flimsy coat. By that time the gelding was starting to sweat. She slowed the horse to a slower run and then to a walk.

When Cindy returned to the stable, she was no longer angry, just scared. And saddened by the situation.

"The bank is all powerful and Herb France is a total jerk," she said aloud, as she was unsaddling.

"Are you talking to me, miss?"

Cindy looked around to see the mystified wrangler standing there, obviously unsure if he should be offering his help again or not.

"No, just talking to myself Buzz. You can wipe this horse down for me if you have time." She pulled the saddle and blanket off the animal and left the rest to the wrangler.

CHAPTER 44

OF A MORE PRACTICAL NATURE THAN HER FATHER AND being perfectly willing to do whatever had to be done to protect, or better the Lazy-S, Cindy began asking herself questions of the ranch's operating practices. Seeing no opening for the kinds of major changes that were required to satisfy the bank and save the ranch, she looked in a totally different direction. Over the next two days she formulated a plan. Her plan was pushed forward by a trip to High River.

Stopping for lunch at a popular café, she noticed a familiar face in a booth across the room. Amelia Beauregard was a well-known lady rancher. She and her husband started a mid-sized operation far back in the foothills, shortly after their marriage. That had been, perhaps, twenty years before. They were becoming well established and gaining some financial comfort when a misstep on a rocky hillside trail hurled horse and rider to the bottom of a small canyon, and Amelia into widowhood.

Always known as an outstandingly beautiful, as well as

determined, lady in the district, the widow stayed with the ranching dream. Determined, stubborn, capable, Amelia worked as hard as any man. The heat of summer or the biting cold of winter were one and the same to her. The A_A ranch grew and prospered, and the widow became well known as a success in ranching circles. But clearly, there was a price to pay.

Cindy hadn't seen her in several years. Trying not to stare, Cindy took several brief glances across the room. She felt judgmental. But she also knew her assessment was honest. The beautiful Amelia still showed indications of her original beauty and grace, but you would have to look beneath the sun and wind-wrinkled skin to see it.

Her hair was chopped off short, as if to simply get it out of the way. He hands were big and bruised and chapped raw, her knuckles twisted with injuries and arthritis.

When the lady rancher completed her meal and walked out of the restaurant there was no sign of gentleness or grace in her walk.

Cindy was well aware that none of those external things indicated anything about the woman herself. Still, Amelia couldn't be more than forty-five years old. She had paid a heavy price for being a lady rancher.

Even with a good crew to rely on at the Lazy-S, Cindy knew she would have to follow somewhat in Amelia's steps. And pay the same price.

No, she couldn't run the Lazy-S herself. She couldn't, and she wouldn't. She needed a better answer.

She returned from that short trip in a reflective mood.

Cindy met with Big Mike. Together they examined the records for the animals on hand. On a ranch as big as the Lazy-S, there were occasional animal deaths, and animals not performing, which resulted in them being shipped to market. There were a few new bulls purchased over the summer and a few new horses. These small, singular transactions were not reported to the bank. Cindy needed the records to be exact and supportable for an audit.

Next, she examined all the recent sales records she could locate. Auction house sales. Published private sales. Sales at the fall agricultural shows. She created a table showing the prices for cows, calves, feeder stock, and horses. She knew the horses would not enhance her presentation to a city banker, but she put them in the table anyway. She used average prices. To use maximum, or peak prices would leave her open to the suggestion that she was padding the facts.

To complete her table, Cindy listed the cattle futures and stock market quotes. Her goal was to approach a new bank with all the information, leaving no loophole that would weaken her argument or embarrass her.

The last thing she did was drive the few miles that separated the Lazy-S from the B/B. Hank Griffin, the B/B owner was a long-time neighbor and close friend to her father. With a slightly larger ranch than the Lazy-S, Hank had proven himself to be an excellent cattleman and businessman, as well as a loyal friend.

The one slight complication in Cindy asking for advice from Hank was that Hank's youngest son, Blaze, had been rebuffed in his efforts at courting. Cindy hoped she had handled his attempts gracefully, but he seldom talked to her since that time, so she wasn't sure.

Cindy found Hank in the stable, grooming a horse.

The animal already shone like the full moon on a still lake, so she wasn't sure what more he hoped to accomplish, but she didn't challenge his actions. Hank greeted her warmly and asked about her folks. She kept her answer short and then said, "I'm hoping to ask you for some business advice. I'm kind of left alone on that end of things and I find myself over my head a bit."

Hank put the grooming brush on a shelf and pointed at a couple of curved-back chairs placed along the wall. They took their seats and Hank said, "How can I help?"

Cindy told him what bank they were dealing with and explained about the large loan and how the bank had tied up the entire Lazy-S. Briefly she outlined her research and her hopes of securing a loan that freed up the land.

Almost under his breath Hank said, "That miserable…"

They were quiet for a moment. Then Hank said, "Sorry Cindy. I shouldn't talk like that. Don't normally. But I know that twit, France."

They were quiet for another moment.

Hank said, "Let me guess at your question and tell you my answer. You've got to get away from that bank and that manager. I know him. I don't trust him. You don't want to be dealing with him."

"Who should I be dealing with?"

Hank took a slip of paper from his pocket and found a pencil in another pocket. He wrote down the name of a bank, followed by a man's name. "You make an appointment with this man Cindy. But wait until I have a chance to call him. He's a good man and a good banker. Handles all the banks' farm and ranch work. He's all business so go prepared. Let me know how you make out."

As Hank was walking Cindy to her car he said, "We received an invitation. Thought you were getting married."

Cindy tilted her head in acknowledgement of that fact and flashed a sad smile. "I thought so too. But now I have a ranch to manage."

Hank didn't push the subject.

CHAPTER 45

THE PHONE RANG IN THE CABIN BEFORE TERRY WAS up for the day. He answered and waited a few seconds before a tentative voice said, "Terry? It's Cindy."

More silence followed this announcement.

Slowly getting his wits about him Terry said, "Cindy? What's wrong. It's not six in the morning yet. Is there news of your father?"

"No, nothing new on Dad. I wanted to catch you before you left the cottage. I miss you Terry. You can't imagine how I miss you. And now I need you. I know how selfish that sounds but there it is. I need you. I need advice and a favor. If I drive up can you come to the city and meet me for lunch."

Terry didn't hesitate. Although so many thoughts and hurts had swirled through his mind over the past weeks, he pushed them aside and answered, "Of course. Do you know where the Highway-Two Hotel is? I'll meet you in the lobby at twelve."

"Thank you. And Terry, do you suppose your father

would be able to spare me a bit of time after? I would value his advice too."

Puzzled, but not unduly concerned, Terry said, "I'll arrange it."

The two young people met just before the agreed-to time. Terry was unsure how to act. But then, he had never been sure in social situations, even with this girl he loved.

Cindy had no such inhibitions. She threw her arms around Terry's chest and lay her head on his shoulder, seemingly oblivious to all the people around them. Not saying a word, the two stood like that for a while. Cindy finally pulled back, looked up at Terry and said, "Terry, I don't even know what to say. But it is awful good to see you."

Terry responded, "It's good to see you too. C'mon, they have a couple of private, corner booths. We have one reserved."

Cindy felt there might be just a bit of aloofness in his greeting, but she couldn't really blame him.

Tucked into the private booth with cups of coffee before them, Cindy fiddled with the menu. She finally looked up at Terry.

"Terry. I'm not as strange and unstable as my recent actions would indicate. I said long ago that I loved you, and I do. More each day. I miss you terribly. We were to be married next week, but we both know that can't happen until I solve some problems.

"Most would-be ranchers grow up praying and hoping that someday they'll have a ranch like the Lazy-S or the Double C. Only a few ever get that far. But we now have both ranches, and we can't let go of either one. It's not even close to what we pictured for ourselves and I don't know what to do about any of it. We can't live as husband

and wife, being five hours apart. Plus, I have troubles on the Lazy-S that I have to solve. If I don't solve them, there won't be a Lazy-S. Until the accident I was content to leave the troubles with Dad, but…"

In a move that he was still uncomfortable with, Terry laid his hands over Cindy's. He leaned forward just a bit. "Tell me."

The waitress slipped quietly into the enclosed booth and accepted their orders. Cindy then launched into her story.

Briefly covering the last medical report on Adam and moving on to the troublesome loan, and what she called, 'that horrid man at the bank', Cindy laid out the situation.

"On top of that, neither of my older brothers has shown the slightest interest in taking a hand, and the two younger kids are away in university. Neither plan to return to ranching.

"Mom is so deep in melancholy and depression that I can't even get her out of the house for a walk or a visit, let alone discuss ranching matters with her. She says she doesn't care what I do with the ranch. But I'm not totally convinced of that.

"I have full power of attorney, but that doesn't give me the right to be careless with three generations of family work."

"What do you want to do?" asked Terry.

"I can't give you a decent long-term answer because I don't have one. I can tell you this much though. What I want more than anything in this world is for you and me to be married and happy. I just don't know how to get there.

"So, I've decided to concentrate on this single big problem right now and deal with the rest when the time comes. I have to secure the future of the Lazy-S. Either that or find a quick, clean way to make an exit. That may mean finding a buyer. I'm not sure how I'd do that. One thing I know for sure, it means cleaning up this bank mess Dad left me with. That's where I need advice from you and your father.

"The way I have it figured, short of selling out, I either have to find new financing or sell off enough stock to pay out the loan. I'm not sure that would leave us with enough stock to keep the ranch going.

"And then, the bank has us so tied up I'm not even sure if they'll let me sell stock. It's a brutal agreement father signed."

When their meals arrived, they ate in silence.

They were just enjoying the last of their roast beef when the waitress quietly said, "You have a visitor."

Terry stood, to move over beside Cindy. "Great, show him over please."

Willard joined the young couple, and Cindy repeated her story.

After Willard looked over the documents Cindy had put together and asked some probing questions that Cindy had good, prepared, answers for, he said, "I couldn't have planned it any better than you have. I don't see how a banker can fail to be impressed with the numbers, the plan and with you, yourself, Cindy. I wouldn't hesitate to show this to a banker.

"If you thought it would be of any assistance, I'd be pleased to drive down and meet the banker with you. You would still do the talking but I might be able to discuss any tax issues or support your contingency plan."

Terry turned his mind in another direction, blocking out Cindy's voice as she laid it all out for Willard.

Willard asked a few more questions and finalized his advice. "I think any competent banker who's familiar with the ranching business would go with this Cindy. There's one thing you need to be aware of though. Bankers hate providing loans that are used primarily to pay out other loans. That detail will be against you. But if this is what you really want, I would say go for it. And again, I'm offering to meet the banker with you."

Cindy rolled her small sheaf of papers and tapped the table with them. She looked over at Terry, hoping he would say something. Eventually, he did.

"What about your two brothers. Cindy. They each have a debt free ranch provided by the Lazy-S. You've said they're not interested in managing the Lazy-S, but what about financial help? Can't they do something for the family now?"

Cindy leaned back in the booth and groaned. "I'm embarrassed to even tell you this. I talked with them both. I'm not sure which is the dumbest. Dumb dumb – A, or dumb dumb – B. Dad set them up debt-free, as you say, but they didn't stay that way for long. They could have been content to sell their finished stock, bide their time and enjoy watching their assets grow. But, no. Neither one was content with that. They built up their herds with borrowed money, wishing to join the big ranchers right away, I guess. They're both up to their eyeballs in debt. Hopeless. Completely hopeless. The dumb dumb's."

Terry was studying the ceiling. Both Willard and Cindy watched the gears go around. Finally, he shuffled out of the booth. He took the papers from Cindy's hand and said, "I'll meet you both at your office, Dad. Give me a couple of hours." With that he was gone.

CHAPTER 46

IT TOOK NEARLY THREE HOURS, BUT EVENTUALLY Terry arrived at Willards office. Cindy was holding down a chair in the waiting room while Willard had returned to his normal responsibilities. Terry tapped on the office door. He and Cindy were beckoned in.

Neither Cindy nor Willard asked any questions, knowing that Terry would get right to business.

"Cindy, The Double C is offering to buy out the Lazy-S. Everything but the land. By that I mean, everything on these sheets of paper. This, plus the hay and straw stacked up. We'll pay the mid-range prices, just as you've listed them here. We'll arrange for trucking, count the stock out as it's loaded, and you'll save the brokerage fees.

"We'll work it all through the Double C and Lazy-S lawyer's trust accounts. The Lazy-S will be left with debt free land and whatever cash there is, in excess of the loan. You'll lease out the land. That will provide a long term, generous income for your mother and you'll be free of it all. I suspect you'll have to keep the power of attorney and manage the finances for the family, but that won't be too big a job."

Terry stopped talking and studied Cindy, waiting for a response. No response came. The room was silent. Willard started tapping his pencil on the desk, as he studied his son. He then looked across the desk at Cindy.

Willard simply said, "Cindy?"

She shook her head as if waking from a dream. Or perhaps it was a nightmare. Still she hesitated as she let her eyes flit between the two men. After what seemed like a long pause she said, "I never once considered that possibility. How? I mean, that's a lot of money. Can you really make this work?"

Terry looked very serious. Willard had watched his son change gradually, since he took over ownership of the Double C. Part of the change was maturity, but a bigger part was responsibility, knowing that whatever happened on the ranch, was on his shoulders. He waited, giving Terry the time he needed.

"I couldn't make it work," answered Terry. "No, that would be asking too much of the bank. But between Eli and I, we can make it work.

"I drove to the ranch. I showed Eli your numbers. I went through my thoughts with him. I didn't even have to complete the story. The old man was way ahead of me.

"Long story short? Eli called the bank manager. He set up an immediate appointment for me. Without going into the deal, he told the banker that we were in it together. My meeting with the banker took only a few minutes. He took copies of your numbers added in the value of the stock on the Double C and approved the deal."

"So, yes. The Double C can make it work."

After a pause Terry said, "If it makes you and the

family feel any better, you need to know that the reputation of the stock delivered year after year by the Lazy-S is what finalized the banker's decision. That's a real compliment to the Lazy-S and the Stocker family."

Cindy looked excited and troubled. She picked up her pages of notes and rolled them so tightly they squeaked. She looked at the floor and then at Terry. "That would solve the problem, but it would also be the end of the Lazy-S. The family would freak out and be all over me. I'm not sure how I would face that or fight off their accusations. They'd probably accuse me of selling out to my fiancée at a bargain basement price."

The three of them sat silently for some time before Cindy spoke again.

"I thought of selling, of course. But I had only considered the sale of the entire spread. Selling just the animals hadn't occurred to me.

Cindy hesitated and then added, "My thoughts of selling out have never been shared around the family. I was afraid of their reaction.

"It seems they think I can do magic. I can't. It might have looked like Dad could do magic sometimes, but that was all a charade, make-believe. It isn't until now that anyone was forced to look behind the smiles and the big hats."

She was silent again for some time while the men waited. "Oh, I see so many problems, but I also see an end to the threats from the bank, which is the biggest problem."

Cindy looked at Terry for a long time again. A tear trickled down her cheek. "Father would climb right out of his sick bed and take a strap to me if he knew."

Willard saw a retort forming in his son's mind. He

spoke before Terry could, hoping to avoid a confrontation. As gently as he knew how, he said, "It's your father that caused this to become a crises Cindy. I think he might very well see that and understand that he led the ranch into an almost impossible position."

Cindy nodded and wiped her tears with a tissue. She unrolled the pages of notes and appeared to be studying them. Willard watched her carefully. He figured all she could see on the page, through the new tears welling up, would be a blur. Again, the men gave her time.

Cindy started to cry. Terry was embarrassed and troubled. "Cindy, you don't have to do this. You're under no pressure from me. Dad has offered to help you negotiate a new loan. You could still go that direction."

Cindy waved him off without looking at him. "No. that won't work. I can see how unlikely it is now. And even if it did, it leaves me stuck with a ranch I don't want to run."

She said this through her free-flowing tears. She was still looking at the floor.

She blew her nose and picked a new tissue from the box on the side of Willard's desk. Idly, she wondered why an accountant kept a box of tissues on his desk.

Wiping the last of the tears, she quietly said, "The bank gave me thirty days. No more."

"Then we had better get started."

When Terry said that, Cindy seemed to pull it all together; the deal, her feelings, her resolve, her relief. She raised her eyes from the floor and looked at this man she loved. "Yes. We need to get started."

CHAPTER 47

THE NEXT WEEK WAS A BLUR OF MEETINGS, PAPER exchanges, negotiations and counter negotiations. But at the end of the week the trucks started rolling.

Terry had a construction camp company install a twenty-man bunk house and kitchen facility. He offered employment to the entire Lazy-S crew, advising them that after the fall auction sale, the crew would be reduced. To a man, they took him up on his offer.

Well before the bank's thirty-day time limit, the animals were moved, taking great care because the cows were heavy with calf. The loan was paid out and the Lazy-S, after three generation of ranching, fell silent. But the Lazy-S land was again free and clear of debt.

Cindy moved a considerable cash balance to another bank in High River, happy to see the end of the big, impersonal bank in Calgary.

Cindy couldn't explain how she could feel relief, sadness and joy, all at the same time. Her emotions were strung to the limit. She added to this weird collection of passions by visiting her father in the hospital. She went alone, wanting the time to be just for the two of them.

She laid her hand on Adam's unresponsive arm and studied his face. He seemed so at rest. But was he really? Who could tell? Perhaps he could hear more and knew more than anyone was aware of.

Wishing for a few minutes alone with this good man who had raised her and taught her the cattle business, setting the pattern for her life, she stepped back and closed the hospital room door.

Speaking quietly, wondering again if he could hear, she told her father about the sale of the breeding herd, and why it was necessary. Ending the story without tears of remembrance and regret, would have been impossible.

She closed with, "I love you so much father. I know you wouldn't have had to do this. But I'm not you. The bank just wouldn't listen. All they could see was that you were no longer in charge. To the bank, the Lazy-S was Adam Stocker, not Cindy Stocker. I know that with three or four more good years you would have had the loan under control. But the bank wouldn't wait. I really had no choice. I'm so sorry to lose the business, after all the years."

Her voice faded. She paused and gulped for air. Her next attempt at speech came as an unintelligible croak. Wiping tears from her eyes and cheeks she gathered her thoughts and her courage. "I'm sorry if I've disappointed you. But we are debt free again and we still own the land. Mother is financially secure."

Cindy didn't know what else to say, so she said nothing more. Her temptation to blame her father and her brothers was almost overwhelming. But saying all that would do nothing but put her emotions on a high wire again. She lifted her hand from Adam's arm, kissed him on the forehead and left.

Cindy, with the desultory help of her disinterested mother, purchased a small home in Calgary, so her mother could be close to the hospital. Her brothers helped her clear out the old ranch house and sort out a few things to keep. The generations-old antiques and keep-sakes the family kept and treasured over the years were moved to her brother's homes.

The boys seemed to feel no regret or responsibility for the actions their father had taken on their behalf, or the follow-up actions Cindy was forced into. But true to Cindy's prediction, she was accused of favoring Terry and the CC in the transaction.

Her only response, which she tried to remind them of, without creating an even bigger family rift, was that she had offered the deal to the brothers first. Neither of them could swing another loan or increase the ones they already had.

Moving their mother to Calgary was nearly as upsetting as closing out the Lazy-S.

Carolyn alternated between silent melancholy and screaming and crying about the loss of the ranch. Her favorite targets were the shame Cindy had placed on the family with her decisions, and anger at her unconscious husband. Some days Carolyn's depression was so deep Cindy was concerned she might never recover from them. She started hiding her mother's sleeping pills, for fear of what the distraught woman might do during one of her low points.

A consultation with Carolyn's doctor offered no solution to the depressions, other than more pills. Without comment, Cindy thought her mother was already taking too many pills.

With each of her mother's rants, Cindy's guilt dug itself deeper into her soul. She longed for escape. To anywhere.

Some days the little house was simply too small for the two women.

Cindy wasn't sure how much longer she could or should do this. Renting a room would be a welcome relief. Moving to the Double C to be with Terry, and among friendly faces was an attractive option. But her mother couldn't be left alone.

The two younger kids were living in residence at the university. To move them to the new house, with all the drama of the situation, could easily cost them a school year.

Cindy was trapped and she knew it. Knew it and felt it. And was starting to resent it.

In spite of the guilt heaped on her by the family, Cindy believed she had done what had to be done with the Lazy-S. She wished with all her heart that her mother and brothers could see that. But guilt and wishing don't always offer entirely rational outcomes. Her mother's actions were so totally out of character that Cindy wondered, some days, what more could be done for the stressed woman. Did she need more medication? Or, perhaps less? Was her head injury more serious than the doctors knew? Was the constant pain from the concussion and the whiplash more than she could endure? Was the loss of her husband and the ranching business weighing so heavily on her? Did she carry some guilt herself for not speaking up when Adam was making the deal for the boys?

Cindy had no answers, but she finally admitted that the accident had, in reality, taken both her parents from her.

No matter what else might be true, Cindy reconfirmed one thing in her mind: her mother could not be left alone. Before the accident Cindy wanted nothing more than to be with Terry for the rest of their lives. In one part of her soul, that desire was still dominant. But without even realizing what was happening, her family's constant blaming, on top of her mother's illnesses were pulling her away from Terry. She was a strong, ranch raised woman but even a strong person can only stand against the wind for so long, without bending.

"What has happened to our family?" Cindy asked herself. "We were so close and loving. Now it's all fallen apart."

She had no answers and, in truth, had quit seeking for answers. Now, she just wished for something, anything, to happen that would bring an end to the situation, and free her to live her own life.

In an idle moment she thought about Sid. Competent, self-assured, happy-go-lucky Sid. A cougar hunting for its next meal changed Sid's life. Changed it in a fraction of a minute. From riding the range as the go-to man for the Lazy-S crew, he went to riding a worn-out couch in a darkened room, hiding and wallowing in self-pity. In a time of need Terry sought out his old friend and rescued him. Could this same Terry come riding in his beat-up pickup truck and rescue her? Then she remembered that Terry had a new truck. Old – new. What did it matter?

With her arms wrapped around herself she started to giggle at the thought of Sir Galahad-Terry riding to the rescue in a worn-out truck. She giggled until she started to cry.

She was exhausted. Stretched to the limit. Torn between two loves. She wanted Terry and marriage. But she didn't want to lose her own family. Some days her shoulders simply couldn't bear it all.

On a particularly grim day, with both Stocker women dragging themselves through the hours, Carolyn said, "Take a couple of those pills the doctor gave me. They'll make you feel better."

Cindy's answer was immediate and harsh. "Those pills put you into a hopeless dream world. You'll never get better taking those pills. If you were smart, you'd dump them down the toilet and never take another one."

Without a word, Carolyn went to her bedroom and lay down.

Terry and Cindy saw each other a few times over the spring and summer but never for long, and never often enough to reaffirm their love or to re-plan a wedding.

Hank Griffin leased the many miles of Lazy-S ranch land. He had two sons wishing to stay in the ranching business. The Lazy-S would become an extension of their B_B.

CHAPTER 48

ADDING THE MUCH LARGER LAZY-S HERD TO THE Double C ranch turned the calving season into a frenzy of activity. The two herds were kept separate. Terry and Sid decided that would be easier than separating them later.

The heifers that were purchased for breeding purposes were kept apart.

The work was non-stop, stretching the efforts of the combined crews to the limit. With Terry busy on management, and planning for the summer and fall activities, Sid was put in charge as the manager of the Double C.

Big Mike was left in charge of the Lazy-S crew.

Sid found work for Scotty where he could be kept away from the whirl of activity, but still play an active role. Scotty was particularly valuable during calving season. He seemed to have the knack. His calm and quiet manner had a way of settling anxious cows.

Watching from a distance, Terry wondered if Scotty had always been like that or was his calmness a result of his own breakdown.

On some days Terry was tempted to find a couple of

additional men, to reduce the strain of long hours in the cold. Big Mike, still chewing a toothpick said, "It's over in a few more days. Slows right down after calving. We'll make out."

In early April the crew awoke to warm winds and melting snow. A giant chinook arch showed over the Rockies. By that afternoon the temperature had risen forty degrees. The snow melt was making a welcome mess of the Double C ranch yard.

Sid got out the tractor and pushed as much slush as possible from the bed grounds. The crew spread a clean layer of straw over a portion of the space. It wouldn't last long but it would give the calves a bit of a break from lying on the wet ground.

Eli made his careful way to the shed and drove out on his new four-wheel toy. As much as he had enjoyed his three-wheel trike, he felt safer on this one. The additional wheel provided stability the trike lacked.

Eli hadn't been outside in some time. Being engrossed in the history of the Double C and the Big Valley country, combined with the miserable March weather, he was content indoors.

He sat on the four-wheeler outside the bed-ground fence and looked in awe at the size of the herd and the hundreds of calves. He smiled at the antics of the newborns, watching as they alternated between nudging their mothers for another sip of milk, and romping with the other calves.

Scotty rode past on a circuit of the herd. He looked down at Eli and grinned. "Quite a sight eh boss? If we can keep them healthy, they should show you a good return. Still, I'm not sure I want to go through another calving like that, not without more space to spread out in anyway. It was fun, in a way, but still…"

Eli nodded his agreement. "Not to worry, Scotty. This was a one-off. We get this behind us, the Double C will return to normal and stay there."

Scotty rode off thinking, "Well, I'm not so sure of that. Terry's a mite more aggressive than anything seen on the Double C before now. We'll see. We'll see how it all works out."

CHAPTER 49

ON THE TENTH DAY OF APRIL ADAM STOCKER DIED. Cindy phoned Terry the next day. If she had been crying or grieving, Terry couldn't detect it on the phone. If anything, she sounded a little too matter-of-fact about it. Almost as if she was relieved, a great stress gone from her life.

"Are you alright? Do you want me to come down? Is there anything I can do?"

Cindy heaved a deep sigh, as if releasing something unpleasant. "No, it's all under control. There really isn't much to do. We're holding a service at the folk's Baptist Church in High River two days from now. Right after lunch. Come, if you wish. I'd love to see you. I'm not sure what kind of a welcome you'll receive from the rest of the family though."

Terry had no way of understanding why the family was taking their anger out on him. He let it go. For now. The timing didn't seem appropriate for getting into it. "I'll be there. I'll turn the crew loose too. Might be some that will want to make the trip down. Could you and I break away for dinner that evening?"

"Dinner together sounds lovely. I can't promise, but I'll do my best to get away."

Terry hadn't gone to the big house for afternoon coffee in a while. Knowing Eli and Bea were there alone, and wishing to talk to them, he took advantage of the opportunity. But first, he found Sid in the stable, working with the horses. He shared Cindy's news and asked Sid to take it to Big Mike and the others. Only then did he go to the house.

With coffee poured and a plate of snacks laid out, Terry took his accustomed seat. Looking across the table at these two old friends, both aged enough to be his grandparents. Terry felt a comfort and contentment he couldn't have imagined in his own family home.

No one spoke, almost as if Eli and Bea somehow knew that Terry had something on his mind.

Terry fiddled with his coffee mug for a moment while he stared at the table top. Without looking up he said, "Adam Stocker died last evening. Cindy just phoned."

Eli offered no words. Bea said, "Such a shame. My, what that family has suffered. But perhaps it's good to have it over. There seemed no hope of recovery. But they'll still be hurting from the loss."

They talked about attending the funeral for a minute or two. Neither Bea nor Eli were interested in making the trip.

Looking troubled, Terry said, "I'll drive down. But I'm not sure how that will go. The family have somehow found it convenient to blame me for their troubles, and for the loss of the Lazy-S. Cindy warned me to be cautious, and not to expect too much.

"Seems to me the Double C took a big risk to bale them out of the situation that crazy loan backed them into. We gave them their full asking price and paid for the trucking. Now the risk is ours. And the risk ain't settled yet, either. Won't be, till the fall sale. And then, only if we get good sale prices.

"I didn't cause that accident and I sure didn't put that loan on their plate. But the whole thing is sitting between Cindy and me and I don't know what to do because I don't understand any of it."

The two old timers said nothing for a bit. Eli took a noisy slurp of coffee and looked over at Bea, as if urging her to say something of comfort. She didn't.

Finally, Eli spoke. "Many reasons behind a person's actions. What makes good sense to one man will be a complete mystery to another. Every man has his own snakes he's trying to kill, and his own failures he's trying to hide. And every man has his own pride."

Terry and Bea sat quietly while Eli fortified himself with more coffee. He then looked directly at Terry.

"You ever wonder why I made the deal with you for the Double C?"

Without waiting for Terry to speak, he answered his own question. "I couldn't imagine the Double C disappearing off the Big Valley map. Pride, I guess. Or honor and respect for my parents and grandparents who started the operation and who brought it through the really hard years. Been a Double C spread here for a century, near enough.

"Might could be I should have married and fathered my own sons. Time I seriously wondered about that I was already sliding into old age. Couldn't imagine a woman who'd have me anyways. And them nephews of mine wouldn't know a cow critter from cloud in the sky.

"Now, it's true I've enjoyed my closeness with your family since your father was a tyke. It's also true that you showed potential as a cowman early in life. And if I was to make a deal with anyone it's logical I'd look to your family.

"Now I don't want you to take this wrong. I knew you'd make out no matter what you did; raising cow critters or going to university. No, it wasn't really my concern for your needs that drove me. It was my need to know the Double C would still be here after I'm gone."

It continued to be quiet around the table as Eli seemed to be thinking what to say next.

"I understand how the Stockers feel. The Lazy-S, three generations old, is gone. It's gone, and it didn't have to be gone. They know all that. They killed it their own selves with greed and pride. And deep down, they know all that too. But that don't matter. None of that matters. It's still gone. And it's not coming back. There's no one in the family strong enough to bring it back.

"You and Cindy together could have done it. But before that opportunity came up you were tied in here, on the Double C.

"The old lady and the other kids were left facing two hard truths. They could either own their decisions and their loss and take the blame, or they could find a scapegoat to throw the blame on. And everyone in the ranching community knows that the Lazy-S animals now belong to the Double C. So, what it comes right down to is the Stockers are embarrassed by their own mistakes.

"None of that make a particle of sense to anyone but themselves. But there she lays before you, right across the path you and Cindy hope to travel. And that poor girl is stuck between her love and loyalty to her family and her love for you."

Terry had never heard Eli speak with such clarity of thought on any subject but cattle. Bea, too, looked at him with new respect.

Terry twirled his mug, messing up the coffee rings that were already on the oilcloth table covering. No one spoke. Finally, Terry lifted his hat off the chair beside him, and stood. "Thanks. Thanks for the coffee, Bea." He hesitated for just the span of a breath. He gently touched Eli's shoulder. "Thanks."

The gathering at the funeral was as large as any ever seen in High River. The family was there, of course. And ranchers came from miles around. Over the weeks since the accident the pain had largely dissipated. The family, and those closest to Adam, were mostly acting numb.

Carolyn had taken a pill. Cindy wasn't sure if her mother was even aware of the events enfolding her.

Terry and Cindy had just a moment together in the hallway of the church. Cindy cried while Terry held her, saying nothing. Finally, Cindy pulled her head back and reached into her pocket for a tissue.

She wiped her eyes and looked up at Terry. "I have to get back. Hang tough for me. We'll work this out somehow."

CHAPTER 50

THE SPRING AND SUMMER MONTHS ON THE CC WERE a steady round of work, adapting, and finding a way. The crew hardly knew a moment's rest. There were a few cases of illness among the cattle that required visits from the lady vets, but most of the minor things were handled by the cowboys.

Space was a continuing issue. The CC had enough acreage, but it was not laid out in a way to conveniently manage herds the size of the Lazy-S and CC together.

With the first sign of spring grass the horses were sorted out, leaving enough for daily use in the horse trap. The much larger bunch were turned into the lower ranch, to make out for themselves among the hoodoos and gullies of the upper river valley.

Scotty was detailed off for this work. Along with two former Lazy-S riders he moved the animals to their summer home and closed the gate. The three men then rode a circuit of the rough range, checking fences and water sources.

The same three men were then moved to the range Terry had leased from Bea. They rode the entire fence line, repairing a few spots before declaring the enclosure secure.

Terry approached the county office and asked about driving animals along the roads, using only the grassed ditches. His intent was to put the CC herd on Bea's land, along with the bred heifers and the CC bulls. The young lady on the counter looked at him as if he had lost his mind. She also couldn't tear her eyes away from Terrys scars. That hadn't happened for some time, and his mind flashed back to when it was a daily occurrence.

Sorry that he had stated his intention to the young lady, he asked to speak to the manager. The manager turned out to be a middle age woman, the wife of a small rancher. She tapped her pencil on the desk and studied the young man before her.

She finally spoke. "The situation on the CC is well known. My husband commented just the other day about it. I didn't know you had made a deal with Bea. Bea's a good friend. I'm glad you're working together."

There was another long pause as Terry felt he was under a microscope. "Are you prepared to guarantee you'll keep them off the road?"

Terry smiled. "Well, beef critters have been known to occasionally have a mind of their own. But I'll guarantee that if any venture out, we'll put them back just as soon as possible."

"Just see that you do," she said with a knowing smile.

Terry didn't figure she would be too upset with a wanderer or two as long as it didn't get out of hand.

To keep on the safe side, the entire crew was posted along the roadways to guide the herd. The move took

about six hours. Sid closed the gate behind the last frol-
icking calf and re-mounted his horse.

"Let's go home, boys."

CHAPTER 51

TERRY'S SUMMER WAS SPENT LARGELY ON ORGANIZING the fall auction. He contracted for the same auctioneers and managed to convince BBQ Barnes to again work out the food and entertainment.

Additional runways were built to speed up the movement of cattle. Another loading chute was added, and a newer, larger livestock scale was leased and installed. Additional movable panels were built to create more small holding cells.

By August the advertising and promotion was in full swing. By mid-September the calves were weaned and isolated, ready for the sale. The bred heifers were moved back from Bea's range and isolated away from the other animals on the CC. Again, young people from the neighboring ranches and farms were hired to groom and prepare the heifers.

Pregnancy testing all the sale cows, plus the young heifers was a slow and time-consuming task. The vets managed to hire a few vet students to assist.

The last group to make ready was the horses. Logically, it was Sid who took charge of that task.

The sale was set for Oct. 10. It would be a three-day event. The entire Lazy-S cow herd, the Lazy-S bulls, the weaned calves from both ranches, the bred heifers and the horses.

A cold, fall rain greeted the buyers on Thursday morning but by noon it slowed to a drizzle. Friday and Saturday were not hot, but the rain stopped, and the sun played peek-a-boo through the clouds.

The weather, good or not so good, seemed to have no impact on the bidding.

Terry, always in the midst of the action, and Eli, watching from a padded seat on the bleachers, were both satisfied with the prices. The sale went quickly. The buyers were serious ranchers. Many offered the top bids on group after group of the Lazy-S cows.

Some ranchers had arranged for semi-truck cattle haulers to be on site and ready. Other truckers were lined along the shoulders of the highway early on Thursday morning, posting signs announcing their availability, ready for a haul.

The cattle trucks started loading and hauling shortly after the hammer came down on the first offering. No sooner was one truck loaded out when another took its place. With three loading chutes available the animals were moved in a hurry.

Friday and Saturday, with the heifers and feeders needing to be weighed out, the loading would slow down considerably.

BBQ Barnes brought an additional crew along, antici-pating a big weekend. With him never passing up an opportunity to tell people how good the food was and how fortunate they were to have him cooking, the crowd was both fed and entertained.

Cindy drove up for the weekend. The situation with her mother had not improved. If anything, since the death of Adam, Caroline may have sunk deeper into melancholy and depression. The fact that the pain of the concussion, on top of the whiplash, had never subsided was troubling.

To ease the situation with Terry's family, Cindy took a hotel room in Red Deer. Although she and Terry found a few minutes, mostly over meals, to share quiet times together, those times were short and jammed between the many demands that required Terry's attention. Their only real together time was Sunday evening, after all the visitors were cleared from the Double C ranch yard.

In a private booth at the Highway-Two Hotel Restaurant, they sat silently. Both were exhausted; Terry from the summer's work and the sale, Cindy from the non-stop stress and frustration of dealing with her mother, and her brothers, who had never backed off from their accusations of favoritism in the sale to the CC.

Cindy finally took Terry's hands in hers and looked up at him. "It's over and done Terry. You took on a great load and a great risk. Are you reasonably happy with the outcome or are you sorry you ever got involved?"

Terry had no problem answering. "It was months of turmoil and hard work. But we had a good crew. Sickness among the animals was held to a minimum. Calving went well. Overall the weather cooperated. We ran up a lot of expenses getting through the summer, with wages and other things.

"But the sale prices were good. We won't have the accounting done for a while, but there's no doubt we got our money back and will realize a profit. So, overall, I would say it worked out for both ranches.

"My one regret is that it drove a wedge between the Stocker family and me."

Cindy squeezed his hands. "I need you to be perfectly clear on this Terry. That wedge does not include me. I can't answer for my family, especially for the two older boys, but I can speak for myself. "I love you and want you. What's more, I respect you. I respect you and Old Eli both. You took a huge risk baling out the Lazy-S. I'm glad it worked out financially for you. Now you and I have to find a way to work it out for us."

The evening and the conversation drifted on pleasantly, but no firm plans were made, or even suggested.

CHAPTER 52

OCTOBER SQUEEZED INTO NOVEMBER. DECEMBER was only a few days away. Terry turned down Boyce Nugent's urging to attend the Cattlemen's Christmas gathering.

With the CC crew reduced and the ranch back to normal, Terry settled into his accustomed routine. Except that nothing was really normal anymore. Or if it was, Terry wasn't sure he liked it.

The delayed wedding date was now almost a year in the past. Did he still want to be married? And if the answer was 'yes', was it Cindy he wished to marry? Was Cindy ever going to tear herself away from her squabbling and angry family, her clinging mother?

The phone rang in the cottage one evening as Terry was reading, with his feet propped up on the edge of the warm wood stove. He answered, to hear Cindy say, "Can you talk?"

With the assurance that he was alone, Cindy said, "I've arranged an early, family Christmas dinner. I want you to be here. It's next Sunday afternoon. Dinner will be at four but come early to visit if you wish. Mother has promised to be on her best behavior. The younger two kids are looking forward to seeing you again. I have to trust that the others will use some common sense. Please come."

Terry felt trapped, but he also felt there might be an opportunity here for a fresh start. With all the financial stress removed from both ranches he couldn't see any reason to carry on hard feelings. It was true that the sale of the Lazy-S stock showed a handsome profit for the Double C. But that would have been true for anyone taking over the heavily mortgaged herd. Making a profit was the reason for all the work. Why else do it? Surely the two brothers could see that.

"I'll be there. And I appreciate you thinking of me."

"Terry, I think of little else. But I can't seem to find any solution to my entanglement with my mother. Her situation seems almost hopeless. I'll admit that she's not doing much to help herself, but I'm still really torn between two loves. And two loyalties. You and my family. There are strong pulls in both directions. For one dinner, at least, I'm determined that we'll set all of that aside."

The week seemed to crawl along as Terry looked forward to a time with the whole Stocker family. He had never met the two older brothers' wives or their children. Perhaps the women would hold a dampening effect on their husbands' emotions.

Arriving at the Calgary house on a snowy and blustery day, Terry rang the doorbell. The door swung open almost immediately as Cindy welcomed him and reached for his hand. Stepping into the warm living room, the first voice he heard said, "Well, looky here, if it ain't the stable boy, all dressed up and pretending to be a rancher."

Cindy looked across the room at the brother who had spoken. "That's enough. No more."

"Why sure, little sister. You go ahead and tell us all what to do, tell us how to fix things, just like you fixed things on the Lazy-S. You're so smart."

"That's not fair or true." This comment came from the younger brother.

Terry stood with his hat in his hand. He hadn't pulled off his boots yet, nor hung up his coat. Cindy was holding back tears, looking defeated before the visiting or the dinner even began. Her hopes for family peace were dashed in less than one minute.

Wiping her eyes with the tea towel she was carrying when she left the kitchen to answer the door, she looked at Terry with a hopeless look on her face.

Terry placed his hat back on his head. "I'll be leaving now. I'm sorry to have barged into a family gathering."

Carolyn spoke for the first time. "That might be best. And maybe leave Cindy alone from now on. She belongs with us. She's a Stocker. You've been trouble ever since you first walked onto the Lazy-S." Just what she was referring to was anyone's guess.

Terry looked from one to the other of the people sitting and standing around the room. He reached for the door knob and, without further comment, stepped out into the snow-covered yard. No one said anything as the door closed.

Over her crying and the pounding of her heart, Cindy heard the truck start. Slowly it crunched through the snow as Terry turned it around in the wide space before the garage. She looked over at her mother and then at the others in the room. Her family. So good. So tight-knit. So loving. A beacon to follow to those who knew them.

But that was before. Before the accident. Before Adam's death. Before Carolyn's head injuries. Before the bank. Before the Lazy-S went quiet.

Cindy couldn't imagine losing even one of her family. She stood paralyzed at the thought. Her loyalties ran deep.

As the truck started rolling down the drive Cindy's mind cleared. Perhaps for the first time since the accident. She glanced once more around the room. These were all adults with lives of their own. They could do as they wished. Why not her?

"No! No! I will not be trapped in your hate and stupidity."

Yanking the door open, she flew across the small porch and down into the snow-covered yard. She had put on neither coat nor boots.

"Terry. Terry," she screamed.

The truck was moving slowly, as if the driver was reluctant to leave. Cindy ran across the yard, oblivious to the snow and cold. She reached the truck and banged her two open hands on the driver's side window. "Terry. Terry, stop."

Terry's mind had been somewhere else as the truck rolled slowly forward. As Cindy's hands rattled his window, he automatically put his foot on the brake and turned to see what was happening. When the truck stopped, Cindy slipped and slid around the front of the vehicle and grabbed the passenger side door handle. She yanked the door open and dove inside. With her foot braced against the door post she launched herself across the seat and grasped Terry around the neck.

"No. You're not getting away from me. You're not. I don't care what else is happening. You're mine. And I'm yours. You're not getting away."

She hung on so tightly Terry was having trouble breathing.

The rest of the family was gathering on the small porch, watching the happenings at the truck.

Cindy's youngest brother stepped down the stairs and made his way along the driveway. He stood in the open truck doorway, holding up Cindy's warm coat. "You forgot your coat."

Brother and sister looked at each other for a few seconds. The brother finally said, "Have a good life, you two. And God bless."

With that he closed the truck door.

Cindy turned once more to look out the rear window at her family. Speaking to Terry, she said, "Go. Go."

Terry took his foot off the brake. The truck started rolling down the slight grade. "Where are we going?"

"To Big Valley. But first, stop at one of these churches along the way. There has to be a minister somewhere who can marry us. Today. This afternoon. Now. No more waiting."

"I don't think it works quite like that. I'm pretty sure I heard something about needing a license. And then, I owe it to my family and friends to tell them and give them an opportunity to be there when we give our vows."

The truck was rolling north, towards the highway. Cindy was sitting quietly.

Terry said, "What about your turkey?

"They can put its feathers back on and turn it loose, for all I care."

A bit later, Terry said, "You didn't pack any clothes."

"I'll go shopping."

For the first time since arriving in Calgary, Terry laughed.

One week later they were nestled comfortably in a beautiful room in the Banff Springs Hotel. The wedding had been small, intimate and lovely.

Following a series of phone calls, Cindy's mother and the two younger siblings attended the wedding. She received no reply from her overtures to her older brothers.

Cindy was gracious to her family, but cautious, hoping the event could be the beginnings of a re-building of the Stocker family.

Terry welcomed his new in-laws without being falsely exuberant about their presence.

The drive to Banff was followed by a memorable dinner in one of the several dining rooms in the huge hotel.

Back in their room Terry felt a quietness, a reflective mood, come over him. He thought of his mother. Of how she longed for stability that was never to be hers. He was conscious of the steadiness in the family that came from his father's determination to hold it all together.

He repeated to himself the words he had said in silent prayer, several times during the past week. 'Lord, I vow to put nothing ahead of this marriage. We will have a stable family, no matter what comes.'

Terry brushed his teeth, cleaned up, and wrapped himself in a fluffy, white, terry cloth robe, supplied by the hotel.

Cindy took her newly purchased make-up case into the bathroom with her.

Terry heard water running. He had never known nervousness like he was feeling right at that moment. He paced the floor for a minute before flopping into the big, wing backed chair placed beside the window.

Humor had never been Terry's strong point. What

possessed him right at that moment he couldn't have explained.

"Throw me your shirt."

Through the closed bathroom door, he heard, "What?"

"Throw me your shirt."

There was a scream of laughter, remembering. The door opened a crack, a hand sneaked out and a warm pink sweater flew through the air.

Terry caught it and thought, 'it's not a flannel shirt, and this isn't a grassy hillside, but close enough. Close enough'.

RAISED IN POVERTY IN MISSOURI, MAC IS determined to find a better life for himself and the girl who is still a vague vision in his mind. Work on the Santa Fe Trail, and on a Mississippi River boat give him a start, but the years of Civil War leave him broke and footloose in South Texas. There he discovers more cattle running loose than he ever knew existed. Teaming up with two ex-Federal soldiers, he sets out to gather his wealth, one head at a time.

While gathering and driving Longhorns, Mac and his friends meet an interesting collection of characters, including Margo. Mac and Margo and the crew learn about Longhorns, and life, from hard experience before they eventually head west. Outlaws and harrowing river crossings are just two of the challenges they face along their way.

AVAILABLE NOW

REG QUIST'S pioneer heritage includes sod shacks, prairie fires, home births, and children's graves under the prairie sod, all working together in the lives of people creating their own space in a new land.

Quist's career choice took him into the construction world. From heavy industrial work, to construction camps in the remote northern bush, the author emulated his grandfathers, who were both builders, as well as pioneer farmers and ranchers.

Quist's writing career was late in pushing itself forward, remaining a hobby while family and career took precedence. Only in early retirement, was there time for more serious writing.